OTHER PUBLICATIONS BY ZOE KEITHLEY

Write Yourself Well

3/Chicago, 11:59 Press

Crow's Song

The Calling of Mother Adelli, Create Space

Of Fire, Of Water, Of Stone, Jophile's Story, Balboa Press

RECOGNITION

"Hide and Seek" Zoetrope All-story 2001 competition finalist.

"The Second Marriage of Albert Li Wu, Illinois Arts Council Fellowship (1997); finalist American Fiction, Vol. 9.

"The Only Thanks I Wanted" Hyphen Magazine finalist.

"There Will Be No Problem, Dr. Rhenehan" placed first in Emergence IV's "First Chapters" competition in Pigeon Magazine

THIRTEEN

Stories for Earth Travelers

ZOE KEITHLEY

BALBOA.PRESS
A DIVISION OF HAY HOUSE

Balboa Press books may be ordered through booksellers or by contacting:

Balboa Press
A Division of Hay House
1663 Liberty Drive
Bloomington, IN 47403
www.balboapress.com
844-682-1282

Because of the dynamic nature of the Internet, any web addresses or links contained in this book may have changed since publication and may no longer be valid. The views expressed in this work are solely those of the author and do not necessarily reflect the views of the publisher, and the publisher hereby disclaims any responsibility for them.

The author of this book does not dispense medical advice or prescribe the use of any technique as a form of treatment for physical, emotional, or medical problems without the advice of a physician, either directly or indirectly. The intent of the author is only to offer information of a general nature to help you in your quest for emotional and spiritual well-being. In the event you use any of the information in this book for yourself, which is your constitutional right, the author and the publisher assume no responsibility for your actions.

Any people depicted in stock imagery provided by Getty Images are models, and such images are being used for illustrative purposes only. Certain stock imagery © Getty Images.

Print information available on the last page.

ISBN: 979-8-7652-3114-2 (sc)
ISBN: 979-8-7652-3116-6 (hc)
ISBN: 979-8-7652-3115-9 (e)

Library of Congress Control Number: 2022912747

Balboa Press rev. date: 01/18/2023

Dedications

With unending gratitude to Elizabeth, Clare and Christopher, and for Fiona, Ian, Steve, Tristan, and Kayla, too. And with special love for Kathy.

With unending gratitude to my brothers and sister, Byrne, Allen, and Martha, and to our beloved parents Edward Marhoefer, Jr. and Isabelle Byrne Marhoefer.

With boundless love and gratitude to Joseph and Fran; and to Michael and Angel and their beautiful children, of whom all I adore.

I am forever grateful to all of those to whom this book is dedicated.

Contents

Acknowledgements

I wish particularly to acknowledge the staff and students of the Fiction Writing Department at Columbia College, Chicago, for their life-giving inspiration, education and support. Many of these stories were "first draft" in workshops there. My thanks also to C. Michael Curtis, retired fiction editor of The Atlantic Monthly, for his perceptive readings, teaching and encouraagement. One tale in this collection was inspired at a Bennington summer workshop he led.

My thanks to Michael Marhoefer and Andy David without whose technical assistance this collection would still be in the computer on my desk.

My thanks to my daughter Elizabeth, for the cover photo.

The following stories have appeared previously in slightly different forms:

"The Only Thanks I Wanted", Hyphen Magazine, #12, fiction finalist; Chicago;

"Mama's Boy", Hyphen Magazine, #3, Chicago;

"That Dinner At The Smith's", The Wapsipinicon Almanac, Anamosa, IA;

"The Second Marriage of Albert Li Wu", American Fiction, V. 9, New Rivers Press;

"There Will Be No Problem, Dr. Rhenehan", Emergence, IV, Chicago, and <u>The Calling of Mother Addelli</u>;

"Hide and Seek" appeared in The North American Review, and <u>The Calling of Mother Addelli</u>;

"What The Daughter Owed", in Emergence III, and <u>The Calling of Mother Addelli</u>;

"Jophile's Story, A Short Story", <u>Of Fire, Of Water, Of Stone, Jophile's Story</u>, (Balboa Press)

The Second Marriage
of Albert Li Wu

Albert Li Wu trudged home through the gloom of an overcast February sky in Chicago's Chinatown to tilt against his first floor apartment's front window the sign he had made at Premier Printing on their hand press: ***Wife wanted. Apply within.***

It was 1983.

He prepared his usual tomato soup along with a grilled cheese sandwich in the iron wok his dead wife Amour had favored. At the breakfast table with his chop sticks, he sat then to scan the sports page of Saturday's *Chicago Tribune,* dipping pieces of the sandwich into the soup and overseeing the sports page. Tomorrow or Tuesday, he knew, a widow or spinster would ring his doorbell. (Well, his real preference was that she be a widow.)

As opening gambit, he would prepare tea and, to become comfortable, make small talk about the weather, the neighborhood and rising prices. He would detail his current circumstances: Bereft these two and a half years, in his early seventies and with a good pension from Premiere Printing where he still made money from special print jobs, as well as from his hand-carved ivory chess sets, known all over by serious chess players, including state champions! No close family ties. In excellent health! He would smile widely to show his still-perfect teeth.)They would tour his living room, bed chamber, kitchen, pantry, bath and back porch.

That evening, he watched the late news, a detective show, then a movie. Since his wife passed a year and a half ago, he didn't sleep well. At one a.m., he lit the usual stick of incense before the dust-covered Buddha seated upon the discrete altar just outside the livingroom door, mumbled a short prayer, andthen blew the candle out.

That night, his dead wife K'uan Lai came in his sleep wearing a wedding robe of red satin and with a lotus in the topknot of her hair. In her hands, and rising like the sun, was the gold bridal fan of her grandmother!

"Why you advertise for wife?" she had asked in the Chinese they shared--had spoken directly into his mind through the mask of her face, and in a voice so cold as to make his scalp flock! "I am your wife!" she drew herself up.

"And since when do you speak so to your husband, or to any man!" he retaliated. "You are dead. Now *I* must cook! *And* clean--*and* carry my shirts to the laundry! And," Albert Li Wu drew himself up, scowling, "I have no one to talk to."

And at that, a wicked light scampered across her eyes--she, who for twenty-seven years had never raised so much as an eyebrow over all his foolishness! But now she drew herself up further, and asking, "Since when do YOU ever talk?" And she swept her closed fan across the half-formed knights and pawns he sat carving then in his dream; and with a final stroke with her fan across the air, she dissolved completely--like color washed from paper.

Well, and Albert Li awoke, then, enraged that his dead wife should tilt her head so as to look down upon him; and worse, should *dare* to scatter his work, his carvings! But oh how his heart had blistered at the sight of her, so fresh, so young--perhaps eighteen--and even more radiatnt than the day he had married her!

Well, he had waited late to marry--waited until his income could command a prize of traditional family; and one his friends' eyes would catch at when they came around to smoke and play *mah-jongg*. And, like any husband, he had expected excellent meals, a tended shrine, and at night the comfort of her breasts and thighs under his roaming hands.

When Albert Li stepped from his door to fetch the Sunday paper late next morning, the sudden clatter of female voices greeting him ceased suddenly like a ribbon cut as the female eyes took in his pressman's hump, hole-infested sweater, flattened bedroom slippers, outsized ears and wisps of greying hair moving gently on the field of his pale and otherwise naked scalp.

Immediately, and as though they had just been bilked, the younger women bolted from the queue to stomp up Twenty-sixth Street--and leaving their scorn to crawl up his stoop to glare at the balding pate, wrinkled shirt and flattened bedroom slippers of the filthy old bag of bones! And a neighbor, out early walking his dog, had telephoned the Chicago Sun-Times about women all doodied-up and lining Twenty-sixth Street on his block since seven a.m.!

Just then, (and taking in Albert Li Wu's sewing thread mustache and beard), a punk news reporter had cocked his hat and stepped forward. "You Wu?" And he'd tapped the sign. "This for you, or are you starting some local business?" And the reporter had leered around, then, chest shaking as another man came huffing up, video camera upon his shoulder.

Albert Li Wu, appalled and secretly and mysteriously humiliated, slammed his front door.

Well, after all, he had pictured one or two older Asian women drifting through his afternoon, chatting, drinking tea, admiring his front room, bedroom, bath, kitchen and back porch. But now, and slumped in his over-used easychair, he felt angry all over again that his dead wife K'uan Lai had not outlasted him. Why, he had required of her only household duties any monkey could perform--and with no children to wear her down with ceaseless crying and new demands every five minutes! But by now, he stiffened up, the Buddhist priest ought have found a widow or two for him to consider! And Albert Li Wu had shut his front door thinking, "What good was religion, anyway, except to placate your ancestors day in, day out, as if they were the landlords of your life?"

Disgusted, he peeled the "Help Wanted" sign off of his front window to throw it into the wastebasket while female eyes continued to pry about the edges of the apartment's curtained windows; and while the chiming of his front and back doorbells drove him from room to room, hands over his ears!

Finally, after twelve hours, the dragon had returned to its lair. Now Albert Li Wu could lift his shades again and lounge about in his bathrobe drinking tea from the oversized cup whose stains he did not know how to remove.

That night K'uan Lai, appearing in her late twenties, gazed serenely upon him as pinching her fingers she stripped away the black thread curling along each shrimp's pink body. "I knew you would never take another wife," she smiled sweetly, and dropped the newly stripped shrimp into a pot of boiling water.

Well! And next morning, Albert Li Wu pulled himself to hisfull height, the memory of the appearance of his first wife still burning a hole in his heart. And since when did K'uan Lai know anything of a man's business? he spread ginger marmalade upon his toast. Why, when K'uan Lai was alive, he'd had to count out into her hand the exact money needed for the shopping list or she would buy a lamp instead of a roast! He bit through the cool sticky sweetness of his marmalade toast. And, had his mother passed on first, his father most certainly would have married again! He snapped open yesterday's Chicago Daily News. Well, *If* and *when* he, Albert Li Wu, ever wanted another wife, he *certainly* would have one!

It was that next morning, then, about ten a.m., when Albert Li Wu heard urgent rapping at his back door where a large shadow filled the pebbled window glass. Mr. Gillespie, the building manager! What day of the month was it?

Albert Li Wu opened the door a crack.

Well, and she was *huge*--and with a plowed-field kind of face under that straw hat squashed flat and holding its own against the black wiry hair nearly two-fingers grey at its roots while the undergirth of chin sifted into the collar of a discouraged brown overcoat; and all the while the woman's eyes took in not only him, but the scarred kitchen cabinets, outdated gas stove, slumping refrigerator, feathered linoleum, drooping white kitchen curtains and large (and nearly empty) pantry.

Not waiting on introductions, the woman pressed a family-size covered casserole towards him.

"No, no!" he backed away. "No wife. A mistake."

"I seen you many a time at the Bumble Bee, Mr. W—."

But he had already slammed the door before she could finish, locking out the small brown eyes scouring his kitchen walls and floor, stove and slumping frig.

And Albert Li Wu waited an hour before carefully lifting a corner of the backdoor window's curtain; and then opening the door a crack onto the back porch where sat a covered casserole dish!

Well, except for the sauce, it might have been Oriental food! And it was his first home-cooked meal in he didn't know how long! Albert Li sighed and chewed, relishing the fantasy of someone in his kitchen and tending to his needs. Afterwards, scraping the bowl clean with his fingers, he washed then set it onto the stoop with this note under its lid: "Very good! No wife. A mistake. Albert Li Wu."

Yet every few days she came again--a different day, a different time. And when he didn't answer the bell, she'd leave something new, tasty and fresh and take-away the dish of her previous offering, it having been washed and set out on the back porch. And it was through a narrow slit between the two kitchen curtains that Alber Li Wu would see her retreat, her body rolling like a ship of trade, and until he could snatch the new meal inside. Later, along with the washed dish, he would leave a note: "Very good. Thank again. Albert Li Wu".

And after the first week or so, the woman began to leave notes of her own. "I am a trained housekeeper, Mr. Wu." "I am looking for a live-in position, Mr. Wu." "I have references, Mr. Wu."

And it came to be daily, then, that Albert Li Wu would pick at a pawn with the tip of his carving knife while turning over in his mind matters concerning this bandit woman-- arguing that, after all, she would be employee--so no woman-minded silliness! Oh, but from no important family from earlier employment! And not even Chinese! So, what to say to the ever-watchful Ancestors? And bringing in with her white-people smells and English words like rocks!. And a fat at old woman for everyone to see! Oh, but good cook! And *BIG* woman to change sheets, wash floors, carry out garbage--even shovel sidewalks and coal to the heater, if needed.

And this way every day now, Albert Li Wu would pick at this piece and then that of his carving, pursing his lips to blow off the pearly flakes of ivory and keep his hand-carved game pieces progressing. Three or four nights later, Albert Li Wu's first wife, K'uan Lai, her pitch-black hair glittering with silver, came climbing, lugging a scrub bucket through the shrouds of his sleep.

"I warn you," she aimed her words well, "this *how li* Irish will never leave if you eat her food! And she is NOT allowed my kitchen, my house!"

Spitting like a peasant! his mind boiled. And speaking to him as if he were a common street vendor! And why was it that the Ancestors could not control his first wife K'uan Lai, when he had always found her perfectly easy to control? He rattled his pillow under his head. And how was that this house suddenly was *her house* when she knew perfectly well that houses always belong to the husband!

He rolled onto his side, staring and absently hearing through the closed window the oncoming chatter of the three a.m. elevated train to the Loop. Oh, but in his mind, it was his wedding day.

"This yours now," his father had drawn the ivory "cards" and "money sticks" of the ancient Chinese game *Mah-Jong* with which he had grown up from its brown wooden box, its pieces of play inlaid with cut ivory word symbols. "Keep your wife as you do your *mah-jong*," his father had advised, then, and nodding deeply.

"What do you mean?" Albert Li had asked, opening and closing the shallow teak drawers, fingering the flat ivory sticks and quarter-inch deep rectangular ivory and bamboo-backed pieces, identifications carved and painted in their appropriate "suit" colors.

"In *Ma-Jong*," his father wagged his finger, "you keep track of your own pieces and all pieces other players "discard" (throw away) onto the table. This gives you the resource you need to win. And a lucky thing is that you draw from the throw-aways as well as from the four-sided "Wall" we build at start of game. And the first person to complete a "family" of all the numbers from this "Wall" wins!"

Well from then on, Albert Li Wu kept track of *everything,* down to the last spoon, dishcloth and scouring pad, determined he would show that meddling ghost of K'uan Lai he *STILL* gave the orders here! And he WOULD see this woman if he wanted to! And this was *NOBODY'S BUSINESS* but his own!

"Rose Malone" was the name she gave out from under her black pie-pan hat while the two of them sat balancing teacups in the front room and the dragon-clock on the mantle dealt out the mid-afternoon as a school bus coughed, then rumbled off to leave behind the footfalls and voices of school children to tatter the air.

"So I says to mi-self, 'Why, they must mean that dignified Oriental genelemen comes in for our stroganoff! I seen you many a time through the kitchen door window Mr. Wu. Well, everybody knows Mr. Wu, "extra noodles"! And I wager his must be a mghty fine home to keep!' I says to mi-self."

Albert Li Wu flushed. He felt his walls stretch, his household furnishings modernize and gleam! He blew across his steaming tea.

"Now I'm an honest woman, Mr. Wu," Rose Malone set her cup carefully onto its saucer, "--on my feet early morning to night cooking and cleaning--. Well, at my age, it gets to be too much sometimes. Oh, but they won't see the likes of me again at that kitchen, I can promise you that! And that boss there, Mr. Rench'll be on his knees and beggin' me to stay!" Rose Malone tucked a strand of grey hair behind her ear. "And don't you worry none, Mr. Wu. I got plenty of work left in me, yessiree!" She paused to give him another look, a frank look.

"--and plenty of good meals for the right customer, too!" And she straightened her hat. I mean "GOOD meals!" she repeated. "And anything else a body might require!"

Albert Li Wu's neck grew hot. "My place one bedroom only. So where I put housekeeper?"

Rose Malone shrank, then perked up. "Why your nice pantry would be perfect!" "You got one of them cots?"

He paused, eyes coursing the bulk of the woman. "You be—comfortable?"

"Lord, once I fall asleep, twenty mules draggin' my bed through the doorway wouldn't wake me up!"

That faint dark shadow above her upper lip, the slough of neck skin, hams for arms, coal-hods for feet. Well, sex would be out of the question. He combed his fingers through his mustache. Well, who's to say, but he might have a woman friend visit from time to time. After all, he wasn't dead yet, was he? He turned to the Irish woman.

"This room-board only. What you do for money, then?"

"Oh, the Lord be praised," she threw her hands up, "I have my poor dead husband's pension these twelve years. And then that Social Security will help some-- sixty now, and no family. And just wantin' to live quiet now, and see Imaybe see reland again!"

A professional cook! He couldn't believe his luck! Well, and what harm could there be if she stayed the night, then next morning fixed breakfast? He certainly would have to sample her work before anythinng could be final! And if he found he didn't like her or her work? Well, then he would get rid of her. This was *business*, after all!

Albert Li Wu wrestled open the old cot and tacked a pillow case acoss the pantry window while Rose Malone called to quit her job and do up the cups before hurrying off for her belongings, and to find a shower curtain for the pantry door with the twenty dollars the Chinese gentleman gave her for that purpose.

That night, Lau Lo Wu--Albert Li Wu's dead mother-- appeared in peasant dress. "Everyone will think you take her to your bed!" And tears glistened upon the ancient crepe of her cheeks as she hunched over working a mound of rice upon a cloth into the familiar riceballs of Albert Li Wu's childhood.

"--and not even Chinese!!!" the old mother went on. And behind her, the mountains of China rose black and white and green. "You have wife! She wait for you!" her old eyes wavered and watered. "We all wait for you!"

The rice balls vanished last.

Albert Li Wu woke popping his knuckles. Why would his mother, now she was dead, care about what people here might think? And what was he supposed to do until "his time came", dry up like those monks in those dusty ancient temples? Anyway, it was the Irish woman herself who suggested that she use the pantry overnight so that the next day he might see her cleaning work!

And that night, through his bedroom door came the smell of that Irish woman--as if she were looking for him until found him, finally, in his bed. Oh, alright, he would get rid of her, Albert Li Wu growled after the woman fixed his breakfast next morning. At least then K'uan Yin and his mother would be happy, then, and would hopefully be satisfied and mind their own business!

Next morning, AlbertLi Wu woke to find his tea already steaming and full-bodied upon the kitchen table. And a little tune from his childhood began to carousel away every unhappy thought while he drew in the perfume of fresh-squeezed orange juice, scrambled eggs and just-baked coffe cake dough decorated with white icing. Oh, and he had not felt so happy in years!

"Good morning, Mrs. Malone," he half-rose from the table.

"Mornin' to you, Mr. Wu!" the woman replied, spatula gleaming as the sun strode brilliant between the kitchen curtains. "Well, and isn't this a lovely day!" she chirped, large face beaming.

In the afterglow of breakfast, then, Albert Li Wu carried his taut belly down the hall to his bedside table, there to rummage in the drawer for the bank box key concealed in the deck of playing cards.

"And shall I do up your bed with fresh linens now, Mr. Wu?"

Albert Li startled. Big as she was, he had not heard her coming!

"Don't have to be now," Rose Malone held up her hand. "I'll be going out for pork roast, like we talked about--and them cherries you love for a fresh-made pie for your dinner! And I'll be using the back."

He rummaged in a Chinese porcelin box upon his bureau.

"Back-door key," he held it out; then dug into his top drawer for four ten-dollar bills Rose Malon peeled apart and give two back.

"Well, we won't be spending all your money, now!" she raised her chin. "A good housekeeper don't need that much money!"

And before Albert Li Wu knew it, the snow of early March had turned to slush; and April rain begun weaving itself into the air. Now, when Rose Malone called, Albert Li came to the table. When she cleaned, he went to his old job or to the movies. During shopping or her "personal time", he worked at his carving. And when, bellowing Irish ballads or cowboy songs, Rose Malone prepared their food, Albert Li Wu turned up The Six O'Clock Evening News.

And soon enough, life before Rose Malone began to fade from Albrert Li Wu--and might indeed have been forgotten altogether if, regular as sunrise, his dead wife K'uan Lai, either bending to perform some distasteful and humbling task or silky bedroom attire open, would appear and train upon Albert Li Wu steely eyes of accusation.

And then one night, her pitch black hair buckled by tortoise shell combs, she appeared at a writing desk upon which rose a multi-tiered pagoda made of the engraved blocks of a *Mah-Jongg* set.

"You give her all money she like; but you never give me money except you count every dime," she thrust forth the accusation, then positioned an engraved ivory Mah Jong tile tile high to complete a narrow structure of tiles wavering dangerously as she touched it.

"You spend money like a child," Albert Li came right back. "I give you money; you bring home colored fans or tortise shell combs!"

"Oh, but I have mind for more than money," his first wife pivoted toward him sharply, her face a polished gemstone. "No one learn sitting in corner--or find out what she think with her tongue tied up in knot." And she opened her hands upwards, then, as if to conjure that very pagoda before her. "And if I make this, tell me then what else could I make?" And she leaned forward to pinch a brick from the very bottom of the structure which, in turn, shivered, wavered and then collapsed. "I warn you, this Irish you take in, he bring you down," she hissed, "like tower of tiles!".

Next morning, Albert Li Wu, at the bathroom mirror and combing through his mustache, couldn't help but admire the arch of his eyebrows; and couldn't help but be tickled, now, to see his dead wife K'uan Lai jealous now, and over the *how li* Irish woman! But every night that week, his dead wife's litany of injustices hacked into his peace of mind. *Well, but wasn't that marriage?* he would punch his pillow. *And hadn't he always taken care of everything when she was here?*

Now Rose Malone took care of everything. And for Albert Li Wu, the giving-over of the care of himself, of his household, was like dropping stones from his pockets! And each week he kept track only of what he withdrew from the bank, marvelling at how he could live with a woman so large and so loud!

Before, at his job, he had both seen and come to be soothed by the clattering racket of the huge printing presses as they rolled the newsprint back and forth like cat's cradles. And amazingly, it was beneath that racket that he had made the improbable discovery of all the solitude and all the silence he could ever need! And so it was that the Irish woman's clatter and bang about his house now came to swaddle his days!

After some weeks, Albert Li Wu found that the giant pillows of the woman's breasts pulling at her housedress, the expanse of her hips rising and falling as she lumbered about the kitchen and even the maternal shape of her stomach as she sat preparing vegetables for dinner began to stir within him a fresh, surprising and nearly-forgotten yearning!

So, following a Perry Mason television re-run one night, he remarked that it seemed a shame to use the pantry as a second bedroom now they had twice the household supplies that needed shelving. Giving no reply, Rose Malone dropped her eyes modestly while her darning needle winked, winked.

"You think you be comfortable in my bed, Mrs. Malone? I small gentleman!" Albert Li finally asked the question one evening, then flashed his teeth.

"Call me 'Rose'," she replied, and bit off the dangling thread.

Well, and it was from above his bed that night that K'uan Lai stepped through boiling yellow clouds iin a gown of black silk edged with red knots of eternity; and her face pale with rage.

"First, you bring home *how li* Irish, take her to your bed!"

"I was faithful husband!" Albert Li raised onto his elbow, his face stiff. "--and you leave me, go to family in Heaven!" He swallowed; then threw his head. "And what *I* do now," his voice wobbled, "*NOT* your business!"

And at that, K'uan Lai, her painted eyebrows raised high, pulled the gold wedding band from her finger. "You shame me before parents, before gods. You shame me before ancestors and hungry ghosts!" her voice shook. "And I divorce you!" Then, with a grunting sound, she pitched the wedding band at him overhand.

And Albert Li Wu waited to feel the cold metal strike him. But no, nothing. And then after a moment, he opened one eye, then the other. And in the grainy light of early morning, he made out the bulky landscape of Rose Malone next to him on her back and enjoying a good snore.

That year, the April rains came on cold at first, but then turned warm, and slanting across Lake Michigan while the cigar-shapes of infant plants pushed aside the sodden earth to reach outward with first leaves, first flower petals.

One evening, Albert Li took down from the closet the antique box of dark walnut wood holding ivory blocks inscribed with Chinese letters, the back side of each letter block covered with bamboo and ivory sticks, sharp edges rubbed off and red dots indicating amounts of Chinese money engraved into each end. He placed the set carefully--reverently-- upon the coffee table.

"This Mah Jong. Come from Emperor in China long, long time ago! My great--great grandfather Chang his chief steward, then. Handle," and he stretched his arms wide to indicate a national and continental expanse, "*everything!*"

Rose Malone pawed timidly through the carved ivory-and-bamboo-backed pieces, each the same rectangular shape, each incized with a letter of the Chinese alphabet and painted with one of four colors: red, green, yellow or blue. And, stacking them, there came a clicking sound, soft and gentle and very pleasant to her nervous system. "Is it worth a great deal, do you think?" she asked.

"Maybe five thousand, maybe more." Albert Li shrugged grandly, and then, with his thumb, caressed the piece he held. The pieces nested each in one of four pull-out wooden drawers. And Albert Li explained each figure had its own meaning in the Chinese language.

"Is it worth a great deal, do you think?" Rose Malone asked.

He shrugged. "Maybe ten thousand. Who know? Oh, but I never sell. I *STARVE* before I sell!"

Rose Malone drew an ivory piece beneath her nose, taking in the perfume of its bamboo backing fixed to the hard white of the ivory, so cool feeling; and with a remarkable sense of softness. She ran a fingertip against its identifying mark, (much like that of a playing card) carved deep and then painted the color of the suit. Oh, and how she loved the click-click, like music, of the pieces as they struck one another loading and unloading the drawer, or against the surface of play.

"And NOBODY think to look for Qui Gong game in old noodle box!" Albert Li, seeing the important impression the set had made, told her proudly, then.

That night after his bath, and looking into the mirror above the sink, his defenses relaxed, Albert Li Wu saw with surprise an old white-haired man with skin of deepening yellow, oversized ears, small grey eyes, young-girl breasts and a bumpy bowed spine. And startled at what had become of the body of his youth--how it had worn itself away under the load he had, year after year, piled upon it -- he gaped while the sly idea scampered across his mind *"Well, you used it up. You used it all up!"*

At first, he shut that observation out, slamming the door of his mind! But then, fascinated--and studying it further--he found himself, then, required to be open and to admit that, yes, he *had* used his body up, *"Used it up just like a wife!"* another part of his mind chimed in. *"--Just like a wife!"* the ideal repeated itself.

Startled at such honesty so unexpected and bald, Albert Li Wu grabbed a towel and began rubbing his head hard, *hard* trying to drown out that voice with its frightening opinions (along with the memory of it already burned into his mind). Oh, but the thought went right on anyway and until, finally, he had to turn with a groan from the sink and shut off the light.

Well, and there had been others, too, hadn't there? some uninvited part of his mind carried on, nevertheless. Free women, they had been, who knew about politics, merchandising, special sex practices. And, years passing, he had increasingly found within himself a growing appetite for younger bodies, a younger smell. And wasn't it also that he had wanted to show that he could afford these high-toned public women whose unfettered arrogance drew married men like flies!

Well, and wasn't it true that if K'uan Lai had in their life shown such fire, such an unfettered tongue and unashamed display, why he would have worshipped her then, cwould have ourted her with jade, draped her in silk and set her among carved ivory, colored lacquer, ebony and mother of pearl!!

But *now*? Oh, but it was too late for such things now!

Albert Li Wu mopped the bathroom mirror with a hand towel, then shut off the light above the sink wondering whether Kuan Lai had been such a woman as that all along? He sat upon his bed; began to button his pajama top. Well, how could he have known, then, he who had neither wanted nor approved that his wife even have opinions!

In the bedroom, he turned back the covers. Oh, but now, *now!*, she was so alive! *But too late!* Oh, and how he felt the barbed irony of it! And "All those years and I never knew you!" some part of him whispered to her, wherever she was now. And it was through the walls of his mind that he spoke those words, now--and through the walls of the room out into the starry night and across the far skies where she waited. Then, in the bathroom, Rose Malone dropped a cold cream jar into the sink. And at the clatter, he shrank beneath the bed clothes, and wishing to God he had the bed to himself!

And soon it was May.

Albert Li Wu and Rose Malone ate with the windows open to their neighbors' backyard barbecues, native lingo, yapping pet dogs and the pitch and drop of neighbors' outdoor cooking until one breakfast morning, Rose Malone turned to him from over the spitting skillet of ham and eggs to tell him she'd be needing an extra fifty dollars that week.

"But you need extra money last week too. What happ'ning?"

"Money don't go so far these days," Rose Malone shook the pan and turned the burner off. "And we can't be always using fancy ingredients, dear as they are. We'll have to eat more plain now."

She shoveled the potato and Polish slices onto his plate; and then dumped the fry pan into the sink to plop down upon her chair and take up her fork.

"Them politicians puts a stranglehold on everything these days. And it's always us poor what suffers! In Ireland, them kind 'ud be held robbers an' strung up over a tar pit, then the lines cut!" she told him around her chewing.

That afternoon at the bank, Albert Li Wu withdrew three hundred-fifty dollars. As he stuck three tens into Rose Malone's purse, his eyes picked up the gold trim of a savings book, one with the name "Rose Cullen" showing in the slotted window; and some-thing cold knocked within his chest; and he slipped the savings book into his trouser pocket. Later, when the woman had left for the store, he sat upon the couch turning the small pages, his eyebrows high at the four months of climbing weekly figures. Why, in April, the monthly deposit nearly matched the whole food budget!

"Who Rose Cullen?" he asked her later at dinner that night. He pushed the savings book across the table.

"Oh," the woman opened a wide smile, "why blessed be Jesus, you found the book! My sister's savings! I been upset all week!"

"Dates start end of February. Latest one this week?" Albert Li set down his fork. "You never tell about sister."

"Why, in Ireland."

"Your sister name Rose too?" He took a bite and chewed slowly, his eyes never leaving her face.

"Now would you believe it, our dear Ma named us both Rose! Myself was Ellen Rose; her, Mary Rose--after our Gram and our aunt. But when Ma died, we each wanted to drop our names we never liked and each just use Rose instead--me here, her there." She laughed pouring milk into her tea, lacing it with sugar. "And oh, its so comical writing her: 'Dear Rose. Love, Rose'." And she stirred her cup, then, raising her eyes.

"I never see you write any sister--or anyone. And why you have her bank book, make deposits?" He studied the woman, slowly wiping his mouth and then leaning with his wrists against the edge of the table.

"Lord love a duck," she tucked a strand of gray hair behind her ear, "but they're poor as dirt in Ireland! And being on government money, my sister needs any penny she can get. Well, and she can dommuch better from a bank here! So I put together this plan at Washington First for a special account. He says--Mr. Brownlee--and the man's a saint, if he is black as midnight!--he says, 'Well now, I wouldn't do this for everyone, Mrs. Malone.' So she shoots me the checks and I takes them into the bank. It's simple as that!" she nodded, off-hand, smiling; and then leaned to her teacup.

"Well, I never hear of anything like that." Albert Li Wu laid his napkin upon the table. "And why her deposits same as money I give you for house?"

"Well, and are they now?" Rose Malone's greyed eyebrows rose high.

Albert Li scraped his chair back. "No wonder food bad, now," his voice shook. "You send money to sister, not spend for us."

And at that, Rose Malone swelled up. "The devil and Holy Mary!," she glared, "and I'd have a right to it, too, the work I do around here!"

Albert Li Wu banged out the door and into the refuge of the night. Hours later and back in his living room, the dark still strong outside the window, he sat rigid upon the couch and staring again at the wall before him with its ticking antique clock. And then it was just before dawn that he walked down to the Bumble Bee, *"Open all night!"* Yes, He would stay out of the house and think what to do. For the idea of confronting Rose Malone ("or Cullen--or whoever!") set loose behind his breastbone a pack of howling hyenas.

The serving girl him brought a waffle, its yellow pat of butter glistening and running. And at the sight of it, his throat closed. He called the waitress. "Where manager?"

The man wore a small black bowtie while blue-veined bags hung beneath the eyes he closed. *"R-o-s-e M-a-l-o--ne*. Nope. Been here since '73. Never anybody by that name I can remember."

"What about 'Cullen', then?"

"Cullen? Cullen?" The man worked the toothpick in and out of his back teeth, sucked, shook his head. But then, "Wait!" he snapped his fingers. "Older?" He cupped his arms. *"Real* heavy? That her name? Yeah. Two-three years ago. Lasted maybe six weeks. Great cook, but *slow!* Ran into her at Zorba's, next to the 'el', last year. Man, it's a sin to waste a good cook on a garbage heap like Zorba's." He shook his head and strolled off.

Albert Li stared out the window. When he was young, he had hooted at stories about men--men like himself--older men taken for a ride! Then his fork slipped from his fingers, first bouncing onto his foot, twanging across the floor. And the manager's eyes strayed from his newspaper to the old guy raking his pockets to leave a five on the table, then banging out the door, the thin grey beard blowing over his shoulder like a long tangled wad of string.

Home again, Albert Li jerked open the bedroom's closet door; the empty hangers chimed softly to see the shelf space where the noodle box had been kept vacant!

"No-o-o-o!" He slammed his fist past the hangers and into the closet's wall. *"N-o-o-o-o!"*

Albert Li spun around to the bedside table. Rummaging its single drawer, he found the key to his savings box still hidden deep in the rubber-banded pack of playing cards. However, the what-not tray on his dresser's top was completely cleared of stamps and loose change. He jerked open the top dresser drawer to rummage through handkerchiefs, socks, neckties and cuff links. The three one hundred dollars bills he always kept concealed there for emergencies! Gone!

Albert Li Wu banged open his front door to fling himself into the street, and stomping as if the authority of his footfalls could erradicate his disaster. Why, he would set dogs upon her! He'd mix *Draino* into her coffee! He strode south on State Street, and finally into the heart of the Loop as rain began to fall softly to turn the pavement dark.

Why, that *Mah-jong* set with its carved ivory and bamboo-backed pieces had been honored in his home in China since he was a boy! Why, even to this day, he could see his father Wan Ho carrying the rich brown wooden chest with its carved ivory insets onto the freighter so as to keep it in plain sight with the family and then taking it to bed to secure it beneath his pillow!

Meanwhile, curious passersby huddled under umbrellas or behind Ford, LaSalle and Chevrolet car dealership windows and stared at the bent old Chinaman leaning into the weather, long white whiskers plastered by the rain and wind against his chest.

Albert Li Wu followed LaSalle Street to Grand Avenue, Grand Avenue to Navy Pier. Yes! He would contact Wong. Wong's henchmen could take her in an alley. There might be a few lines in the *Tribune;* but then that would be that, he ground his teeth. Well, but wait! Hadn't he now begun to find in her something like (or *almost* like) a friend?

Oh, never mind! he shook his head. Why, it would be better to strap a concrete block to his back and jump off of Navy Pier into Lake Michigan than to be in the debt of Chicago criminals! *That* much he knew! In despair, he leaned against the cold thick metal railing at Navy Pier while Lake Michigan's grey waves below tugged and tugged at him. Well, why not jump, then and get it over with! Anyway, who would ever miss a bent, worthless old Chinaman but the Southside Chinese who barely spoke English and hid under their beds when police were in the neighborhood?

Albert Li Wu pushed on and on then, until turning, then turning again he finally met Michigan Avenue where, still cursing the old woman's filthy Irish soul, Albert Li Wu f passed under the canopy of the Blackstone Hotel. *Yes! Oh, yes! That was it*! *He would file a police report!* What? And let those *how li* cops bleat about him in taverns all over the nose-in-the-air North Side and shame his father and all Chinese men? He spat into the gutter. *Never!!!*

Four o'clock. Legs trembling violently, Albert Li Wu let himself in at his back door, sodden shoes chirping across the kitchen linoleum to the breakfast table. And there he sat in despair, the muscles in his buttocks thrumming. *My God!How could he have been such a fool, opening himself to a woman he hardly knew!!!* Why, in the twenty-seven years he had lived with K'uan Lai, he had never opened himself so, even to her?

As he flung the antique *Mah-jong* set from his life, a cold rain began at the window. And what comfort, after all, had ever come from all that "keeping of things"? Shivering, but too tire to brew tea, he peeled off his wet clothes, lit incense before the Buddha brought from China and then, teeth chattering, crawled underneath the bedcovers to lie there like a tombstone.

Well, it was within and during the darkness past midnigiht that K'uan Lai came to himin a shimmering white gown cuffed with rabbit fur, her black hair rolled and seeded with pearls; and in her right hand two green olive leaves and a stemmed lotus bud just ready to open.

Albert Li Wu startled, then waited quietly for the tilt of her chin, for the scalding look. But instead, a surprise perfume of wildflowers filled the air. "We should marry." K'uan Lai stepped from the the lazily swirling mists. "This courtship goes on too long." She stretched out her hand.

"But-- you divorced me!" Albert Li couldn't believe his ears.

Q'uan Yin held up one finger. "You thought you bought me." She held up a second finger. "I was an obedient daughter." She raised the third finger. "Both of us were young and blind!"

"Oh," he murmured, then, "you were not much taller than an a new young tree--." Like a doll, she had been--a shadow, a quiet lake. "Oh, but now," his voice softened to a whisper, "I know now that you are fire. FIRE!"

"All women are fire. Men must become tinder!" she raised her chin and her pearls gleamed. "You are thinking that if I had been this way before, you would not have gone to other women."

His eyebrows flew up.

She drew nearer. "Every wife knows. Sometimes I called you 'Stone Man' to my friends, waiting for you to become tinder or clay. All those years, waiting, keeping my place. Ah, that was *my* blindness! And you, seeing only something you thought you bought but not seeing *me*! Ah, but *today*--today I would not hold my tongue for *any man*!" And she gestured toward the mists, then.

"After I died and left this earth," she went on, "I could watch and learn. And when you put that sign in the window, the thought of another woman taking my place with you loosed my tongue and I realized that behind your stiff face you had really come to love me; and that you loved me still.! And it was then," she stroked the lotus bud, "I found that I wanted you more--even *more*-- than I had in life!"

"You want *me? NOW? --an old man?*" His face was wet.

"Yes. *MY* chosen husband!"

He swallowed, tried to find his tongue. "I-I would not go to other women again now," he stumbled, softly.

"No," K'uan Lai smiled. "Now you are tinder. Now you *choose* to be tinder."

Somehow, then, the wedding band with its circle of tiny rubies was there! And Albert Li plucked it from the air to slip over her finger she offered. And then, radiant, she reached to turn back the covers of his bed; and for the briefest of seconds before her breath was upon his neck, he saw the beauty of her naked form; and the warmth of her body stilled the shaking of his limibs then came to rest light as a butterfly upon his most private organ. And a child-like happiness bubbled up behind his breastbone. And drifting off, then, in this warm cocoon, he heard her voice again, and saying, "In the morning, call Dr. Chow. You are about to get a cold."

In the morning he had a cold. It came and went. The days came and went. One month, two months. And just so, K'uan Lai, the band of rubies upon her finger, appeared each night when sleep shut down the waking sight of Albert Li Wu, a man happy and lost in the arms of his wife!

Oh, but night after night of this pure bliss ran out, finally It just evaporated, somehow. Oh, but the memory of that ecstacy returned daytimes to set each cell ablaze in his body. It began finally to wrack him awake early to himself alone in the dark in the solitary bed, and facing the luminous hands of the clock. And disappointment would pile up inside his chest, then, like rocks to crush the air from his lungs.

Mopping up his kitchen, dragging bulging pillow slips to the laundromat where women undid hair rollers only to put them in again, impatient and angry and studying his underwear gymnastic in the dryer, he would try his own case: Well, it was fine enough to turn spiritual when he was dead; but now, *today*, he still had a body, and a life! Yes, but no proper wife to tidy up the bathroom, to set out his clean shirt and sox, to do up the dishes after a meal.

And so it was that, sun up to sun down, the silence of his house whined, prowled gnawing his bones! And he would swear, then, *swear* to withdraw from this silly nightime folly! Oh, but lugging his folded laundry home, setting canned soup ina pan on the stove, he would rescind: Really, it wasn't K'uan Lai's fault that she was stuck on the other side, now was it? That death slipped into her cold and took her away.

Just so, September stretched into October, into November.

And Albert Li Wu realized that he rarely remembered his dead wife's comings in the dark or eaerly mornings; that now there was no longer the perfumed air to breathe nor acerbic sayingin her voice to savor; but only nightly sleep thick as pea soup; and out of which, mornings, he would stagger to go to the toilet, tongue dry as sandpaper, eyelashes stuck together with the green goop of sleep.

One evening, he came the back way from delivering a cleaned older chess set and there, jammed berween the legs of the porch chair--battered and tied with string--sat the old noodle box.

Eyelids stinging, he lifted the *mah-jongg* set from its newspaper wrappings and searched for a note of apology from the house-cleaner theif.

But nothing! Well, probably the *how li* Irish was afraid he might track her down, or go to the police!

And sliding the box onto the closet shelf, he struck empty hangers with his elbow; and their plaintive cries so wrenched his insides that he ground his teeth and swore he would set the cops on that Irish woman if he ever found her!

And a week later on his way to the green grocer, didn't that black pie-pan hat and squared bulk of the woman come rocking down the street toward him from the far end of the block! And blinded by an unexplainable fear, Albert Li Wu pushed himself through the door into the elevated train station. And it was from there (and frozen to the spot) that he peered through the door's window of waved glass to see her lumber past; but then was knocked aside by two laughing teenaged girls bursting past him and onto the sidewalk.

He followed the girls outside and, hugging business buildings and specialty shops for four blocks, saw the woman disappear through the open door of the Unique Dry Cleaners. Plastered against the building and out of sight, he waited on the sidewalk until--and putting on the face of a distracted older businessman--he rushed past the open door of the establishment to see the woman there behind the counter and sorting soiled clothes for a customer.

That night, K'uan Lai appeared, an empty cook pot upon her lap and growing mound of soybean husks at her feet while her fingers opening the pods moved fast as scissors. "You follow her! Our marriage is not enough?" she hurled the words while the soybeans plinked rythmically into the pot.

Albert Li Wu's face took fire. But from force of habit, he drew his eyebrows into a frown. "If you come at night, I do not see you."

"But you see me now!" And with her long polished fingernail she slit open a pod.

"--and *you* torment me--coming, not coming. And my house echoes like a cave."

K'uan Lai leveled the peas in the pot. "You want what I cannot give now. And it is *your* body keeps us apart!"

"Well," he snapped, "maybe I should run a hose from stove to bedroom! Or they say plastic bag work good!"

But K'un Lai shelled o in silence until the last green pea fell gleaming from her fingertips, and she vanished.

Albert Li Wu awoke in a temper; but after a bit, thought he smelled pancakes baking, tea brewing. Oh, but it was only his old man's mind; for when he looked, the kitchen stood shadowed and empty. He plucked a bowl from the sink to pass under the faucet and then fan back and forth on the end of his arm until it dried a little.

As he chewed his Raisin Bran, he saw Rose Malone, could have touched her bosom and heard her belting out "Mamas, Don't Let Your Babies Grow Up To Be Cowboys", the heft of her upper arms quivering, her broad hips slipping back and forth under her housedress. He forced open his eyes; but she was still there, now piling scrambled eggs onto a plate, pressing it toward him!

No! Albert Li Wu slammed his fist onto the tabletop. *He would NOT think of her, how-li Irish!*

And so November came. Now people took to wearing scarves and gloves. And, most nights now for Albert Li, there were no dreams, but only clouds grey and close: and from which he would habitually open his eyes at six a.m. to dress and hurry to the Busy Bee to escape his empty kitchen.

One Saturday morning, he looked up from his Western omelet and there, three booths down, were the gray bun, thick Irish neck and tilted black pie-pan hat of Rose Malone! Well, and how, he scanned the room, he could have missed her absolutely stunned him! Immediately his body began to shake.

He fumbled into his wallet to throw down a five dollar bill. But instead of leaving, his feet took him directly to the booth where Rose Malone's small eyes widened as they moved floor to hard-clenched fists to his furious face.

"Why you steal from me, Irish?" Albert Li Wu hurled his words. "Where my three hundred dollar; my stamps?" Ears and chin thrust out, the greying sewing threads of his beard quivered violently.

Rose Malone, her small eyes growing ever larger, trying to rise gathered up her purse and clumsy coat, her feet paddling at the floor.

But Albert Li Wu pressed a raised palm outward. "No. *I call cops!*" He raised his voice further. "What you got to say to me, Irish?"

And she threw her hands up to let them fall loose into her lap. "Me? Why, I got nothing to say to you. What I done, I done."

"WHAT YOU DO NOT TOO NICE!," he shouted then, the outer edges of his ears bright red now, and voice so wild that the weekend manager, a thin worried-looking woman in her forties, stopped counting five-dollar bills to stare out over from the cash register.

"--and good thing you give me back my box, or I get POLICE onto you!" Shouting now, Albert Li Wu glared, crossing his arms upon his chest. "WHY YOU DO THESE THINGS?"

Rose Malone sank back to push her plate away.

"Well, YOU be a woman. YOU be sixty-seven and out of work and with no health money, no savings and roaming the streets--and the young bastards ready to drag you into an alley and open your throat for a few dollars and a hairpin." And Rose Malone paused, then, to turn to stare beyond him. "I'm sorry it had to be you," she shook her head, finally, "but I've got myself to think of."

"I give you bed, food, TV. And you lie from get-go! Not even tell real name."

Rose Malone raised her chin. "I told you my real name."

Albert Li blinked. "'Malone' your real name?"

She nodded.

"You lie to bank? Your real name not O"Neil?"

She lifted her chin higher while Albert Li Wu slowly wove his fingers in and out of his beard; then slapped the tabletop.

"You crazy woman!" he crowed. But oh!, how the deception *did* tickle him! And he leaned upon the booth, then, his chest shaking with laughter and him repeating, "*Cr-a--z-y! Craaazy woman!*"

And Rose Malone started in laughing too, then. And now it was the two of them laughing and wiping the tears from their eyes until finally she waved that he should sit down. And he slumped onto the seat while the two of them howled and howled and she wiped with the backs of her hands the tears streaming down her cheeks while he, over and over, slapped the seat. Then things would quiet until one of them would start the laughing up again. But finally he stopped abruptly. His face turned sour.

"You steal from me every month! Tell me lies!"

"Well, because I needed some sort of retirement fund, just in case," Rose Malone shut down a bit, looping her hands. "My Social Security's a pittance. And with my legs going on me, I can't work like I used to."

Three boys nearly horizontal on their bicycles bled across the window while at the same time speeding across the mirrors above the counter, jumping the interruption of the kitchen door.

Albert Li's eyes narrowed. "You have husband's pension!"

Rose Malone lifted her gaze to look him full in the face. Albert Li raised his eyebrows high, "No husband either?"

"Died of drink before he was thirty. Then my last boy friend cleaned me out, like the dirty crook he is. Got my pitiful money all tied up in fake antiques; then got busted."

"You figure you clean me out, then skip," Albert Li, angry all over again now, raised his voice and began to pull himself out of the booth. "You find foolish old Chinaman--." He was shouting now; and the manager hurried over, worry crowding her mouth. Albert Li raised his hands before she could speak. "O.k. I leave, I leave."

Against a cold wind, he boiled down Clark and up Wentworth, the rims of his ears turning to ice; but once at home (and with his rubbers off and the kettle on), he calmed down, sipping tea and dropping oil onto the grinding stone carefully to hone his carving tools, one by one. It was while wiping at the grey burr of the fairy-like metal that the thought came of Rose Malone fooling the bank; and a high happy laugh he couldn't help erupted his work. *That woman!*" he shook his head, then over and over.

Deep into the same night, K'uan Lai, wearing a tunic of Jewish design stepped through the restless drapery of his sleep, her shining black hair set free against her pale neck.

"I must tell you, I have been in another place," she cradled her arms, "very small, and with a woman holding me. More and more now I am there." She paused and dropped her eyelids. "That is why you do not remember me. I forget to come."

"You tell me we are married, then forget me," he cried out jolting upright; and not knowing if he was awake or asleep.

"You know what it is. What the priests have told us. It is all true!" And she looked at him even more deeply, then.

Albert Li Wu swallowed. K'uan Lai had begun an incarnation, a new life. "But can't you wait for me?"

She shook her head, no. "I have finished my work here."

"You trick me!" he hissed, then. "You seduce me, marry me to finish *your* work!"

"Yes. And because I wanted you as the husband of my choosing!" she replied. And the gold keystones of her dress gleamed. "Now we have no karma with one another. And what we have built between us is forever! For myself, I have learned to know my own heart, to speak my own mind. What have you learned?"

Albert Li Wu looked at his wife, the radiant spirit who had already left him, this talk trailing like the train of her dress.

"*LEARNED?*" he exploded. "*Nothing* is what I have learne!"

And he turned his face to stone, then, to withhold from her; and also to cover his terror of the dissolution he felt deep in his bowels to be at hand. "What I learn is not to love!"

"Oh no," K'uan Lai threw her head and opened her lips to let a gentle laugh tinkle forth. "You learned something else. What is it?"

But he scowled, then, and shook his head "Nothing". His brain felt as if filled with melon seeds. "Nothing, nothing!"

"The ancestors tell me we have been together before--and that perhaps we shall be together again. I hope so! I start a life; you finish a life. Together we carved a marriage. The ancestors say each person has many lives, many marriages. Perhaps we shall carve togeher again." And so saying, she folded her hands in the old gesture of respect, bowed to him, then vanished into rose light.

But for weeks on end, Albert Li Wu would think he heard her moving about the kitchen, or felt her brush against him in the bedroom. And, frustrsted, lonely and disconsolate, he would picture a plastic bag from the supermarket over his head, then. Oh, but how to stop himself, then, from ripping it open?

Some weeks later, and carrying three days' garbage out the back, he found the covered casserole with its note set upon the kitchen porch's single chair. "Mr. Wu," it read, "Here's thirty. Will give some every week 'til paid off. And for them stamps, too. And I know you could always use a good meal. R. Malone."

Albert Li Wu stripped away his jacket to sit upon the porch chair to turn the money in his hands, moved in spite of himself. Back in the kitchen, he looked at the calendar. In a week she would come again! Oh, but this was might be a *how li* trick, next time to steal his clothes, dishes or Grandfather Chang's antique clock!

Back in the house, he took a few steps toward the front room, but turned to the bedroom to throw himself upon the spread. Finding that woman's bank book had spoiled everything! Oh, and why couldn't he have just left it alone in her purse--it would have been so much better not to know! Well, but at least now he would have a little company!

He stared at the ceiling, tracing the cracks in the plaster. All his life he had been a stiff old Chinaman--and never hearing anyone's voice but his own!

And now here he was at seventy-three! And how could he change now? He threw his arm over his face. And what could K'uan Lai have done-- what magic could she have worked-- against such great spiritual forces? Well, and wouldn't they scoop him up one day, as well? He drew a deep breath, then; and something moved inside him and he let go and forgave K'uan Lai everything.

The next day, he sat listening, watching at the back door with its small window. The moment he saw Rose Malone's black hat and Irish forehead rise into the window's frame, he would fling the door open. And when, after a bit, there was the real clump of footsteps and the black hat through the window, he did just that.

"Why you spoil everything?" he barked before the woman could steady herself. "I happy, you happy. Why you not leave things alone, Irish? We get along fine until YOU mess up!"

Immediately, Rose Malone went rigid, her eyes sweeping the man's stitched face, his angry tense body right down to its closed fists. A step or two more, then, and she had set the dish upon the seat of the porch chair--and with such force that its glass cover chattered in its rim. She turned to him.

"Sure! FINE for you! HAPPY for you with that pension of yours! Me? Some new chickie comes into Zorba's and I'm out on my tail, I'll tell you! And hey, I promised myself that wasn't going to happen to me again. No, sir! And listen, Mr. Albert Li Wu, there's plenty of broken-down women like me! We're a dime a dozen! I was just trying to buy myself some protection, that's all."

Albert Li Wu shook his head hard. "No!" he roared, "You no *buy*, you *steal!--STEAL,* and build yourself up out of me!" And oh! how Albert Li Wu's eyes snapped then! But after a minute, why, he calmed down; he cocked his head. "Why you do this way? Tell me."

"Tell you what, sweet Jesus?" Rose Malone slapped her sides. "Tell you I got nothing and nobody but myself? Tell you I want to see Ireland again before I die?" And she lifted the lid of the covered dish on the counter, then, to pick in silence at the fragrant brown crust.

Well, and the way she came right back at him with that sharp tongue of hers just stirred his blood; and he smacked his palm with his fist. "*When nobody talk, nobody know what happening!* My wife, she never talk." Well, and before, when he was married, to be fair, he had never really *wanted* to know what she--or anyone else-thought! But now? Now his curiosity just ate him alive!

"You really from Ireland?" he asked, his voice softening.

She waved her hand. "Long time ago."

"You have sister there?" He pulled the kitchen stool over to sit.

"Dead now! Years ago." She popped a potato bit into her mouth, chewed, swallowed. "Malone's my married name. But *HERE, NOW?* Well, I got nobody. Just like you." And she looked at him straight on, then. "Listen, I figured here was a nice old China guy living all alone. What was he going to do with his money, leave it for the government? So I figured you'd be better off having someone to help you spend it-- someone like me, would cook good for you. I thought them things when I was at the Busy Bee and seen you through the kitchen window. So when I heard about the sign—" She flung her hands out.

Well, he looked at her a long moment; and then shook his head. "It too bad I can't trust you. I start to like you. You too big and noisy; but I like you anyway."

Working in silence, Rose Malone stripped browned potato bits from the casserole's edges, then sucked her fingers.

"A person could make a mistake and learn from it, Mr. Wu," she said finally in a low voice, and not looking up; and then shook her head. "I just couldn't sell that fancy box of yours! Would have set me up proud, too; but I just couldn't bring myself to do it."

Albert Li put the tea kettle on so that the woman would not see the feelings flood his face. He offered her an empty cup; and when she nodded, set one out for himself. On the street, someone laid upon a car horn three or four times while the late afternoon sun emerged softly through the curtains to warm the sugar bowl, the salt and pepper, the tired flowered cloth beneath them.

"If a person knew a person liked having her around, it could make a difference--" Rose Malone leaned back and, folding her arms, continued when the horn stopped, "-- in how a person behaves, I mean."

Albert Li set the teapot between them. "You not know I like you around?"

Rose Malone shook her head, "no"; sniffed, then ran her finger under her nose.

"Oh," he nodded. He lifted the teapot's lid to peer past the steam. "Not ready," he chinked the lid back into place.

"I figured anybody'd put me in the pantry and didn't want to offer no money was looking for real cheap help, that's all. Big older woman like me, what else would it be? And here I was, stuck, so I'd have to make it work. Figured I'd do you good, but get what I could for myself along the way. Thought I might even drag you off to Florida one day to warm our bones," Rose Malone laughed, then sobered. "I got greedy. I'm not proud of it."

Albert Li Wu picked up the pot, but held it without pouring.

"I get greedy, too," he said. "I want cook, housekeeper—" the blushing of his neck glowed faintly through his tan skin, "--other things, for nothing." Pouring, he glued his eyes to the spout. "I treat my wife same way."

The tea rushed out dark and heady. He filled her cup, his own; then sat to blow and sip, his eyes upon her face.

"You--" he shrugged, "comfortable where you live now?"

Rose Malone set down her cup, pushed the casserole dish off.

"Well--a few of them roaches." She shrugged. "It's what I got money for."

Albert Li nodded, amber beads of tea clinging to the grey threads of his mustache and beard as he watched Rose Malone's upper lip feel its way delicately over her cup's rim. Then the soft sucking sound; and he watched her swallow.

He took a sip from his own cup.

Say, she comes back--say, tomorrow or in a few days; and with at least *some* of the money. And say, she comes again the next week with a little more of the money and maybe a covered dish or plate of cookies. And say she tells him she'll bring more of what she owes, say, each week or every few weeks--or what they agree upon. Well, and then what harm could there be if he would, say, invite her to stay for, say, a cup of tea or a bite to eat?

The Only Thanks I Wanted

I had just spent my lunch hour getting a haircut and beard trim at "Danny's Best For Men" a few blocks down; then pulled up to the curb on Randolph near the elevated train station. I'm locking the door of my Toyota when I hear the soft click-click of his wheelchair as he comes to a stop and reaches to rap at my passenger window.

Could I give him a ride south on Michigan Avenue? he wanted to know.

I'd seen this guy back and forth piloting his "Friend of the Odd Fellows" motorized wheelchair sleet or shine from behind dark sunglasses' and wearing that stained tan windbreaker unzipped, a navy and white checked shirt underneath, a cowboy bandanna and his feet stuffed into beat-up loafers piled onto the chair's metal footrest.

One time, I saw him chase a dog into the street in the midst of relieving itself; and just as the animal began to accomplish its business, this guy lets out a ringing whoop and opens his wheelchair's motor full-blast heading straight for the startled animal at its most awkward moment.

Well, the pup heard human shrieking, saw long arms waving wildly while huge spoked wheels came spinning straight on; and he let out a yelp and, leaping high as he could, bolted straight into the street where a Yellow Cab had to swerve not to make hash of it.

Hey, to have a perfect stranger ask for a ride, now *that* was the last thing *I* ever expected! And because I was so surprised, I said, "Sure!" and opened the front passenger door, without ever thinking- how do I – what do I – he will tell me won't he -about his chair. Hey, it was only a few blocks; and on my way back to work. I could do that much for the guy!

And just let me tell you, this guy turns out to be an expert at getting quickly and comfortably into my car! And he *did* tell me what to do: "That chair'll go in your trunk. Folds in half.," he informs me briskly, then. "Careful how *you* handle it! Odd Fellows' Wives got it for me with bake sales!"

Watching from the open car door, then, (and seeming quite amused!) next he digs out a mashed-up pack of cigarettes from his shirt pocket to select one while I struggle to fold the wheelchair. "-- locks at the back; then folds forward," he finally tells me briskly, then turns his head to mutter, "Great God, it's not a puzzle!"

So, I wrestle the wheelchair into the trunk; and then, mopping my face with my breast-pocket handkerchief, I tie the handkerchief, like a flag, to a wheel of the chair, then squeeze back into the front seat.

"MICHIGAN AND MONROE," my hitchhiker tells me briskly, then exhausts his cigarette smoke into my face. "What-the-hell time is it, anyway?"

Well, I gritt my teeth and ignore his question. And, as always at such moments of moral faltering, my dear dead mother's words come full-stereo into my mind: *"Always be gracious to a stranger! And it could be Jesus His very Self askin' for yer help! And remember all that HE has done fer us!"*

Hey, by now, my awe of the guy's troubled state had pretty much evaporated. Again, I gritted my teeth; this time while my hitchhiker scrutinized his fellow citizens scurrying down the street.

"Boy!" he crowed, "Ya sure see some freaks loose these days, eh?" and turned his mirror-like sunglasses upon me like cameras "Just look at that old doll there with her orange hair and supposed-fur jacket! And thinks she's gonna turn a trick on every corner; and all she has to do is wink! Hey, and no one's gonna notice her monster BEhind--eh?" And exploding with laughter, he first wiped his nose on his sleeve, then ground out what was left of his cigarette on the interior handle of my right front door.

"There's the ashtray," I pointed dryly. My hitchhiker nodded absently, then flicked his ash on the front passenger floorboard as he turned back to the goings-on out the window.

Well, the fifteen minutes' drive to Monroe Street seemed interminable! I must have hit a red light on every corner while my coarse new friend, fingers drumming dixie on the rolled up car window, shifted from ham to ham sighing. Me? I just wished to hell I was at my crumby desk at my crumby job.

Then finally, the stone blocks of Chicago's Cultural Center loomed and passed; and I could release my pent-up breath. Only one more block to go! I cheered myself. And three minutes or so later, signaling, I eased my car over at the corner of Michigan and Monroe Streets where my hitchhiker opened his door immediately; but then closed it again.

"I haven't eaten today," he informed me.

"What?" my head spun towards him.

"I said, 'I need something to eat!' How about ten bucks?"

Well, I swear to God that I couldn't believe I'd heard him right! And because I didn't respond right away, he raised his voice further, as if I were deaf!

"*I SAID*, 'HOW ABOUT TEN BUCKS?'"

"NO!" I blared back; but then, determined not to lose my cool, dialed myself down. "Listen," I said, "I don't even know you! And besides, I don't have ten bucks. I don't have any money on me," I lied through my teeth.

Well, my hitchhiking pal scrutinized the car's front window. Then he turned to look me up and down. Then he stared out his side window a long moment.

"I'll take a check," he decided.

Hey, and that was it! I bolted from my seat, my mind somewhere behind my eyeballs raised to a boil! And without a word, I climbed out my car door and threw open the trunk so hard it swung back to bounce off of the wheels of the stowed wheelchair I was about to pull out. The lid-bounce, in turn, left long vertical streaks of black grease across my hands and the lower part of my suit jacket as I tugged his contraption onto Michigan Avenue.

Still, my false friend made no move to leave the car. Instead, he lit another cigarette and began smoking it with great intensity, flicking ashes over his legs and shoes and looking furious. Well, and you'd better believe that like lightening, I opened the door on his side of the car; then I stood aside while traffic bulleted past.

But he moved not a muscle. Instead, he sat staring straight ahead until finally he threw his nearly-finished cigarette out his window and into the gutter.

And then, his face, filled with bad feeling, seemed to be working itself like potter's into some definite form. Finally, and beckoning with his head, he indicated I should roll his wheelchair close to his open car door.

Well, I pushed the chair close as possible; then set its brake and extended my hand to offer help. Oh, and you'd better believe I was able to be patient at this moment: Bickering with him as I stood in the gutter was the last thing on earth I wanted to do!

By now, pedestrians, curiosity standing in their faces, slowed to watch this guy finally come out of my car and into his wheelchair I had parked locked next to the opened front passenger door. Because, you understand, at that point to see his back disappear as he exited down Michigan Avenue was the ONLY thanks I wanted!

Well, he strapped and locked himself into his chair, then gunned its small electric motor. I slid quickly back into the driver's seat to fit the ignition key into its slot and turn the key.

My engine roared. And then, the split second before I shifted into reverse, mixed with the rhythmic throbbing of the motor there came a great thud at the right rear of my car, while at the same time a sharp piercing scream split the air.

Well, my heart dropped right into a deep freeze!

Okay. I shut the ignition off, whipped my head around to see framed in the rear window his brown head bobbing wildly, the rhythmic bobs accompanied by long, loud, drawn-out moans that kept time with my hitchhiker's long, wild fly-out brown and grey tangled hair.

And, as if the *car* were on fire, I automatically scrambled onto the street where a woman at my right kept crying out, above the on-going well delivered pitiful moans, "*OH, ARE YOU ALL RIGHT? ARE YOU HURT? DO YOU NEED A DOCTOR?*"

And you can believe that my heart clenched like a roll of spiked fencing as I bent over him to stutter out, "Whatever on earth happened?" Well, and a crowd had materialized like magic--and in the eye of it sat *my* wheelchair man, bawling and holding his stomach, head thrown back and reflections of surrounding skyscrapers dancing drunkenly upon his mirrorlike dark lenses!

"Oh. O-H-H-H," he rocked back and forth holding his stomach like an injured pet. "SOMEBODY!!! HELP!!!"

And it was then that a woman (early forties, tasteful dark green suit, briefcase and Donna Reed hairdo) threw her arms into the air and, her face flashing fire, turned upon me struck dumb there behind the steering wheel!

"Oh! You hit this poor man--ran right into this poor helpless poor man! Too important to look around and notice anyone but yourself, I guess! Couldn't even take the time to see him trying to cross!" And righteous horror gushed from her as she pointed at me.

No!" I defended myself. "Hey, I never even moved the car!"

My--now "our"--victim stopped his rocking at that.

"Oh, *yessirree*, you did too!" he waggled an accusing finger. "And everyone saw it! Look! Here's the mark, right here on my chair!" And triumphantly,--no, *gleefully*--he pointed out a stubby set of the thinnest of bright blue lines from the car's paint upon the vertical end of one wheelchair handle. "From YOUR CAR!" he trumpeted. "Right here!" he pointed again. "Your car! *Yessiree!!*""

Reluctantly, I stepped out for a closer look. The blue paint on one wheelchair fender end was broken by a set of blue threadlike lines, each about an inch long and crossing a fresh, quarter-sized dimple in the car's left rear fender.

"From your car!" he hissed, his tongue slipping happily over his parched lips. " Yessiree-bob, *you hit me!*"

"Oh dear!" the accuser began clucking. "Someone get a doctor! Someone get an ambulance! Someone call the police!" But not one person in the small gathered crowd moved a muscle. "Wait! I'll find a policeman," she decided, then. "Oh, and will you be all right while I go for the police?" she bent tenderly to search the raised complaining face while the wailing man gathered his stomach into his arms like a flock of chicks. And he took up rocking and moaning the more.

Really, I was sure I hadn't hit him! But who was going to take my word for it; and with all these spectators buzzing like flies over a dead horse? "Ran right into the poor man, can you believe it?" a gossipy type carried on. "-- backed right over him, I guess. Too busy and important to use his rearview mirror! Well, maybe some people who can't be careful because they're *SO important* just shouldn't be allowed a license, no matter WHO they are!" a balding business type told the man next to him in a loud voice.

Well, and you can imagine that I broke into a cold sweat and wished to hell I'd given the sonofabitch the five dollars! And why in God's name had I ever even offered him a ride in the first place?

I leaned in despair upon my car's rear fender, then; and my life flashed before my eyes: Cut off financially in my early thirties, never to rise beyond a second class exterminating company; and later, no matter how hard I work, never to walk into a shining office at the top of a beautiful skyscraper and greeted by an admiring staff; but just debts unceasing hanging like a noose around my neck!

Oh, and I saw too, the courtroom, the horrified jury, my friends turning away while the police lead me to my cell until finally, in my seventies, grey-haired, grey-skinned and with a mind so dimmed as to be unable to figure the simplest math, I saw myself with a tin cup, fodder now for the streets, plucked up or struck down by bad humor or whatever natural sloth marked the day.

Well, and it was at that very moment (and like an apparition from Lourdes!) that a man in a brown business suit and muted beige tie touched my arm. Twirling a toothpick across his teeth, he offered me his business card.

"Oh God," I thought, " this creep's got ambulance chasers tailing him for their daily business!"

"Hey," the man grinned, "I saw the whole thing! You never touched him! The guy ran his wheelchair into you full blast! I hear he pulls this act all over town! Just never got to see him do it before, though. Quite a show! Here, take my card. I'm with the City Attorney's Office. Call if he--or anyone--gives you any trouble."

Oh, and the relief poured out of me!

You saw it? I didn't hit him? I shook his hand too long while he, like a big brother, patted me on the shoulder, then dissolved into the noon-hour traffic.

Well, I turned to my scamster friend, then, still busy rocking and moaning in his wheelchair at the right front wheel of my car.

"Hey, you can stop all that, now," I told him. "That guy saw you run into me! He's with the City Attorney's Office; and he's calling the police right now," I lied. "They'll be on their way any minute!" And I couldn't, I couldn't help grinning, then, like a kid stepping off his first rollercoaster ride at Riverview Park!

The well skilled scammer stared at me long. "Shit!" he said, finally.

As he dissolved into the traffic pulsing along Michigan Avenue, I started to laugh. "Well, and God speed!" I sent after him dryly in my mind as his wheelchair disappeared to a lunch hour crowd thick as cheese and bobbing along Michigan Avenue.

Annie Doesn't Mean No Harm

Walter swung his forty pounds of overweight across the community dining room, empty salad plate in one hand, spoon in the other, and heading toward one end of the horse-shoe table where the old woman with a long narrow face and steel-gray braids flattened atop her head sat ignoring her food as Nurse Rose watched.

"O.K., Annie, no dessert now, unless you eat your beans!"

This was "Nurse" Walter's voice pealing from farther down the room. It was early March in the Sacramento Valley where the sun had just disappeared behind a blanket of gray clouds heavy as rocks.

In the Golden Triangle Guest Home, a stone's throw off Interstate 80 near Vallejo, thirty-six "elderlies" on state aid faced plates of chicken slices with gravy, mashed potatoes and a fistful of canned string beans. Seventeen of the some forty oldsters remained in their wheelchairs to eat.

"Nurse" Walter, as people sometimes called him with sarcasm behind his back, was not a registered nurse but brought on to handle the heavy, bulky and awkward equipment and furniture needed by the establishment's elderly "guests". At this moment, he was scraping an old woman's mashed potatoes from her paper "meal mat" on the table's top, and then clattering plate and silverware into the bus cart.

"Hey, for just once I'd like a meal in peace!" he muttered aloud to no one in particular. "Mealtimes are the only time I get to smell something besides piss, bleach and bed pans."

Bald except for the greying black rim of hair and fluffy sideburns looping his extra-large face-forward ears, Walter Griggs, "floor assistant" to the nurses, is in his early forties and heavy-set with skin the shade of under-baked dough. Rose Stevens is one of the three registered nurses for the establishment. Griggs, a "certified professional aide", is on call mostly for "heavy work" noon to eight p.m., Monday through Friday, plus wo weekends and their over-nights per month.

Walter Griggs would tell you that Nurse Rose's keys to "La-la Land", double pay check and perky "nursey bonney" were the only differences between them; otherwise, they "slopped the same decks" three p.m. to eleven p.m.--an "easy shift" Walter called it because "all the Big Shots leave by four; and then Staff has the place to themselves."

Nurse Rose would, on the other hand, would tell you that Walter's ideas of "elder care" fell into three categories: Lifting, Pushing and Laying Down The Law. What Nurse Rose will not tell you is takes in the droop and shudder of this man's cheeks as he chews; and how he's "all appetite" in a way that both fascinates and disgusts her!

"Oh, you'd have all these old people in restraints!" she told Walter, once; "and you could get paid for watching t.v. re-runs the whole shift, then! And Annie can't help it that she doesn't eat her potatoes because they make her think of dog poop. She told me last time we had them they give her 'the willies'.

Nurse Rose, in her early thirties, has Clara Bow lips, hair peroxided and bobbed, and wears with her nurse uniform fuzzy pink slippers that slap along the corridors. Nurse Rose told a friend after her first month at Golden Triangle "and hey, this isn't Mayo or whatever! And like our helper-man Walter says, 'Old people like these can't see well enough to tell a sink from a waste basket!'"

But now, Nurse Rose knows all that to be a *gross* exaggeration. Actually, the whole Golden Triangle Nursing Home "staff" is given to such exaggeration that their work and its atmosphere seem more like something from a nineteen-forties' movies on late night t.v.

Well, and "the Nursing Business" hadn't turned out to be what Nurse Rose had expected when she graduated from the Crestwood School six years ago where she attended classes nights and Saturdays while also working near by handling the desk at the Ford dealership in Thousand Oaks. Another surprise for her, was that it turned out the patients weren't cute and spry like Nurse Rose's Gram; but instead, were poor; and some dribbled or drooled on themselves and didn't even seem to notice! And actually, it also turned out that the pay was nowhere; but like she'd told her cousin Lerna, this was "a lot better than 'ward work'. There weren't any cut-open people you had to sop and turn over. And meanwhile, she, Nurse Rose, was keeping an eye out for something private and closer to Hollywod or L.A.

When she was hired a year and a half ago, Nurse Rose had told her friend Lerna about those bedroom eyes of Walter's; about how he, at sixrteen, being tall for his age, had lied his way into the Navy; and that still to this day, he wrote to his old captain on the *Iowa!* Oh, and these many shifts later, she had seen how these last two years had crept in to ballon his belly; and that she personally had experienced his short fuse--that he really meant it that he would never pick a scrap up from the floor that he wasn't paid for!

Sometimes he had taken her in the linen closet, against the stacked bath towels, his hands so hot--just like Uncle Vinnie's that time when she was fifteen and they'd made Mama's jelly jars ring; and she had found that she could make a man's porker grow long and stiff and wet. Uncle Vinnie had begun to cry out in a funny high-pitched voice like one that crawled from her own throat as well; and while banks of invisible stars seemed to explode inside and around her. And even after she'd gotten her blouse buttoned, she'd felt that glitter settle into her very bloodstream so that--and with the least look from the right man--that same glitter would start up again, sparkling and crying out; and she, herself, helpless against it! But since then, she had learned about "right timing" and that you could always "pull the plug", if you needed to.

"You know that new night man, Ingalls?" Nurse Walter had paused to sop gravy with a chunk of bread. "He told me that Annie pissed all over her bed last night! Said she'd had a nightmare. Well, I told him that couldn't possibly be right, because with what Annie's on now, *nothing whatever* could be moving up there!" And Walter, whose own life had been both narrow and dark, orchestrated, tapping at his temple with his forefinger and loving his joke!

Under the light from the room's chandeliers, heads of hair white and sparse (if not balding) bent in silence to their meal while outside and the wind moaning, pawed its way up the long narrow platter of the Sacramento Valley towards Marysville, Chico, Redding; and further on, to snuffleing about rocks, trees and bushes burrowing into the breasts of the Trinitys.

"'Ingalls asked me, once," Walter, still unused to a job requiring a sense of delicacy, would go on to Nurse Rose (but nodding now and again at Annie or someone else like her), 'Does that old guy/gal ever say more than two words at one time?' 'Oh yeah!,' I'd say, 'I think it was five years ago; but the phone rang so I missed them.' And he'd let out a laugh, then--a kind of stuttering like a round of bullets until--and dragging air--he'd wipe his eyes, finally, with the backs of his hands. You know, that man never could get over his own wit!"

And Nurse Rose would shake her head, grin and say, "Oh, you're full of it, Walter! You weren't even here a year ago!"

And outside her job, she'd tell close friends, "That Walter! He'd never even seen a urine bag before! And I wouldn't put it past Golden Valley Careful Care to slip us someone'd been kicked off a ship or something! Oh, and the guy is STRONG! I have to give him that much! There's real iron there under all that flab! And he makes up these wild names for the 'guts', he calls them--'Paperclip', 'Brown Bomber', 'Squeaky Wheel', 'Sexy Softy'--. Answering the business phone nights, he'll pinch his nose and say, 'Go'len Valley Gut Home. What kin I do fer ya?' Hey, and he'd come to me that he couldn't WAIT to get off of that night shift! 'There's times I didn't get two hours' sleep! 'And I'm not gonna' be just sittin' here all hours, either!' he'd tell me after he'd had one or two," Walter faced the old woman, then, "and all 'cause you don't eat your plate, Annie! *Now get that chicken in your mouth!*" Then Walter would turn to Nurse Rose for suppport, saying, 'Hey, that dame must have the brain of an angleworm. And I'm no goddam baby sitter, either--not for this money! No sirree! I do my work; then I'm outta here!"

And the old woman Annie had turned her head slowly, then, to blink as though she had never seen the man addressing before--his yellow 'aide's shirt and emblem. Next, she had blinked at the woman across from her with a fleshy coin purse beneath her chin. And finally, she blinked at the woman with the purple knob above her right eye while, once again, the odor of cold chicken fat came crawling up her nostrils to reach a long finger down into her stomach to tickle it awake. And Annie would push her dinner plate to the center of the table, then; and wouldn't hear the nurse lady tell the gangster-looking waiter and room-cleaner guy, "Go and sit down, Walter, before you blow a gasket. I'll take care of this."

The sound of bedroom slippers, then; and Nurse Rose would *flap-flap-flap* over to Annie one more time.

"Okay, Annie. Right now, everybody here will get a nice dish of chocolate pudding! Oh, and I'm sorry, but not for Annie because Annie hasn't eaten her chicken, her potatoes and green beans! And *we-all* know that Annie knows that she *must* eat her plate before she can have dessert, don't we? So here, I'll help you'"

And Nurse Rose would turn to the hunched old woman frozen over her dinner plate, then, and pick up a fork. But despite the gentle approach, Annie always pulled her head away to shut her lips so forcefully against the impending fork that her long thin body, arms and hands would begin to shake.

And this particular night was no different, Nurse Rose lowered her fork "Now, just one little bite of each, ok, Annie?"

Meanwhile, Walter, moving table to table, began collecting dinner plates. Since four o'clock when he'd finished moping the wood-paneled hallways and dumped the last washed bath and kitchen towels into the steaming hamper, Walter had been looking forward to this cake with its dark drum, its smooth white top bristling with chocolate shot and crowned by a fat glistening red cherry. "Oh," Walter thought, "and Mr. Pauly is allergic to chocolate!" That meant an extra serving of desert tonight!"

Cook emerged from the kitchen drying her tan hands upon her stained white butcher's apron; and, the dinner plates cleared, she bore two steaming pots of coffee from the kitchen to begin the filling cups, herself at one end of the long looped table, Walter at the other.

Then, cups raised by trembling hands to lips old but eager, Walter picked up the knife to slice the cake, dawdling over curls of frosting left behind each cut while Nurse Rose carried the slender slices to the dinner table and, amidst the tinkle of forks like a Spring rain, a comforting silence settled deeply within the room.

"Lucky for us about Annie and Pauly," Walter was commenting around a dark mouthful when three serving staff finally seated themselves at the small staff table in the corner." Why, that kitchen never does think to include us. Sometimes *we* get any desert left-overs, if we get anything at all!"

But now, Nurse Rose paused at her own plate, her eyes sifting the room, table top to old people to floor linoleum to table top to old people again. She set her fork down.

"Annie's crying."

"Oh, for Christ's sake!" Walter waved his big hand in disgust. "Annie's a cry-baby. Five minutes after dinner she won't even remember the cake! *And don't look at her!*" he hissed to Nurse Rose. *"Looking at her is just what she wants!"*

Annie's pale angular face with its delicate web of glistening pain-filled tears was pointed direcctly toward their small staff table now.

"DO *NOT* LOOK AT HER*!!*" Walter repeated, this time. "And KEEP EATING!" he forced the words through his closed teeth. Still, Nurse Rose set down her fork. Oh, she couldn't bear to see people cry--especially old people!

"Annie can have my piece," she decided, then, and got up.

"The hell!" Walter hissed. *"OKA-A-A-Y!* And why don't you put that nursey bonney of yours on her head, too? Oh, and give her the nursey pin you got on, too!" he sneered.

Nurse Rose's eyelids flickered, then dropped while, at the big table, Annie continued to bawl and Albert emptied his fingers of his fork to leave his own slice of cake still untouched. Beverly, seated across from Albert and watching, pushed her own plate aside as well to fold her hands upon the tabletop while other guests, in perfect peace (and having heard crying before!) receded into the comfort of their sweet.

Meanwhile, Walter's eyes roamed to the marichino cherry still gleaming like a wet jewel, and beckoning from the cake on the sideboard. And it was then that Albert, white hoar-frost eyebrows knotted above his narrow nose and trembling body, appeared at the staff table, and at Walter's elbow.

"We think Annie should have cake!" the old man insisted in a voice of surprising authority.

"What?" Walter rotated his trunk, then, to draw back as if aghast with disbelief, his fork frozen over his own piece of cake.

"Beverly and me think Annie should have cake." the old man, now on trembling legs, insisted firmly.

"Well," Walter lowered his fork, "first of all, Albert, who asked *you* OR Beverly what *you* think? Oh, I get it," he sneered and drew back, "by some magic, you and Beverly are in charge now! Well, there *is NO talking at dinner, Albert!* Otherwise, *nobody* eats. Otherwise, the meals go on *forever!* Then obody eats. Then everybody gets sick! You old people get sick aand the Doc blames *us*, families blame *us*, the State blames *us!* Secondly, you *heard* Nurse Rose: *Annie is NOT* to have cake! Annie didn't eat her dinner! So f*inito!* Besides, there is no more cake!"

Albert opened his mouth, then closed it, his eyes searching back and forth. "Beverly and I think Annie should have cake!" he announced again, finally.

And Walter paused, then, as if taken aback; and then, the side of his fork but half-way through the dark slab and white frosting upon his own plate, he let his cake sit triumphant while he helped himself to a long draught of tea.

"Listen," he clinked his cup back onto the table, "*THIS* is not any of *YOUR* business, Albert! *WE* don't care what *YOU* think! *WE* are the NURSES!. *WE* know what's best! AND *YOU* GO and *SIT* in your chair!" And Walter pointed toward the horseshoe table with its burden of the wrinkled, the bald and the white-haired.

Hearing Walter's words, hearing such disrespect for these elderly and *especially* for gentle Albert, Nurse Rose felt her stomach turn; and a sudden personal authority she had neither before recognized nor called upon rose up.

"Oh!" Nurse Rose thought, and didn't that "Admiral Griggs" decide that he was always in charge of anything and everything! And yes, sometimes, (and perhaps too often out of her own laziness) she would allow 'Admiral Griggs' to do just that. Well, except for *certain* times that you just couldn't step around!

And to be honest, had she, *Nurse* Rose, felt she could have found any better path forward when she graduated eight years ago from The Crestwood School of Nursing just south of Chicago, why wouldn't she absolutely have grabbed it; and for the very reason that it automatically made her too sad, *too*--and *too sad* to be around old people--too sad for them; and sad for herself, for what her own future could/would look like? And besides, she had *never really wanted to be in charge of anyone or anything*--nursing degree or no! Well, and for a woman--one wanting to be self-sufficient and just graduated from nursing school, and now breaking in--. And well, didn't that Walter just L-O-V-E to be in charge! And didn't he just L-O-V-E to make up new rules so as to LORD it over the patients and (whenever he could get away with it!) with the help as well! And now, *at this particular moment*, the only problem was that Walter had (Nurse Rose knew well enough!) that kind of fuse that could be lit by the very least of sparks; and that his fuse could--*and certainly might* ---"blow" at any moment, and about anything!

And hadn't she, Nurse Rose, years ago learned about "forgive and forget!" (and found since, practically speaking, there was usuallly nothing else to do, anyway!) Well and so far she haad found ways to forgive Walter. Well, he had been a U.S. sailor-- Korea and all!

And at the current moment, Nurse Rose was now keeping watch (and warmly!) as the old white-haired gentleman Albert wavered across the diningoom. Eighty-seven and still with a necktie, just like her Gramps! And that Albert certainly could warm her heart, like so many of these old people did!

Meanwhile, Walter shoveled great gobs of cake and frosting into his mouth as he told her between forkfuls, "Hey, we can't give Annie cake now! Not *after* we just told her 'No'! Then every old fart in the room'll give us a fight over *whatever*! And these old ducks here have their mouths open every second minute about something, as it is!"

Walter and Nurse Rose chewed on in silence. And amidst the soft chink of china, murmurings of the old people and muffled clatter of Cook and her helper in the kitchen, darkness came on outside, the wind thrashing treetops and breaking fragile lower bushes against the windows of the dining hall causing an "OH!" or a shrinking-way gesture in deep silence from edlderly guests in their chairs.

Walter, seated at the staff table in the corner, daubed at his empty cake plate with a wet fingertip. He turned to Nurse Rose.

"You gonna want that cherry there?"

"No. It's bad enough I eat desserts at all. You can have it. I don't need the inches."

And it was while at one end of the sideboard, then, that Walter, refilling his coffee cup and about to step down to the other end of the food service table to pluck the cherry from the cake, caught in his peripheral vision the sight of a chicken-claw hand closed over a fork, the dark red cherry awobble there upon the tines.

"NO-O-O-O!" Walter spun around, steaming coffee sloshing over his fingers. *"OH! GODDAMN IT!!!* 'he bellowed again, dropped the cup clattering to the sideboard while the coffee jumped wild and scalding onto the white tablecloth from which the spreading brown liquid dripped like practice notes onto the diningroom floor. Three strides, then, and Walter was facing down the frail old woman.

"We TOLD you, 'NO cake', Annie! NO CAKE!" And he closed his fingers over her ancient sculpted wristbone to force the burdened fork away from the old woman's mouth, Annie first letting loose a long plaintive cry, but then halting it abruptly as her tongue, pale pink and cracked along its edges, stretched after the bit of cake while the fragrance of its dark chocolate filled the air.

"NO!" Walter's voice split the air. "NO CAKE, ANNIE!" And he grasped the old woman's wrist to shake it hard so that the dark morsel lept from the ends of the tines and into the air to fall to the table's top where it bounced hard scattering dark bits over the white cloth, then rolling to the table's edge to plummet off and explode upon the hardwood floor below.

"WALTER!" Nurse Rose called out as her eyes flew to the small old woman seated next to Albert and nearly hidden now behind the standing Walter's broad backside while the startled, Walter threw his fist down upon the tabletop so hard his empty cup rattled, slopping coffee onto its saucer.

"AND YOU LEAVE HER HAVE THAT!" Albert was shouting then, half-risen from his chair. "THAT CAKE IS HERS; AND YOU LEAVE HER HAVE THAT, YOU BIG BULLY!"

And at this, at first, Walter froze as if an ice-cold wind had blown water over his naked body; but then spun back, a yellow light breaking over his face.

"O-H-H-H!. And this is *YOUR* piece of cake, isn't it, Albert.? *YOU'RE* the TROUBLEMAKER here, eh? Well, OKAY, then! NOW *NOBODY GETS CAKE! AND I HAVE TO TAKE HIS CAKE FROM ALBERT, NOW, TOO.!"* Walter carried on, while the old woman in front of him whimpered, the end of one grey braid standing atop her head and waving like a warning signal upon the high seas.

"And Albert shouldn't have stuck his nose in where it doesn't belong, should he now, Annie?" Walter carried on, unabated. "One of these days, Albert just might lose his *nosey* nose, sticking it where it doesn't belong--eh?"

And Walter plied phantom scissors then, snipping close between Albert's thin old nostrils and sprouting chin.

And it was then the ever-silent Beverly rose up; and staring hard at Walter from beneath the purple knob over the left eyebrow of her farm-wife face, she shoved her own cake plate out in front of Annie and declared, huffing in her scratchy voice, "Well, if Annie can't have cake, then I don't want mine neither!"

"Oh?" Walter raised his chin high; and then, sighting the old woman along his nose, called out, "Well, what do we have here, now? A mutiny?" And he reached across the table to push Beverly's cake plate back in front of her.

"Well, and I can give her mine if I want to!" Albert raised his eroded face to carry on. "Besides, you don't have any right to pick at her like you do—you and that other one. Why, Annie doesn't mean no harm! But you two just pick her down to nothing! You're a *BULLY*, that's what you are-- just a BIG BULLIES, the two of you!"

"And we're just sick to death of it, too!" Beverly joined in then from under her braided steel-grey hair and weathered face. She pushed her own dessert plate in front of Annie as well, then. "Here, Annie," she said, "You have my cake, too!"

And how Nurse Walter glowered, then, his balding head starting to sweat. "Hey, don't you get in on this too, Beverly," he warned, and shaking his finger, "'cause *you* just might be next!"

"--and it's not like Annie's the only one, either, "Albert clambered on anyway, his head trembling above his purple tie. "It's always *SOMEBODY* does *SOMETHING* gets your back up! But more'n anyone, it's Annie. And Annie hasn't done one bad thing yet!"

The guests around the old man, eyes being riveted to their own dessert plates now, chewed on in silence. But some laid down their forks. And here and there, an elderly "guest" reached for a sugar or a sip of tea so as to shoot a guarded look at Nurse Walter, his belly straining against his white medical aide's jacket and towering above Albert 's age-shrunken head and shoulders. And under this back and forth of talk, Annie's fingers stole toward her cake plate.

"Oh, I'm a bully, am I? I pick on Annie, do I?" Walter backed off, blowing his chest out. "And if *you* KNOW *so much*, Albert," he sidled back, "how come no one *ever* asks *YOU* for advice? And maybe it's because you have to take pills five times a day to remember how to knot your tie." And Walter reached over to flip albert's necktie's ends into Albert's face; and then turned smartly upon his heel toward the sideboard to claim the cake's cherry; and was just lifting the cherry by its stem toward his opened mouth when, in his peripheral vision, he caught sight of a fork near the chin of the old woman Annie's mouth! And Walter spun around, his face black with rage.

"*N-O-O-O-O-O!*" he thundered then across the floor while the dining hall slid into a rigid silence. "And how many times am I going to have to say it, God damn it! How many times?" he bellowed standing behind Annie's chair and dwarfing the old woman's thin shoulders, narrow head, parted hair, pink scalp and wiry steel-grey braids. And Walter drew his arm back, then; and with an open palm, slapped the old woman's fork and morsel of cake to hell-and-gone.

The fork chimed thinly against the dining room wall while the bit of cake shot across the dining table barely missing Virginia (now nearing ninety-three)m to speed on, bounce off a wall and shatter upon the floor beneath.

Annie, her mouth open and forearms protecting her face, stumbled to her feet while Nurse Rose, whose eyes suddenly grew to the size of half dollars, bolted from the staff table to assist the astonished and now deeply disturbed elderlies. Oh, but it was Albert who sounded their call, then, directing the words to Walter.

YOU PIG!!!" Albert clambered from his chair, red-faced and shaking, his legs pumping like someone walking in sand. His right hand gripped a wobbling cane while Annie now having slid to one knee, buried her face in her chair's woven back while Walter boomed over the old woman's shrunken head and shoulders, "--and when are you ever going to listen to me, old woman? When are you ever going to do what you're told?"

"Hey!" Albert stepped forward, "You just shut up and leave her be!. "And haven't you done enough already, you Gutter Filth?"

And the guests at the long dinner table saw Albert's white hair was standing up and out like snowy thistle; then saw him draw the oak cane from behind his shoulder, and then straighten his elbows. They saw his black walking stick plunge downward through the air to land with a muffled "thwack!" straight across at Walter's lower spine.

"*WHAT?*" Walter turned sharply, searching at his backside with his hand while Albert staggered away a second time to lift the cane like a batter at the plate

"Hey! Now you just God-damned better give me that, you old fool!" Walter cursed. Then Walter, his eyes grown big, grasped the end of the cane while eighty-something Albert locked his forearms, elbows and shoulders.

Walter yanked more sharply the second time to see Albert's torso twist and the old man's feet leaveing the floor, cane in one hand, raised cake plate in the other. They saw the bony nose-ridge of the old man's face tilt, plunge forward and bounce against the thick carved wooden edge of the dinner table, his body follow it to the floor while Nurse Rose, her shoulder propped under Annie's armpit, took in the sound of the old man's head cracking like a hard-boiled egg meeting the linolium followed by the sickening thuds of the old man's arms and legs piling up next upon the floor.

"Albert!" Nurse Rose cried out, then. "Oh, Albert!"

And along the horseshoe table, the elderly guests sucked long horrified breath through their open mouths; and after notched moments of silence-- silence still as death--heard Albert's cane clatter after him to the floor and leave its ghostly echo in the air.

And the old people saw Walter's face register shock, and then close. And they saw Walter look upward at the bottom of the plate he'd raised upon his palm and above his head--saw him turn, then, and heave that plate hard and high over the bus cart where it turned upon its side and exploded against the wall to create a wide star of darkness and light to hang a long moment before sliding onto the floor, a concert of nerve-shattering splintering and clattering.

It was from the small oval window on the kitchen door that Cook's startled eyes appeared, then disappeared. And after a few moments, there came the muffled slam of the kitchen's back door. And they looked at Albert to see the scalp beneath the shocks of the old man's white hair turned a parchment color; and a deep dark stain spreading across the front of his trousers.

Walter rushed past Nurse Rose, hissing, "Get a medic! Get a doc! Quick!"

Then sounds of crying took up among the residents.

Nurse Rose planted Annie firmly in a chair before she turned on tiptoe to peer at Albert whose eyes were still closed while blood trickled from his nose. "Oh God, no!" Nurse Rose begged silently. "PLEASE, NO!!!" Wildly she searched her mind: The procedure. What was the right procedure? Oh, *"When a victim is injured, don't move anything. Always support the head!"* And this was all Nurse Rose could drag at the moment from years of training she was still paying off!

She folded her sweater for a pillow, then; and felt, trying to move him just a little, now, how Albert's neck was *loose*, like a chicken's! His scalp was warm; but no movement from his chest! *Oh please let him be alive!* she prayed, then, to Whoever had power over life and death. And she searched the old man's wrist for a pulse. it was then Cook ushered into the room the police she had called.

And at the sight of the uniforms, crying erupted amongst the women guests, while through the dining room's main door there emerged a black male--an Officer Foucalt--and a white female, an Officer Maloney who saw a nurse upon her knees and searching the wrist of an old man stretched out upon the floor. As both stepped carefully toward her, Officer Foucalt felt bits of dishware grind underfoot, and then noticed the strong smell of urine. And Nurse Rose looked up as well just then to see these visitors who sent her eyes to bulging and mind screaming out, *"POLICE! Oh God, the police!"*

Officer Foucalt squatted to take in the victim. "Older man. *blood at the nose,"* he scribbled on a small pad; and then turned to ask the woman attendant, a Nurse Rose, "How long?" nodding towad the crumpled body.

"Not long. Ten or fifteen minutes" *Oh, don't let Albert be dead!*

"Your cook told 911 she heard a gunshot."

Nurse Rose shook her head. "We dropped a dish," she told them, fear, sudden, powerful and cold, cluttering her windpipe.

Above the bus cart, a hunk of chocolate cake clung crazily to the wall. Officer Maloney nudged the shards of dinnerware she'd felt underfoot. Officer Foucalt peeled his hat from his head, knelt and laid his ear to the victim's chest, then pinched the old man's nose and fitted his mouth over those loose lips to heave air once, twice, three times, four times while

"Come on! Come on Pops!" he'd beg quietly through his teeth. Five times. Six times. Nurse Rose had climbed to her feet, wringing her hands; and by then, a small dining room crowd had gathered, each person keeping a respectful distance.

Old Annie tottered up.

"Over here, doctor!" Officer Maloney called out just then; and a silver-haired black physician with spectacles hurried across the room, unsnapping his medical bag. Two aides appeared behind him with a stretcher. And at the sight of the medical team, a murmur like the warning of a storm approaching rose and fell among the oldsters.

"Doctor Jordan here! You the officer called? Lucky you caught me in my car."

Doctor Jordan listened with a stethoscope, thumbed Albert's eyelids, shone a penlight into his pupils, checked his wrist pulse, pressed with his index finger the victim's fingernails.

"Bring the oxygen," he commanded then, and sat back upon his heels while an aide hustled off. Drawing a pocket phone from his uniform, Dr. Jordan looked around. "Where's the nurse here?" And Nurse Rose raised her hand. "I'll need to look at everyone in the room. Please stay close, M'am."

"Yes, Sir." Nurse Rose's heart banged, banged against her ribs.

"All right," Officer Maloney picked up the cue, stepping out toward the old ones struggling onto their feet and craning their necks. "They're taking care of the gentleman now. Please, all sit down; the doctor will want to examine each of you presently."

Reluctant, the onlookers shuffled back to sit at the big table, heads in their hands or eyes riveted to the medical bag, the physician, the aides; and then back again to the prone form.

Officer Foucalt sauntered over to the burly guy in the white lab coat shielding his face with his hand. "Are you a nurse or what?"

Walter shook his head. "Oh no, sir! Not me! I'm just an aide--a worker here."

"Well, you want to tell me what happened, then?" The officer dug into his shirt pocket for a small pad and a pen.

Walter's eyes slid sideways first to Nurse Rose, then to the doctor, then across the room. "Hey, the old guy just went nuts. Started beating on me with his cane!"

"This old man started hitting you? And for no reason?"

Walter leaned to the officer. "Listen, you don't know what it's like here. Half of these old geezers are loonier than hell! And you never know what shit one of 'em's gonna pull!"

Officer Foucalt wrote something on his pad, then. "Yeah? Well what about these broken dishes? This old guy throw dishes and food all the way up there on the wall like that?" And he pointed with his pad to above the bus cart.

Old Beverly tottered up, then, purple forehead knob and moley chin jutted out. "You know what, you're a for-real sonofabitch; that's what you are, Walter!" And she tightened her lips to show her teeth in menace. "This guy here--he pulled Albert down, Officer! Pulled him right down! And picks on everybody, he does. Thinks he's King of the place."

"Oh, and is that so, m'am?" Officer Foucalt turned his big shoulders and tipped his cap. "Now, I'm going to get right to you, m'am. So please sit down 'til then. And I'll want to hear everything! And everything from everyone here, so we get the whole story!"

Officer Foucalt watched her baked potato shape move back to the horseshoe table before stepping across the room to Nurse Rose where the two of them spoke, then, the officer nodding toward Walter. And after a moment, Nurse Rose strode across the room to where Walter sat, his head buried in his hands. And the officer followed her, writing upon his pad.

"Oh for Christ's sake! Everyone saw it, Walter." And Nurse Rose swept her hand out wide to indicate the room.

Yes. The old people saw it. They saw it all. And they would tell everything, starting with Annie and the potatoes, with the chicken, and then with herself, the nurse; and then with the cake. The old people would tell about Walter yelling, and then smacking away the fork. And the police would go on to "day-in, day-out" with their questions, then. And at first it would be like pebbles coming loose; but then--and soon enough--the whole face of the mountain would shudder and slide away!

Walter jutted his chin out at Nurse Rose; then rolled his head, snarling while he piled his fists into his waist. "Well, you were the one told Annie she couldn't have cake, Nurse Rose! And that's what started this whole bloody mess!"

Officer Foucalt raised his hand. "Hold on there," he said; "I can see there's lots to talk about. Where's the manager? Who's in charge?"

"She is," Walter pointed with his thumb; "She's the nurse right now; everybody else leaves for the night except for the cook and regular "overnights" who come on later, just before bedtime."

And she, "Nurse Rose", could feel the policeman's perusal, then-- his deliberative inventory: Chipped nail polish, run stockings, shoe toes scuffed of their white, slip showing below her uniform's skirt.

"Okay, Miss. You go and help the doctor," Officer Foucalt told her, then. "And you," he turned to Walter, "get the manager and owners on the telephone. And *pronto*! Then come find me when you have them!"

Walter swallowed. He stepped aside for the oxygen tank squeaking over the floor. Doctor Jordan fitted the hospital's gray mask over Albert's nose and nodded. The attendant turned a knob. A red needle in a small round window appeared and trembled upward.

"Good. Fine. That's fine, now."

He held the mask in place on Albert's face for a slow count of twenty; then he turned to the aides, raising his voice. "See that the gentleman continues oxygen in the ambulance. And I'll meet you at Emergency soon as I finish here."

"But just a minute, doctor," Officer Foucalt elbowed his way in, then hitched his pants. "There are procedural matters —*police* matters before you can remove the— "

Dr. Jordan held up his hand, eyes snapping behind his lenses.

"Listen, Officer," he tilted his head and lowered his voice, "I know all about your 'procedures'. The question is this: 'Did this man die as a result of head injuries sustained in a fall here, or did he die in the ambulance of such injury? Oxygen or no oxygen, the man *will be dead* when he gets to the hospital." He gestured around the room. "Now, how much more trauma do you want to be responsible for; because I cannot guarantee what will happen if these old people learn that their friend has just died. And neither can I promise that no old person's will have heart failure at such news."

Officer Foucalt took in the elderly huddled at their dinner places. He peered at his policemen awaiting his orders, at Albert so deathly pale.And rubbing his thumbs back and forth over the tips of his fingers, he nodded, finally; and then turned toward the oldsters to address them in a respectful and softened tone.

"Ladies and gentleman, I am Officer Foucalt. And we will want to check each one of you. We are sending for a doctor. Until he is available, this officer here, Officer—," he looked around for the policewoman.

"Maloney," she raised her hand for everyone to see.

"Our Officer Maloney and our other officer, Officer Bryant, will help you to your rooms. Also, more staff to assist will be here any minute. So please rest quietly in your chairs, meanwhile."

Then, as he folded his jacket upon the staff dinner table, then unbuttoned his shirt cuffs, the "aides" (a few police and cleaning staff) stepped in to lift the body.

Albert's head lolled to the right; his thin arms flopped open.

"Please excuse us," one of the aides stepped around Annie as they moved in to lift the stretcher.

Annie made no reply; but walking quickly as she could, her white hair sticking out from its two bands of pinned-up braids, she clutched one side of the stretcher, seeing it out the dining hall door and across the foyer to the front entrance where the bearer at the head pushed the doors open with his shoulder while the bearer at the rear let the doors swing shut behind him. Lifting the body into the ambulance, the wind gusted suddenly and sent the sheets covering Albert so to snapping that the two ambulence staff had to reach down and tie the corners to the frame of the carrier.

And all this time, Annie stood watching at the door, her gnarled fingertips flattening tears against its glass pane while thunder murmured from afar. And Nurse Rose, assisting the doctor, kept an eye out on Annie, one grey braidend raving, as the old woman limped back across the foyer and to the dinner table.

The day Walter Griggs ambled into the Golden Valley Guest Home, she, Nurse Rose Stevens, had felt catastrophe ride in with him; but she didn't know how or what to name the feeling then.

"So, you're the nurse?" he had asked, taking up her hands so as to hold onto her palms with his thumbs so hot; and while with his lush dark lashes and liquid eyes (Those eyes with something barbed afloat in them) he had gripped her face. And the dream that men carry festering beneath their skin had pierced her, the young nurse, then too; and she knew that somehow she would be in that man's bed--be there perhaps many times, and robbed of the will to awaken herself from his spell.

And then a great cold tidal wave of fear with its bite as of sand had dragged through her body; and that urge, like tiny snails let loose to crawl her veins while at the same time something like narrow darting fish with razor-sharp fins streamed through her throat, through stomach and her eyes.

Then Doctor Jordan handed her the stethoscope; and she fitted its cold nubs into her ears.

Soon, she knew, the owners of the nursing home would come. They would ask her, Rose Stevens, *Nurse* Rose *the professional*, just why she had never reported Walter's behavior--reported his explosive temper, his scorn of their elderly guests? And Albert's death would be *her* fault, then! And she could not really say such a judgment was wrong because somebody like her, so clouded and easily controled--someone who had never really wanted to be in charge of others' lives, but hadn't the courage to say so, nor the courage to reject any favors that came her way; but might cost her dearly, later. And she saw clearly now how--even from her teenaged years--that the poison of "need" had trailed her even to this day; and to strike Albert down--sweet thoughtful Albert who always wore a tie and never hurt anyone, not even with a joke!

Nurse Rose followed the doctor, then from oldster to oldster, while the antique voices moved about them, surrounding them like many waters, murmuring and murmuring the grief embedded in the history of growing.

And she saw, too, that Walter would go down. Walter would go to jail, would drown in what he could not control. And she saw that she herself must be the one to open her mouth and send him to those deep waters!

And this not because she had the courage to make right the wrong that was hers. No. Walter would go down because of the old people. Those eyes and ears he had thought so blind and deaf would reach out with suddenly sharp edges to cut the tangled fishingline, that nearly invisible line (she understood now) that cost women, that snatched away their most precious power and fruitful years; and that cost men their nobility, their honor and right to self-esteem!

And she, Nurse Rose, saw now that tether that had held her to Walter, and to men like Walter. She saw how the righteousness of womens' faces, of their voices, would float above her, first high, but then, as the years went on, would fall in a wobbling circle to bring her, too, to her knees and bring her down to go jail where someone would clang shut that door of iron and steel so that she might never again hurt another human being!

And mighty indeed would be the long pitiful cry of those metal hinges, the snapping into place of the steel locks so as to continue the pruning away of that pitiless glitter which, like a mid-summer thunderstorm, could, for anyone and at any moment, turn anything or everything into insignificance.

And she prayed--*PRAYED*--to whatever God there might be, that this might restore to her a life in which she would *never again* dishonor *any* human being, either by thoughtless or selfish acts or by the clever accepted masquerade of hollow custom.

And to this, she dedicated herself.

Mama's Boy

Hanging from a branching floorlamp, the monkey peers across a room filled with shadows and tired furniture to the woman hugely fat and resting upon a couch. Just now, she is talking into the telephone.

"No! And that's final," the woman Mama Louise barks. "And listen, buster, *you've had all day to find me!* Now, Mama Louise is 'quit', 'finished', 'in' for the night'! Ya got that?"

So saying, she bangs the receiver back onto the cradle of the worn twenty year-old instruent set upon the lamp's sidetable. And leaning over the two bulging bags of groceries she's let slide to the floor, Mama Louise chops the air with her hand, continuing.

"--and hey, I damned near break my neck getting to this telephone; and then it's *your* sorry ass again!"

And inished, Mama Louise drops the instrument onto its cradle while turning to rattle her hand into a small cellophane bag of small round milk chocolate candies. She pops one, one more, into her mouth. "Mmmm!" grindsing the sweet, she cocks her head.

"--and how is my Sweetness today?" she coos, sucking the ends of her fingers clean and then, drying them on the underside of the hem of her long skirt, shakes a cigarette from the pack half-empty upon the coffee table. She lights up, draws deep and throws her head back as the exhaled smoke jets toward the ceiling, strikes it and feathers lazily outward like the clouds of late Autumn.

The monkey has a caramel-color face and dark brown mask set with large wet black eyes, a short narrow nose and deceptively small-looking mouth housing teeth, tiny and very white and very sharp.

Now the monkey selects a cigarette butt and tucks it deep into the trench at the base of its lower lip as Mama Louise, comfortable upon the couch, stretches out her arms and calls, "Sweetness, come here! Come to Mama, now, baby!"

And the monkey freezes, fixes its eyes upon her, and then in one sudden leap covers a quarter of the room and lands whisper-soft upon the mound of the woman's over-flowing bosom. It winds its long thin hairy arms about her neck, so soft, pink and fleshy, then; and while Mama Louise pulls her head back to purse her lips to make long tisking sounds.

"And who is it ate all the pretty nummies, and didn't even leave *one* for Mama Louise?" she pets the animal, her voice soft and personal. And its large eyes alert and searching, the small animal studies the movements of the woman's lips; and then watches while Mama Louise stumps out her cigarette to one arm of the couch and then lurch to her feet.

"Oh, but don't you worry now, my Sweetness," she goes on to coo. "We've lots more nummies--oh, *plenty* of nummies for my Sweetness!"

And Mama Louise picks up the grocery sacks to move sideways through the kitchen door, the monkey riding her shoulder now as she moves into the kitchen where a food scraps frame a blue china plate set upon the floor along with a dented yellow nursing bottle left fallen onto its side. The room carries a sharp animal scent.

"Oh!" Mama Louise throws out her hands, "and now my Sweetness made a mess again! Well, I swear I don't know how such a PRETTY BOY can be SO messy! And just look at this!" she gestures with a despairing open palm while the animal skips to the top of the refrigerator to squat and scratch under its arm as it peers down.

"And you didn't use your poopie box again, like you promised!" Mama Louise continues, and tisking now. "Poopies go IN THE BOX!. Your Mama can't be cleaning up Baby's poopies all day long!" And she drops the sausage-shaped clumps into an overflowing garbage container set on the floor and next to a low-sided wooden box filled with sand. "Now, baby *knows* he has to be neat, here--just like is Mama is!" and she shakes her finger, small bright eyes in the mass of her flesh dancing with humor and affection.

Outside, the rain starts up again to pock-pock at the windows' glass while unwashed dishes teeter, piled into the sink. Ahd at the breakfast table, a dark purple sweater hangs from the back of a wooden chair while a foot above the stove, a "My Homemaker" clock --one arm a wooden spoon, the other a four-pronged fork, clucks on. And the kitchen telephone jangles, then.

At the sound, the monkey jumps through the doorway onto the living room couch, next onto the coffee table and then, finally, to the top of the television to rummage with long lumpy fingers amongst the ashes and cigarette butts in the partly-filled glass ashtray.

"Hey, I already told you *NOT TONIGHT!* Are you *DEAF or what?*" Mama Louise bellows into the telephone, then listens, listens. Her voice steely, she finally speaks again.

"Hey, and it's just too damned bad you just can't find the scratch, now, isn't it?" Mama Louise, stacking boxes of Ritz crackers and canned goods, goes on. "And hey," she raises her voice further, impatient, now, "NO! No YOU listen to *me*, buddy: You use, you hurt. Goes with the gig. You ask for it, you get it. Dig?" And she bobbles green grapes into the sink. "And hey, Junkie, I'm no charity here. And even if you HAD the cash, I wouldn't sell to you now--not with *your* mouth! I got my dinner and tv waiting. And hey! you can't find anybody else--well, I just won't be cryin' over *your* problem, y'a know? You use, you get what you get. Dig?" And Mama Louise starts to hang up, but "Oh? Yeah?" her voice hardens, then. "Hey, I got me a few things I could wish on you, too, Buster; and got me a few friends'd be proud to deliver for me, too! Dig? So better look after your own pecker 'fore you think you're man enough to stick a knife into this woman! And listen, you just ask *anybody anywhere* in this neighborhood 'bout Mama Lousie--Is she somebody to tangle with!" And she slams the receiver onto its cradle and heads into the kitchen.

"Let the hustler get somebody else out of bed for his stuff--" she snarls into the open cross-top freezer, then, "and soon enough that narc'll come crawling to me on his belly lookin' for some deal--or with a wad from some old woman he's just hammered."

She rattles raw potatoes and onions into the vegetable hopper, throws the empty sack into the garbage, then spins around. "And now where did my Sweetness go?"

In the next room, the living room, the monkey, atop the worn television console, with its thin fingers blindly searchs its stomach hairs while it eyes the enormous woman as she bangs the telephone receiver into its cradle.

"Oh dear, and your Mama had to go and yell at that stupid sonofabitch, now, didn't she? And we hate slime-balls like him, don't we!" She sets a plate of butternut cookies and can of pop upon the side table; then drops with a grunt onto the couch. "Kissy, kissy. Come to Mama, Sweetness!" she calls, then opening her can of Cocoa Cola.

And the monkey jumps to the floor, then onto her huge breasts.

"Oh, and did Baby miss me?" she reaches up to turn the knob on the floorlamp to let warm mellow light flood the room.

The monkey's lips are black and thin like the bottom seam of a purse. And now it fits them over a roll of fat on Mama Louise's neck to begin sucking with soft, wet sounds while Mama Louise lays a long polished fingernail atop the monkey's small head slowly to trace the curves of its skull, when suddenly the window shade next to the couch clatters itself upward.

Mama Louise startles, then stares at the wildly dancing pull-ring. By now, on the outside of the window, pane is thick with frost. And Mama Louise leans back to laugh, deep and throaty, Oh, that loud old shade, again! Always giveing us a fright, isn't it?"

And calmed, the monkey winds its fingers through the woman's hair to study bright lights appearing and disappearing upon its strands. And then it slides its paws behind her neck to return to sucking there, working in deep earnest now that the jolt of fear and "emergency" has disappeared.

"Oh, and there's a good boy--a *good* boy!" Mama Louise murmurs, combing her fingertips through the short silky hair of the monkey's head, and then softly running a forefinfer down the boney ladder of its spine. "And everything's all right, now. Everything's all right, now, she reassures the pet, "and for our nap."

And she reaches for the squared white buttons on her navy dress, working at them one-handed until the front panel falls away to reveal the peaches and cream of her breasts in the lamplight.

"Here, my sweetheart," she calls softly, "your Mama has something for you!" And she fetches out one breast to slide a forefinger between the monkey's black leathery lips to break their suction while the pet screeches with impatience.

"Now, now," she soothes gently. "Can't wait. Mama's boy can't wait."

And the monkey, its dark lips moving rhythmically, glittering eyes are glued to the fingertip, to its long pointed nail of cherry-red.

"There. Now your Mama has something for you," Mama Louise whispers, finally; and putting her fingers behind the monkey's small brown head, urges its face forward until it takes the nipple with a soft grunting sound, stretching its long arms and sable streamers across the mass of Mama Louise's bosom, its legs and tail curled onto the rise and fall of the woman's warm belly.

And Mama Louise releases a deep sigh, closing her eyes as she feels for the monkey's head to begin to trace rythmically over and over with her polished pink forefinger the geography of its small warm fuzz-covered skull. And "That's right," she whispers; "Mama's boy. Mama's boy. That's right."

And so, cradled in the crook of her arm and with her head thrown back and copper hair fanned out over her shoulders, Mama Louise and the monkey doze while the Micky Mouse clock above the couch points out (with a soft cluck and its pointing white-gloved finger) the ever-passing minutes of the afternoon.

It is perhaps an hour later that the half-full bottle of Jack Daniels whiskey arcs upwards, then downwards and hurtling with a loud shattering *boom* through the closed unprotected side-window of Mama Louise's livingroom followed by a sound like many tiny bells ringing out high and all in one long voice.

And the monkey screams, digging its toenails deep into the woman's arm supporting it; then leaps away as Mama Louise jerks her head upright as the hurtling empty whiskey bottle turns end over end to strike the wall opposite, and shatter into a sudden shower like glittering ice, but with mixed odors as of whiskey and gasoline.

Immediately, and with a loud *whooshing* sound, fire blooms to paint the floor, window's wall and the ceiling with path light-yellow and red with bits of bright blue while grey smoke, billowing first with a loud *whoosh* of air, then with the loud flapping of emerging flames of red, yellow and pinpoints of blue while from the heart of this blossoming display springs gargantuan light, white-hot and blooming a great red, white and yellow-petaled flower whose firey tongues lick upward, upward, then along the ceiling where they melt into one another, crackling, and stabs of white light, with petal tips smoking crawl on across to the hallway ceiling before climbing into the kitche an, then drop only to scale the paneled front hallway door.

And the huge brightness is everywhere now, and scorching the air and older woman's bosom as she digs herself backwards into the couch in the front room. A sheet of red rattles up the walls to leave a fluffy grey-brown waste pulsing further and further onward. And the monkey, eyes bulging and tiny teeth gleaming in its wide-open mouth, shoots through the dense plug in a high arc towards the open kitchen door.

Mama Louise sees it all as if in slow motion: the red wink of flame upon the monkey's head, the monkey tail frozen in an elegant concave arc, delicate nub of each monkey curved toe now stretched to its limit, banners of long sable fur feathering beneath the thin desperately grasping arms and atop small brown ears the winking beads of flame, the waving fringes of smoke trailing, trailing on.

"Oh Sweetness!" Mama Louise lunges to her feet. "Baby, baby! Come here!" she cries as the monkey swings outward from the kitchen doorway; and then, as if felled by a bullet, crumples midair to drop first onto an arm of the couch and from there to the floor while from beneath the small body, liquid hysterical red fingers of flame crawl out, then up and onto the small parchment-color belly with its delicate covering of new belly hairs.

"No! No!" she presses the heel of her hand against each red tongue as it leaps from the monkey's stilled body, absorbing an excruciating music that shoots inward through her hand, then her belly, then into her groin as she cries at the tongues of fire, "Get off my baby!" and pressing the heel of her hand down on the little corpse until the last dancing tongue shrinks to to leave behind from that smoke so hot and dinse naught but wavering black globs with threads of monkey hair and skin from those red dancing tongues, so small and evil!

Then, and hugging the burned monkey to her bosom, Mama Louise, her legs and feet shaking beneath her, pivots through the dense grey smoke, knocking against corners of furniture until her fingers strike the farther wall to feel their way over its scorching face. And "God-damn-it, where is the door!" her mind hisses.

But finally, FINALLY, she stumbles into the pinch of a corner as the TV explodes with a burst of brilliant light and sound that punches Mama Louise back again so that her knees desert her and she slides to the floor, the dead monkey rolling down and off of her legs.

Mama Louise's bosom heaves as she draws in one tiny breath after another, straining the scorching air through her teeth. Oh, the bright burning is everywhere; and, high-pitched and pitiful, comes now a wailing dreadful and lost; and that might be her own voice.

About That Dinner At The Smith's

There was a pause in the conversation, then.

So we women sipped our tea and listened to the grandfather clock cross-stitch the afternoon--six of us women in the "big room" of Miss Pearly Luke's old farmhouse. A Sunday afternoon of digesting cheese balls, celery sticks, and curdle dip. And the newest stories of babies, engagements, graduations, divorces, major and minor surgeries, automobile troubles, bankruptcies, needlework traumas and deaths!

Then, it was Edith Atkins who opened her mouth from over her square of homespun where we all sat. The quilt we worked joining us like an ocean does shores as we plied our sewing needles and opened our ears

"Well, I've brought a sewing story for the pot today," Edith Atkins announced to us, threading her needle. Well, everyone's ears perked right up!

In her sixties, Edith was still working for that same local trucking firm "Gary's Carry Your Load". And I figure that she'd been quilting with us going on three years now, ever since she first came to New Harmony from "her exile on the west coast" (was how I remember she put it!) Her citified grey striped hair, fancy eye-glasses, and fingers with polished nails pulling the needle steady as your pulse! And Edith always brought along her home-made apple curdle dip.

Edith's first year out here "in the boonies" (as foreigners call it), we discovered there'd been a divorce; and that New Harmony was the third place Edith had tried to make "home". Yes, she had a child still living there now, she'd reply and then slide into a long silence. Well, we didn't ever inquire further but just let her be, you know?

Her second year, meeting and sewing with us, Edith broke down about her boss with his under-the-table financial dealings while he scrambled from the attention of government officials--and all this witnessed from her tiny office on the second floor of that crumbling government building on Pearl Street. But this year, for the first time, she added the shenanigans of the truckers and the boss for whom she would, when required, be general secretary, business hostess and jack-of-other-and-all-trades!

Myself, I do admit that by nature we women are a nosey bunch always looking forward to Edith's "business adventures" she'd deliver in installments, with humor dry as a creek's bed. But, you know, we really did care about Edith; and were always glad finally to see her more talkative and sociable!

So this one day, our Edith actually volunteered a story. And while she took off her glasses to polish on her shirttail, you could hear that dog barking from clear over at Younger's Hardware. We women were *that* quiet waiting for her to start!

"Actually, this started out twenty-five years before I got the job at Fulton State. And if Henry or my kids ever found out that I'd agreed to tell this story here, why they'd carry me off to the packaging unit at Sears sayin' I'd finally lost my marbles altogether and should be shipped off to a 'place of care' for such cases."

And well, some of us started in to laugh, then; but Edith didn't; so we stifled ourselves.

"The Art Department was small, those days," she went on, already back there; "and the town was far up north on the godforsaken rocky coast of northern California. Hey, nobody up here but us rocks! we used to say."

"Well, my hubby Henry had just four small classes, but up to his big ears in work every night! Believe you me, Henry didn't *care* that nothing went on in Fulton except for the wind blowing past like the 6:15 express while the Pacific ocean foamed itself up like a mad dog!"

"So there in those days, dinner parties constituted the best type of entertainment we had! And when a couple put on an event, well, it was *their* chance to prove that they really came from other places, and that *they* thought they were cultured, educated, and refined!

And believe you me that to throw such a party, the hostess had to roll out every last living speck of finery the family ever possessed! Well, that was a real pleasure to me because, raising four kids, two dogs and a parrot, Henry and I didn't own squat except for a rag of a quilt I kept under the mattress on that bed that used to belong to Aunt Rita's Grandma Shirley. An' believe you me, Henry knew better than to ask me when we could take our turn at entertaining!

And let me tell you, that in all those years, I managed *never* to put on a single dinner party, but I *always* brought my apple curdle dip; I learned that from Grannie Kay! And whoever my hostess was, she knew that whether Italian theme or Chinese, she could count on me for Grannie Kay's apple curdle dip!"

Well, all of us listening close, we had all picked at Edith's apple curdle dip for nearly three years now; so we kept our eyes to our needlework and zippered our lips!

"About that dinner at the Smith's, that Larry Smith (the big novelist!*)* and his wife Vivien were 'coastal' folks and what-not. And they always seated us at their oval wooden table with its curved legs and mahogany top; padded, then protected by a plain color under-cloth, and followed by the most beautiful white-enough-to-burn out-your-eyes lace-trimmed placemats!

And well, that Viv would carry out glass salad plates with mixed greens and crusty French styled dishes in fancy baking things you bring right to the table. Why, I never had seen the like! Oh, and Vivian had a way of making everyone feel like a celebrity! And she always liked to serve *my* apple curdle dip; I always brought it in grandmother's fluted silver and glass-lined relish dish!

Now, that Larry was a nice enough man, with reading glasses, who'd go around pouring wine into what looked like individual little fishbowls balanced upon glass stems. Once, after I'd had a few, I said 'Wouldn't it be a scream to put a minnow into somebody's glass while they're off in the john! Ha-ha!'

Myself, I was introduced to drinking after Henry and I got married. That's when I found out that alcohol would absolutely unlace me! But eventually, Henry would give me one of *those* looks, and then move my glass next to his own.

"Well, and after all that imported wine and chocolate flambe, even the *Economic* Department chairman's wife 'Peanut' would open up! Even so, that woman never did have a bad word to say about anyone! And her husband Wade was southern, too; and he made a real handsome figure, wavy grey hair and all. Oh, and you could just tell that after their twenty years, those two were still just crazy about each other! And you never saw a nicer thing!

Now Wade, he was usually the big storyteller; but this one night he called out to his wife, 'Peanut, tell these people about Whitneyville, Tennessee where you and your folks come from. Tell them about Gran'mama's sewing thing!' Well, that Peanut *did* tell!

Well now, it seems that Peanut's Gran'mama had belonged to a Sewing Circle down in Whitneyville; and that Sewing Circle was some kind of high society there, if you can imagine that! So I asked Peanut did she mean that the women would bring their household darning, patching and whatnot?

'Why no, darlin'',' Peanut told me, 'it was, you know, fancy sewing'. And by that she meant embroidery, crochet, tatting and other kinds of handwork most people don't give two cents for nowadays--and along with that, telling about who was doing what and how well, and so on. 'And you can just imagine' Peanut went on, 'that all that competition 'mongst those women stirred up some fierce pride and jealousy.'"

"Over *sewing?*" I interrupted. I couldn't believe it!

"Oh you know: how small a stitch, how complicated the knotting and how many different stitches--European or American, how many movements to complete each stitch--. All that."

"'Why heavens, I never darned a sock in my life!" These words just jumped right out of my mouth! "And I can tell you that Five-and-Dime in Fulton rang like a bucket of silver dollars any time I had half an hour to wander there--but NEVER over sewing!"

"'Now, this Whitneyville Sewing Circle was all women from local 'founding families'", Peanut went on, "and I can tell you those women weren't *about* to take on anyone new!"

And Edith took a sip of water before her launch into how Peanut told of how the younger women weren't really interested in needlework, anyway, but only man/woman talk; and that being about ten years old those days, the family called Peanut 'Gran'mama's haint' because she was so skinny and quiet. And she told us, too, how Peanut had *loved* to hang near her Gran'mama, as if that woman had some kind of special magic!

Edith painted Peanut's picture of how once a month, needles would flash and these women got down to scouring out their neighbors and the town real good. And until now, this Peanut hadn't said "Boo!" while those Sewing Circle women would put on "their best" for each other, you'd better believe!--settin' out cucumber disks with radish flowers on silver trays, little apple pies, ice cream rolls--oh, and I don't know what-all.

And this Peanut, growin' up, she had a butler and used to tell us that if "that man" hadn't of been there, why her whole family would've been paralyzed, 'cause none of 'em was taught to do a lick for themselves. And knowing this, we-all thought it was a wonder that Peanut ever got on as a wife! And I give her credit for that, too!

"Now, this Whitneyville Sewing Circle held a Mother's Day Exhibition once a year downtown" Edith continued, "And, to hear Peanut tell it, the race amongst those sewing women was bloody and fierce and spiked with prizes: five dollars for third place, ten for second and twenty for first. Oh, and there were red, white, and blue ribbons awarded, too, and along with an outside judge from the School of Law. But this sewing exhibition was always held, 'public invited', at the Women's Club." Edith looked slowly around for response, with none coming.

"So, according to Peanut," Edith started in, "starting in February, a lot of secret needle-pushing would get going. But the members of the Whitneyville Sewing Circle would not bring the pieces they intended to enter into the competition to their meetings. And some wouldn't even let family members *see* what they were up to! Why, Peanut told me one year that her Gran'mama had driven far as an entire day away to a lady way South who could show her how to do some kind of fancy knots that looked like little mushrooms standing up!

Well, it all turned out to be worthwhile because, three years in a row, Peanut's Gran'mama took the Blue Ribbon for her bridge cloths! And Peanut recalled that over those fifteen years, there were usually three women in the Circle who most often passed first place amongst themselves; and *her* Gran'mama took Blue Ribbon *nine* times! And Gran'mama kept a special wall at home for display of the Sunburst Plaque with her name and year all engraved thereon." Pausing for a gasp or awe at the plaque but met with silence, Edith continued.

"And this time I'm telling about, the 'big event' finally arrived at ten a.m. sharp on a bright day in early July--and with the Women's Club all done up with summer lilac bouquets. And the judge herself arrived in her bun, eyeglasses, business suit to study the entry pieces upon the long exhibit table. Meanwhile, competitors waited outside on the front walk chewing through the fingers of their gloves while peering past one another at the building's front entrance and waiting for the judge and for her final decisions.

"Forty-five minutes later (*and with sweat popping now through the contestants' face powder!*), Professor Sloane would come out and down the steps, her judging completed.

Now the etiquette was that afterward the judge speaks to no one, but just gets into her car and drives away. And then, the judge's car out of sight, contestants were allowed to enter the exhibit hall to face the posting board and learn who got what. And *everything was VERY strict!*" Absent mindedly, we all nodded. Less for agreement but more for acknowledgement at what Edith meant; we could imagine the judging, all the way around!

"So, this one particular day, the women whose work made 'the finals' trailed with their families up and into the Club while "The Blue Danube Waltz" played over the loud-speaker and tea cookies and raspberry punch were set out for winners, their families, for judges and special visitors.

Well, it turns out that Peanut's Gran'mama took Second Place for her "Petticoat with pink parrots amongst green leaves". But '*--and the Devil's own britches!*' Gran'mama had cried out seeing the Second Place ribbon upon her own piece, '*And that Professor Sloane must be too old or stone blind if she can't see that JOKE she gave first place instead of what I put up!*'"

Edith now lowered her voice to us, and we all leaned in, but just a bit as she whispered, "Third place was a white-on-white pillow covering with hand-done eyelets in a bridal wreath pattern--and *real* tedious work! Well, the story goes that, after the decision, the contenders traipsed along the display table to find the First Place blue ribbon taped to Evie Winton's entry.

Well, and you'd better believe that ALL contestants about *dropped their teeth* then! Now Evie Winton was the Sewing Circle's 'loudmouth, as Gran'mama always put it; and if there was any one person those women didn't expect or WANT to win, it was Evie Winton! So, spitting like hot grease, they immediately disavowed any *of her* tatting as being good enough to go up behind glass in the local museum for the year! After all, there were *standards* to keep alive!

Now, Ms. Winton's piece was done with extra fine thread from the lightest to the deepest of greens; and all in a real complicated stitch that took six passes per knot. And those chains of stitches looped through one another to make a fluffy ridge of what Peanut called 'frozen sea foam'.

And seeing the final judgments, then, nobody knew what to say, except for Gran'mama who declared, 'That Winton woman never did do this work! She must've gone across the tracks to that voodoo witch who puts crows' feet and rats' hair into beet soup claiming it'll cure anything from a runny nose to a broken back! And I tell you, she'd better get herself quit of all that *fahl-der-ahl*--and quick if she expects to ever come back to THIS Sewing Circle!'" Edith sat straight up, as if channeling Peanut's words.

We waited, afraid even to stitch, until Edith sputtered out: "Well, the piano played away to an old man and a few children who had strayed in off the street whilst the proud winner pinned the blue ribbon to her handbag and then strutted on down the front steps like the band playin' Dixie! And that would've been the end of the whole blessed thing if Gran'mama's kitchen cook, Mimosa, and Evie Winton's feller who helped at the house hadn't in fact been cousins, of all things!

Now that Gran'mama was so upset at only taking *second* place, that she carried on for *a whole week,* sulking and storming around until it about broke the kitchen cook Mimosa's heart!

Well, so, Mimosa went off looking for Gran'mama under the big bay tree in the side yard where Gran'mama liked to sit when she was simmering in her stew.

Edith, enjoying our rapt attention, clacking her teeth more quickly picked up her voice to retell the story telling, "'I got to tell you something so's you won't feel so poorly 'bout your sewing' Mimosa said when she found Gran'mama stewing in a lawn chair under the bay tree. And wiping her hands upon her apron, she bent to Gran'mama, all clenched-up like a fist. And she told her, 'I seen how hard you worked on your stitching; and then how beautiful it all come out, too! And I know you should have took first prize—.' And Mimosa had to stop to take a breath. '--an' I know, you *would've* took it, too, if it weren't for something not right that Miss Evie done in her piece.'" Edith's face was working hard and she recounted Peanut's tale of the disclosure.

Taking liberties a bit, we imagined, Edith let out, "Now Gran'mama was a real distinctive-looking woman, not quite five foot but with a lean face, high cheekbones, a roman nose, thin fingers and white hair rising like merengue. At least as Peanut reports."

And that Gran'mama pressed her, 'Why, whatever can you mean, 'not right', child,?'

'"Well—' And Mimosa, tried to go on, worried her apron then. Now, she was taller than Gran'mama by quite a bit--thin and supple like one of them Japanese trees you see on the lawns of people with money. 'Well, but I don' like givin' nobody no trouble, M'am.'

'Speak up, child. What do you know?' Gran'mama hissed, then.

But then came the sound of a child's voice and of shoes grinding upon the sidewalk, so that Mimosa held her peace 'til the man carrying a little boy singing upon his shoulders passed by and she could speak up again.

'I know Ms. Evie didn't make no trimming, M'am.'

'You mustn't say that, Mimosa. That's not God-fearing.'

'No, M'am. But yes, M'am, it is true! My own cousin, her house helper, he told me so.'

Well, that Gran'mama stiffened her back then, and squinted. 'Speak plainly, girl. Are you telling me Evie Winton didn't do that tatting? Are you saying that Evie Winton cheated?'

'Well, yes, I am. I am saying that!'

'Well, that piece doesn't look store-bought! Why, I never saw anything like it!'

'No M'am. And it weren't from no catalog, if that's what you was thinking.'

'Well where did it come from, then?' Gran'mama pounded her wicker chair's arm, her fuse sputtering.

'Mmm,' Mimosa dug back and forth with her foot, buying time. 'Well M'am,' she finally said, 'my cousin done and made that.'

Gran'mama dropped back in her chair gasping, 'What? Elmer Green? You're saying *Elmer Green did that?*'

Gran'mama studied Mimosa's face long and good. Next she studied the freckles on the backs of her hands, then the dark green ovals of the bay leaves overhead and then stuck out her shoe to study its crisscrossing laces until finally she shifted in her chair to study once more the features of Mimosa's face; and then to shake her head and scowl.

'No. I don't believe it!' She spat the words out then.

'Oh, yes, M'am.' Mimosa pulled herself up tall. 'He did too do it. Why, Elmer does fancy work as good as any of the ladies—And him, just sitting back there in the pantry with them pots and pans. But he says it feels real peaceful to be back there, doing that. And he gave some of it--of his sewing makings --to his mama and sister. And he gave some to us-all, too, now and again! Me, I keep mine for when I get married.'"

And then, Edith Atkins stopped her story-telling a moment to wet her throat with warmed blackberry tea. We-all in our sewing circle - picked up our cups, too.

"Well, that day we were talking about, Peanut was playing "Jacks" on the front stoop when Gran'mama grabbed her by one of her braids; Gran'mama went steaming down the street without even her hat on! And she ringed that bell 'til the cousin, Elmer Green, come on the run to let Gran'mama into the parlor whilst he got Evie Winton to tell her there was a visitor. But Gran'mama didn't sit. No, siree! And that Evie Winton just stood there like an umbrella in a caddy, just where Elmer Green left her!"

Edith wet her throat again with more blackberry tea, the last of the tea, then started on again, with an uptick in her pace, gaining speed on the story!

"'Why, what a nice surprise!' Evie Winton had said when she seen Gran'mama. 'Why don't you take a seat?' Now Evie was a big woman herself--square and square, her hair all in little waves.

'Never you mind any seat!' Gran'mama told her right back real loud. 'I got business you an' me better do right now! An' standing up!'

'Why, whatever could that be?' Evie Winton raised an eyebrow high. And that there was the last question Ms. Winton would ever ask, because, from then on, Gran'mama was asking the questions 'til finally they brought Elmer Green out the kitchen, a towel tied at his waist, a needle and thread in his big hands.

And Elmer, well, he just stood there giving a few words about how his

Mama taught him sewing. But then, his wrist started to snapping back and forth and faster and faster 'til it outright blurred and showing Gran'mama *the* stitch that took that blue ribbon! And Gran'mama, well she thrust the tatting needle at Evie Winton who admitted she didn't have a first idea how to start in, or do that stitch.

"'An' you oughta be ashamed of yourself', that's what' Gran'mama told her, then, her voice and color rising at the same time. 'You took a dollar and blue ribbon that should of been mine! And I intend to call an emergency meeting of Whitneyville Sewing Circle tomorrow, four o'clock. And really, Evie, your age and telling lies!—and one that ties up this poor boy here! *Shame!* I say. *And shame on you now!'*

"Then Gran'mama shook her head like a turkey gobbler an' turned on her heel whilst Elmer Green leaped up to help open the door. But Gran'mama, she stopped dead still in the doorway right then.

"Now course, she snorted, 'nothing happening to this here boy! None of this mess belong to him!' And as he closed the door, Peanut said she saw Elmer Green roll his eyes towards Heaven." Edith leaned back quickly, laughing more to herself than with us, she collected herself and took a deep breath and continued.

"Well, the Whitneyville Sewing Circle gave First Prize to Elmer Green; and then ordered Evie Winton to attend a ceremony where she was going to give the awards to Elmer Green and the others.

But Evie Winton, she wrote a letter the next day saying, 'You old women are a drying'-up root; and I don' intend to sit around and dry up with ya!' And next day, she joined the *book club,* of all things, at the library because she said she was good at reading. And Gran'mama said Evie Winton was actually good at running her mouth; and she should go to work for them Democrats because they always carrying on about some fool thing!"

Now Elmer Green didn't attend the giving out of prizes. His cousin Mimosa delivered him the five-dollar bill and blue ribbon. And Mimosa said Elmer right away laid both ribbons flat inside his bible saying he really didn't want to look for any other job. Besides, he liked Ms. Winton, that the two of them play penny gin rummy nights; and Ms. Winton owed to him twenty-seven cents, at least!

And when word got around about Elmer Green being so handy with the needle, all the ladies of the Whitneyville Sewing Circle *and* their friends wanted to borrow him. And so, for a time, Elmer had to get up a good two hours early so as to squeeze Ms. Winton's chores into *his* day. And that's the whole story!" Edith sighed loudly, satisfied she had concluded. She drained her cup before retreating behind her eyeglasses.

Well, there came a satisfied silence amongst the lengthening shadows outside. Inside, the old grandfather clock chimed the half-hour while we all went on with our work, while past the windows, the crows launched a great disagreement amongst themselves. And a bit farther off, a truck with a loose-fitting fender clattered over the slats on the old-covered bridge.

"Well, and I just wish Elmer Green would teach my husband Joseph how--" I started; but Edith broke in.

"Oh no! That's not all of it!" Edith held up both hands and took command again.

And that was when we-all looked real hard and really saw her face. Greyed and puckered, it was. And we-all made sure we kept our own faces matter-of-fact, sewing on in silence like we always did for one another; or when our storyteller's voice held something awkward, we made as if nothing happened. And so we sewed on in silence until, after a few minutes, that bulky whatever-it-was for Edith teetered, then slid forward.

"I been coming here near three years now," Edith finally moved her eyes from face to face, "and you women always made me feel real welcome--like every month holding onto my same chair for me; but still not pressing me where I wasn't up yet to being public And now I believe I'd like, for once, to tell you things I couldn't--or *wouldn't*--before."

And with that, Edith nosed her needle into the fabric to let it idle there while we-all leaned deeper into our stitching, but our ears full-blown as sunflowers!

Edith, she looked at us, one face to another. Then she began.

"Well, and the week after we'd heard it, that story of Evie Winton's just kept hanging on there inside me; but I didn't know why. Then one day, scrubbing out the toilet bowl," she went on, "it came to me that *I* also had stolen a prize--I'd lied, practiced wrong-doing! And the only difference between someone else and me was that *I* hadn't ever got caught! So Evie Winton's one up on me, now; because she didn't finish roped to her prize the rest of her life; but me, I'm still roped to mine, my husband Henry!" We not one of us looked at another, the silence still with startle.

"I got Henry in Centralia, Illinois, where we grew up. Nothing in Centralia but corn, soybeans, trees and cows far as you can see! But I liked it, being there plunk in the middle of all that land! Now, Centralia those days was about as big as New Harmony--a few hundred of us souls working acreage outside of town. And though we didn't have much in Centralia, we had our own high school!

Me, in school, I wasn't the brightest bulb--nor the most interested; but I liked hanging around between classes--smoking, nipping beer behind the gym, the usual. Actually, *I* was "the usual"!

Oh, but I had one edge, because about twelve miles outside of town my daddy owned his OWN property! And well, the people who claimed the town would call people like my daddy 'a legendary' to make themselves feel really big. And I finally figured out that it was because, in their hearts, they knew Centralia was nowhere--and well, then *Ha, Ha, SO WERE THEY!*

And it used to just fry me when kids at school would bellow at me across the playground, 'Hey, Legendary! Be my legend!' Those boys with no manners would call me out. And hey! When they insulted me, it felt like they insulted my Daddy, too; and I'd come right to a boil, swearing and yelling at them to erase what they said out of the air; and I'd make a scene about it in public too, to get even with them!

Then, as luck would have it, I got the attention of the "brain" of the class, Henry Atkins. Now, one thing that Henry had was manners! And so it turned out I ended up Henry's "sweetie"—*me*, a farmer's daughter taught to stay out of the way, to stay "put"; and I darned well knew that!

But I'm telling you that every girl at Centralia High had her eye on Henry! Hey, but I was the one who got him even though we were like opposites: Henry towering while I was short; him reading classics, and me at the TV; him listening to Bach; me wanting Western; him wanting to be famous and me just wanting some privacy and peace. And he told me once that more than anyone else he felt at home with me!

And those days, for a lot of us, Henry was the hope of Centralia High. And next he was going to the University become a scientist and make a name for himself!

Now, I won't say I didn't have feelings for Henry; but I might of convinced myself I had a wee bit more feeling' than I really did. For one thing, I didn't give a fig for all those books Henry said were his "teachers", "advisors" and "best friends". Well, but I never let on!

At first, no matter what Henry had to say, I'd brighten up and hang on every word. But after a while, it looked to me like his stuff was like water just running in a curb after a rain and on to nowhere. Me, I really couldn't get excited for it, like you're supposed to. So after not that long, the things he liked, well they bored me; they were like gibberish. And I told myself I just didn't like school well enough to stay on with all that gibberish--and that no one did -- and soon enough Henry would find another path.

When we married, Henry got a part-time teaching position in Decatur, a few miles away from here. And he'd be spouting off at a faculty party quoting So-and-So and So-and-So. Afterwards, Henry would tell me how much he admired that I was "So level-headed," he'd squeeze my shoulder; he'd tell me that one thing he really loved about me was that way.'"

And then Edith paused to look at each of us-- our needles, our sewing materials one after another--and then right in the eye.

"I married Henry because I was young and headstrong." She said as though we asked. She went on defiantly, "I married him because I could get him. I married him because I didn't know what else to do with myself. I married him because I wanted revenge on my Daddy. I married him because he took me to dinner Saturdays before the movie. I married him because he gave me a music box and pearl earrings. I married him because in those days he didn't try to make me do things I didn't want to do. I married him because I never did know what to do with my life. I married him because the girls in my graduating class at Centralia High began to treat me like a celebrity when they heard I was going to be *Mrs. Henry Atkins.*

But Daddy, after the wedding, asked me 'wasn't I going to miss the land?' And I remember I pushed my real feelings down real hard and lifted my chin up and told him; 'Land is land'. Oh, but I felt a great wrenching as he drove off and I didn't say what my Daddy had wanted to hear.

I would find out later that it wasn't true. There wasn't any land anywhere else like I was reared on. And by the time we got to Fulton State, we had kids, and I was up to my neck in diapers and supermarket coupons. Oh, and I missed the Midwest!

"The night of that dinner party, something started pecking at a shell inside me until, a week or so later, the truth broke free and left me on my knees! That's when I finally realized that my Henry, that Henry, was the prize; and that I actually had stolen him."

Well, you could hear the slow *plink, plink* of the faucet in the bathroom down the hall. I anchored my needle to fix my eyes upon the plum tree just past blossoms in the front yard, and breathed deep. Someone blew her nose. And Pearly Luke took off her thimble, tucked the escaping grey wisps of hair behind her ears and said she believed she'd put on water for tea, more tea.

And we shifted in our chairs, then: each of us coming up as if from deep water to blink and stare at one another in the dying afternoon light--and to stare at the lives we had hoped for the way you might at a distant shore--so sorely desired; but far. Oh, too far, now, too distant to be any help.

Doc Bailey Gets Busted

Hardly anything ever happens in our town except stock car races, basketball tournaments and softball games.

But one early morning last Spring, a murder was reported in the Iowa Falls *Gazette:* Juanita Lucinda Gomez had killed old Bradford Bailey in his office--had aimed right at his chest and blown his stomach out.

Well, everybody knew Doc Bailey was no good as a doctor! He would sit in his office and do crossword puzzles and pick his nose; and he'd only see patients when he needed the money. If he didn't need the money, he would tell you he was too busy, then go back to his crossword puzzles and nose picking. And if he needed the money, he would examine you; and if you had something bruised or cut or sprained, he'd tape it up. For anything else, it was a shot, or "Go to the emergency room."

Doc Bailey was a "cash only" doc. And whatever he did, he'd charge at least ninety dollars plus the cost of shots or meds-on-hand. And that comes to plenty of dough in a lumber town where you have the wrecked-from-work, the born poor, and the totally-out-of-luck.

Doc Bailey always did everything himself—temperature, pulse, weight, blood pressure; and he never wrote anything down, except for the shot. The law said he had to do that. And then he would throw the report into a big file drawer with no folders, shrug and say, "Everything's right in here. Just takes a little digging." And hey, we live in a real poor neighborhood; so we could like it or lump it!

Now, this woman Juanita Gomez lived with her four children in one of those "fringe" neighborhoods in Chicago. The husband, Heraldo, ran away when Juanita got pregnant with the third baby. That's what I heard.

And then, mad at being left alone, she got pregnant with the fourth by somebody passing through. And it doesn't make any sense; but when her time came, Juanita walked the six blocks to the hospital.

The next year, she started seeing the assistant butcher from her neighborhood market. They liked each other and eventually, so the story goes, they became lovers, though the guy never moved in because he couldn't stand the noise and mess of the kids. But he was always, as they say, "visiting". And he would fix things around the house and remember her on 'special' days. And each week, he would take her to dinner and a show. Oh, and he'd make sure she had money for rent--that kind of stuff. So when she got pregnant with his baby, she was happy--very happy; but she never brought up marriage.

Then when she was three months along, that butcher she hooked up with (and the father of her baby!) was killed in a car accident! Juanita went to bed and wouldn't get up until finally she became so weak that her children called the neighbors who made her eat and then got a priest. The priest consoled her that, despite the death of the father, she still had the baby; and that she had been allowed to keep something of the man she loved.

So Juanita went back to regular life; but at seven months, came down with a bad flu, throwing up for twenty-four hours straight before she thought to go to the doctor.

Doc Bailey took her money first; then he examined her. He told her he'd better give her two shots: one for the flu and one for the baby. First, he wiped the needle on his shirttail; then he gave her penicillin in the rump and vitamins in the upper arm and sent her home, then. Well, after twenty-four hours, she felt better.

And she began to cook again, to do her housework; but then, a few days along, she started to feel tired and then collapsed and went to bed. She was in bed four days thinking it was the flu back and that the shots hadn't worked. By then her stomach burned and cramped while the whites of her eyes took on a yellow look. Then, in the middle of the night, she started vomiting and bleeding. Finally, the oldest child ran to the neighbors who called the ambulance; but by the time they got her to the hospital, the baby had come, and died.

Now, the hospital doctor was a kindly man who felt sorry for her. He asked where she had gotten the hepatitis that had made her so sick that she lost her baby. He told her that most people get sick from not washing their hands after the bathroom, or from using a dirty needle taking dope. He asked if she used dope. She said no; and then her face went pale; and then it went dark.

She went right to the pawn shop three blocks from the hospital, pulled her grandmother's wristwatch from her wrist and laid it on the counter. (And that watch was the only good thing she had!) The pawnbroker liked the watch with its tiny bits of diamonds and rubies; and knew he was coming out ahead. So he gave her the gun in exchange fori it.

She buttoned her coat over the gun's barrel, then walked the three blocks to Doc Bailey's office where she found him alone in the examining room and sitting upon the examining table clipping his toenails.

"The doctor at the hospital says I lost my baby because someone used a dirty needle on me," she told him. "You was the only one used any needle on me. And that baby was the last thing of his I had." And she opened her coat to pull out the gun, aimed at his chest and fired the way the pawnbroker had showed her. The first shot got him in the stomach. The second hit him in the lower backside. He toppled off the table to take the last blast in the back, face-down upon the floor.

"You shouldn't be a doctor," she told his body; "you're dirty."

And she dropped the shotgun on top of him, then walked out of the office.

The man next door, hearing the gun shots, and so close, in a panic called 911. A police car, in less than an hour, found her wandering barefoot in snow-covered grass three blocks from her home. She had thrown away the gun, her coat and shoes.

Uncle Fun

I still remember that Saturday morning in September when Ma slapped a postcard onto the counter, clapped her hands to her knees, waggled her big hips, and announced, "Uncle Fun will be here in two weeks!" (Our Ma always handed Uncle Fun's name out like a trip to Paris.) "We'll give him your room, Tony. You two boys can bunk together. Eddie, clear out a drawer for your brother."

Well, Eddie and me just stared at each other over the open box of Wheaties. Being a sophomore in high school, Eddie naturally didn't have time of day for a "rat-face" in the seventh grade like me.

"How long is Uncle Fun going to stay, Ma?" Eddie stopped shoveling Wheaties into his mouth.

"'Til he gets his feet under him, our house is his house," Ma sang and then saw Eddie's face go dark. "Oh, come on, Eddie, he's your uncle! Forgive and forget!"

Ever since Uncle Fun slipped my brother pepper gum wrapped like Wrigley's, he'd stopped being Eddie's favorite relative. Mixed with the noise of the faucet running that day, Ma and me heard Eddie crying and spitting. Our Pa was at his union meeting that night. And all Ma said to her brother was, "Oh Tony, you promised! Remember?" We-all knew "family" was "off limits" for mean jokes and things.

"Hey, but did you see it?" Uncle Fun had cackled, anyway. "You see the kid's kisser?" And all Ma did was turn away shaking her head. And being three years younger than my brother, then, I tucked it away that the "rules" can change, depending on who's got the power at the moment.

Now my eyes were nearly level with Uncle Fun's. His were light grey and cool, like stones in a creek bed. My own are brown; but I have Uncle Fun's reddish hair and pale skin scattered all over with light brown freckles.

In those days, I really liked looking like Uncle Fun! Some day, I promised myself, I would travel the world, too; come back with Ma's suitcase all tied up with rope, just like my uncle did--only, I'd come back with with lots of money--maybe even buy Ma her own car!

So when Pa'd get home from work, Uncle Fun (who was staying with us "just until he got some things straightened out!") he'd have the classifieds spread out on the diningroom table to circle ads; or, before dinner, he'd drape himself over the kitchen counter to tell Ma how good-looking she was for her age; and make her light up like a two hundred watt bulb. And I'd see Ma slip him a twenty later, hear her tell him, "That's not a loan now." And Uncle Fun would nod, then saunter off to watch TV. Dinnertime, Ma'd pat his arm and say, "Having you here makes it just like the old days, Tony, after Mama died when you were twelve and then it was just you and me and Pops. Remember?"

"But I don't remember Mama, Rita," he'd tell her, then; and he'd put on a long face, but with a dark twinkle in his eye for my brother and me.

"Why, of course you do, Tony," Ma''d urge him, then. "You remember Mama," she'd tell him, the little tears starting up in her eyes. And Uncle Fun would flash a fast grin at my brother and me, as if he was telling us, "This is how you do it." But myself, well I could never figure out what "it" was.

That Fall, Uncle Fun and I got to sort of be friends, seeing I was the only one home after school because of Ma working at the dry cleaners on Clark, then; and my brother staying Eddie after school most every day for sports. Myself? I was a kind of bookworm, I guess-- my nose always in the Nintendo. But with Uncle Fun staying on, I had company now after school!

Uncle Fun and I would spend hours sitting at the foot of my (now his) bed, our thumbs ablur, the two of us cackling while the weird-looking Kung-fu guys on the TV beat the living shit out of one another! And when I'd win a game (which was most of the time), Uncle Fun'd give a "Dutch rub" to my scalp with his knuckles that would make knots in my hair. Once I said, "Hey, that hurts! And I'm not a kid any more, you know!"

But Uncle Fun'd just clap me on the back and tell me, "Sure you are! Sure you're a kid! I'm a kid! And stay a kid, kid and keep your privilege!" And he'd pound me on the back one more time.

"Privilege!" I'd wave my hand at the room then, meaning: Hey, this here is all I have--or *will* have whenever you decide to give it back. One thing us kids *don't* have is *privilege!*"

"Hey, *wrong*, buster!," he'd carry on. "You kids got ALL the privilege; the grown-ups, they got none!! And why? Because, if you're a kid--and no matter how miserable, skinny or snotty-faced you are--somebody somewhere's going to go weak at the knees over something about you. Usually, it's a woman. And then, you've got it *made! MADE!!!*"

So, one afternoon, and me at home after school, Uncle Fun breaks out a deck to teach me Rummy. Well, up 'til then, I'd never played cards before. And oh how I *loved* the surprise of the cool, slick and graceful way the cards slipped behind one other--and the stiff, goofy-looking people in weird costumes looking out from some them! Well, and the longer we played, the faster I'd meld and knock to leave Uncle Fun with a fistful! And you'd better believe that he'd be watching me *real* close until finally then he'd ask me, "Sure you never played this before, Kiddo?"

"Gee, no, Uncle Tony," I'd shake my head. "Honest!"

Well, and it got so that we'd play every night, sitting on the floor beneath the bedroom lamp, and hunched over the little pile s--slapping cards down, picking them up--and myself learning really fast about keeping an eye on Uncle Fun's socks, belt, shirt sleeves, and trouser cuffs--oh, and *always* to watch for any slow creep of his cupped hand.

"Hey!" I'd point.

"See quicker little man!" he'd crow at me., then About eight-thirty, I'd hear Pa's step upon the stairs; and he'd lean in at the doorway, then, for a long time, just watching us.

"Hey there, Steve-o!" Uncle Fun would look up. "We're going to make a *professional* out of this kid; and bail you outta that sweat pool you call a job! Right Beaneroo?" he'd bob his head at me, his nearly invisible freckles stepping forward under the glare of the lamp.

"Wanna play?" I'd ask Pa, "You can have first 'cut'."

But Pa's eyes would hang upon Uncle Fun a long moment; then, "Light's out," Pa'd say, turning away. And I would hear his steps upon the stairs again; then, from the TV, the shrunken male voice of our local evening news, still a miracle in those days.

And "Big man, your Pa," Uncle Fun would always nod at me, then; "--a real hard worker!"

Uncle Fun taught me *Goofenspiel*, *War*, *I Doubt It*, *Crazy Eights* and *Michigan*. He'd always tell me, "You play cards, kiddo, you can go *anywhere* in the world!" And I'd feel, then, that by some incredible stroke of luck I'd stumbled into some secret club where I fantasized the silence at "breaking of the seal, shuffling and then dealing of the cards while veiled women passed sweets and us men picked up our cards, anticipating the play and one another without speaking.

Then one night, I heard Pa's voice angry from the kitchen. "Well, I don't care. It's too much time together. The kid's only twelve."

"And how much time do you spend with him?" Ma came right back, then.

Like always, my parents were deciding my life.

"Well, you work at that mill ten hours a day. See what kind of butt you've got left to drag home!"

"I work, too!" I would hear Ma's voice go watery. And in my mind, I'd see her, knuckles dug deep into her hips, chest pushed out while she went toe-to-toe for her boy!

Silence, then.

"O.k., yeah, yeah. You 'work'," finally, from Pa. Then silence again except for the refrigerator door opening and closing. And then from Pa, "--the question is: When is *he gonna*?"

"When he's good and ready!" Ma'd come right back. "He's my *brother*!" she'd draw her trump card as if it were a position of royalty.

The pop and hiss of a bottle, then. The faucet again. And then, Pa's voice, weary and caving in. "Yeah, yeah. He's your brother."

One afternoon a week or so later, I came out into the schoolyard to find Uncle Fun there, his fingers hooked through the diamond openings made by the wire fence; and a cigarette dangling over his lower lip. Well, as I came closer, I had to gasp seeing a knife handle and lower part of a blade sticking out of Uncle Fun's chest; and with a bright pool of blood welling around it.

And a bolt of fear pushed me into a sprint until I heard Uncle Fun's cackle; and dug my heels into the cement of the playground.

"Hey," I barked at him, "you'd better watch it around school grounds--" passing it off that I hadn't been fooled by the fake knife and blood. "because Mr. Grey, our principal, calls the cops on anyone here with a knife!"

And then, remembering my manners, I turned to the kids who had come out of the building with me. "Uh, this is my Uncle Tony," I waved my arm. And well, afirst they stopped dead; and then began to move off walking backwards and staring at the bloody handle and partial blade of the joke knife Uncle Fun ripped from his chest to jab at me through the fence. Well, and to save face, I picked up the game, buckling my knees, gurgling, clawing at my chest and finally falling to my knees sideways against the fence.

Oh, and how Uncle Fun loved that! "Hey there, kiddo" he barked happily, "Got me some people I want you to meet. Let's go."

Well, I thought about the platter of brownies at home; I shook my head. "Can't. Got to leave a note, first for Ma."

"Hey, kiddo, I already stuck one on the fridge we'd be home for supper. So c'mon" And he wrapped the knife with its fake too-bright blood in a kerchief and stuffed it into his trouser pocket.

So we walked further into East Rockford by way of the bridge crossing the Northwestern railroad tracks and then past Rockford's sagging apartment buildings, hamburger joints, gas stations, dime, drug and hardware stores, hospital, churches and schools.

And with every third step I took I would crane my neck at the unmowed front yards, the driveways with scattered automobile parts, sagging shops with presently boarded up windows, small grocery stores with chicken bodies hung in the window while the smell of rancid ice and the sounds of cowboy music flooded from open tavern doors.

"Who do you know over here, Uncle Tony?" I finally asked.

"You'll see. C'mon." and we turned a corner, then.

I followed Uncle Fun through a worn front gate, then, and scarred unlocked front door and up dark sagging stairs, my legs throbbing. On the third floor, Uncle Fun stopped to knock at the apartment marked "B" displayed by a tarnished metallic letter. A pause. Then the tiny "spy" window in the front door slid back; and a human eye filled its empty space. Another pause. The window closed. The worn door opened.

Uncle Fun told "his friends" there sitting at the round table that his nephew had never played in a "real poker game" before. He was "baby-sitting" his sister's kid. "The squirt's got 'the touch', though," he said, nodding strongly. "I can tell you that!"

Uncle Fun explained to "his friends" that he wanted to "break me in" with "professionals"; and that he'd like to get things going for me with, say, Seven Card Stud--or whatever they were up to. And he looked around the table, then, holding off lighting up his cigar while he met each pair of eyes and, by a silent and mutual consensus, they sat down to pick up the playing cards upon the heavy old-fashioned wood table like the kind you see all the time in "those special stores that sell old things," Uncle Fun explained in a whisper to me.

Well, I looked around.

Behind us, the off-balance kitchen faucet leaned and dripped *plop*, *plop*, while the scarred refrigerator rattled off what seemed like a doze; and the room, poorly lit and sagging-feeling room smelled of beer, cigar and cigarette smoke hovering just above in grimy sheets. Well, the place felt to me like it was sinking! And the gathered men, seeming to know Uncle Fun and to need no further information about me, shuffled over to the big round heavy-wood old fashioned play table, a green shaded lamp centered low above it.

And Uncle Fun claimed a seat for me next to him.

"Don't coach him too strong now," the guy, Fresno, who'd opened the door, a black patch over one eye, waved that we should take a seat at the table with the others there. A moment of silence; then Fresno began raking a jumbled pile of playing cards toward his chest. And I gathered, then, this was *his* apartment; and he didn't look like he cared that much for Uncle Fun.

Silence fell, then, amongst us-all. Then Fresno started dealing. And Uncle Fun bent toward me, a raised hand to shade what he would say.

But "Hey!" Fresno burst in. "Let the young man learn hisself what he need to know. Right, sonny? Meanwhile, us folks'll have us our game." And as Fresno opened his mouth wider, then, to replace his cigar, the brilliant pink of his tongue leapt into the room.

Well, and I couldn't believe they were really going to let me play--*me*, a kid! And I leaned over to Uncle Fun already patting the table for his cards.

"Hey, they don't care how old you are," he whispered back. "The point is, if you've got money, they want it !"

"Hey, an' somebody give my man a beer!" Shotgun, in an undershirt, loose tie and wide-brimmed hat, piped up then while I stared at his long pointed fingernails. "Can't nobody play pokah dry."

Uncle Fun broke in. "--but his ma don't want him drinking."

Starch came right back. "— Oh, but don' min' he play'n poka'!"

And at this, everybody hooted while Uncle Fun grinned. Then then Lotto, in overalls and dreads, hustled me up an RC while, beyond the drawn-down shades, I could hear the cross-town bus wheeze, then lumber on up the street.

Uncle Fun put up ten dollars for red, white and blue chips for me; and then bought twenty dollars' worth for himself.

During play, he would lean close, coaching me with arranging my suites, coaching me to watch for what was dealt, reminding me about four of a kind, full house, and straights and, despite all the other players' eyes scrutinizing him, managing to keep his own cards to himself.

Face-down cards were "in the hole"; "streets" were rounds of play; and on each round you could place a bet that you had the winning hand. Finally, then, came "show down" where everyone throws out their two weakest cards, then turns over the rest of their hand for everyone to see.

At one point, Uncle Fun got up to go to the fridge; and I was about to ask him for another RC when Starch, the Chinese guy, tugged on my sleeve.

"You in high school now?"

I shook my head. "No, seventh."

"Seventh!" his eyebrows shot up. "Baby Buddha." he nodded around the table.

And "ha, ha," Shotgun pruned his cigar against the edge of the ashtray at that. "Baby Boodah playin' poka!"

I heard a chink of glass, then, and the refrigerator door close with a sucking sound; then footsteps again, and Uncle Fun was in his chair. And I saw, as he let his head fall forward and onto the table, the knife sticking out of Fresno's back.

Well, the table exploded with hoots, then.

"Somebody done you in, Fres'," Lotto whooped; "you a dead man, Fres. Th'o in yo' cards--an' gimme them chips you cain't use no more!"

And Fresno felt up his back. Then leaned on one arm toward Uncle Fun who was cackling away and wiping tears. "Hey, that kid stuff, man!

Don't you make me no fool, man. I done tole you 'bout bringing them toys aroun' befo'. You ain't deaf is you?"

Well, and at that, my breath suddenly wedged like a stone in my throat; and Uncle Fun, he sat with this smile frozen upon his face while Fresno reached back and pulled the fake knife away and then threw it across the table saying, "Hey," and I ain't tellin' you 'nother time, Man."

The knife, its blade gleaming with fake blood, wobbled in the air, then dropped until, bounce/flop, bounce/flop it lay directly in front of me. Then Uncle Fun grabbed it up to slap over his own chest, then, and drop his arms and let his head loll to one side. Then, for a moment, there was only the drip, drip of the faucet until Shotgun's voice broke the silence.

"Hey, he 'pologize enough, now?"

Well, everyone shuffled out a laugh, then, except for Fresno who drew his eyebrows hard as he tilted his head to pull at his beer bottle, but never taking his eyes off of Uncle Fun. And I tell you that it felt that the very near the edge of hatred hovered there, then.

And Uncle Fun looked around quickly, still cackling and playing it light as he folded up the knife to jam into his pocket, then picked up his hand. And so play settled down again. But, I tell you, it made me really nervous the way Fresno looked at Uncle Fun all the while. And after an hour, Uncle Fun cashed in our chips saying, "Well, better get our boy here home."

And Lotto turned to me, then. "Come on over anytime yo' mama let you out, hear? Let us win some our groceries back. And mighty fine playin' fo' a beginner. You sure you ain't no dwarf?"

Then they all laughed; and each man shook my hand. But Shotgun squinted through his cigar smoke at Uncle Fun.

"Hey, next time y'all come, we gon' have some poker-playing dwarfs our own, hear?" And he leaned close, then, and with a lowered voice told Uncle Fun. "--an keep yo' pockets clean, dig?"

Then Fresno came along behind us to close the door; and as his eyes glanced off the top of Uncle Fun's head, I saw hatred in them!

So we stepped out onto the sidewalk, then, and into the gloom of a late Winter afternoon. And I drew the chilly air down hard into my lungs like a curative. I really hadn't realized how nervous I'd been.

Uncle Fun finished counting, then. "One hundred-five dollars!

"Man," he chortled, facing the heads all in the same direction."-- s'nothing like taking money from people think they're better'n you! You talk to 'em in the bars, they think they're a morally superior race or something—and like everybody owes them, and *Big Time!*"

Moving from foot to foot, the bite of February on my ankles, "It made Fresno really mad, that trick knife of yours."

"Hey, keeps him in line! I don't take orders from nobody, especially from guys with an attitude. Besides, all that rooster does anyway is to peck and squawk."

Hey, and really I didn't like my uncle calling people names. "I've got friends who aren't white. And they're just as nice to me as White kids. --sometimes nicer!"

"Hey, because they *want* something from you, Bozo," Uncle Fun threw his head and yipped. "Don't you get it?"

And I told him that they didn't want anything; but Uncle Fun was already turning away, jamming the money into his pocket as he steered me into a dingy hamburger shop to push me into a booth.

"Listen, kiddo," he blew across his coffee with thin rose-colored lips, slightly blue underneath. "How'd you like to end up the year with money in the bank—say, two thousand, maybe more."

My mouth dropped open. *"Two thousand? Dollars?"*

"Maybe more! Get something for your Ma. Buy yourself something."

My mouth hung open. "Could we do that?"

"Yeah. You and me. I've got ideas. But I'll have to figure it out!" He sent up a long stream of smoke. "But it's our little secret, right?"

Well, whatever "it" was, if Uncle Fun thought I could do it, *hey!* So my uncle was weird about other kinds of people; well, so were Ma and Pa and most of my friends' parents.

We talked about stuff I could buy for Ma; and I let my imagination rip while Uncle Fun paid the bill.

Outside on the sidewalk, a newspaper skittered across my feet.

"You know," Uncle Fun lit another cigarette, "I was about to split this Nowheresville; and then I've find I got a brilliant nephew, *a real gold mine*--and sleeping right next door to me!" And his eyes started shifting, then, like he was reading. "Rockford's spread out. That's good. We'll take our time; start small." He came around to me again, "Have we got a deal?"

No grown-up—not Pa of Ma, not my uncles, no teacher, no priest—ever took me into his confidence like that before, or showed such faith in me.

"Sure." I shifted my schoolbooks and stuck out my hand.

And Uncle Fun pulled his own hand from his pants' pocket to meet mine and electricity crackled into my palm, then up the inside of my arm. And I jumped away and cursed myself: *I knew better than to shake hands with Uncle Fun!* And he flung his head back and yodeled, "Never take your eyes off the other guy, kiddo."

Well, I'd brought in almost all of the hundred and five--and in under three hours! Welll, something in me had a feeling about the cards, about the way play moved around the table-- like music or those surfer guys on TV riding the waves. Yeah, more like them. And I hugged it to me that Uncle Fun thought I could do this! And that grownup men would play cards with me! That *I* could win; and--.

That's when I realized the streetlights had come on! "Oh my gosh! What time is it? Ma'll kill me if I'm late for dinner!"

"Hey, I'll take care of your ma." Uncle Fun waved. "You never have to worry about her."

And I relaxed a little, then because I had an uncle who knew how to handle everything!

Ma was just carrying the meatloaf to the table when we came through the door. Pa looked up at me. "Where you been? You didn't get the garbage out to the alley. Eddie had to do it!" he glared out of his square face and drew a breath. "And you stink of cigarettes. You better not be smoking!"

Well, my insides froze; and as I opened my mouth, a big apologetic smile spread across Uncle Fun's face.

"Hey, my bad habits, Steve-o," he interrupted. "I had a few smokes on the steps with the guard, the beaneroo and me and him chewing the fat about baseball after the beaneroo got through inside there." And then, never missing a beat, he spun out this story about a paper I had to write on Egyptian tombs. And hey, he'd been to Egypt; so why not help me?

Well, I *did* have a paper to write, that much was true.

And Ma, well she lit up like a Christmas tree! "Here," she passed a basket of rolls, "fresh-baked. And I've got some of that pie you like, too. It sure was nice of you to help your nephew out--and with all your experience from traveling."

Myself, I kept looking at Ma. And I could feel the hundred and five we'd won as if it were in my own pocket! I wanted to wave it in the air, to dance around like a maniac, to crush it into Ma's hand and say, "Here. Buy something! Buy anything you want!"

Well, after a bit and we cleared the plates; and Ma brought out the chocolate dream pie and put it on the sideboard. She cut two slices. Then, turning toward the table and still glowing over the fake homework deal, Ma set the first plate in front of Uncle Fun; but then froze, picked it up and set it in front of Pa, a blush crawling up her cheeks because in our house, Pa was *always* served first. But Pa, he didn't say a word; but just stared at the piece of pie and then picked up his fork.

"Mighty sweet woman," Uncle Fun said, then, and in this really soft voice but loud enough for everyone to hear--and looking straight at Ma. "Sweetest woman. Best cook! Best sister I ever had!"

And that's when it hit me that Uncle Fun had a hook in Ma's heart, and was working it in deeper every day!

I stared at him, then. Well, because it seemed like something a kid would do! But then for all I knew, the whole grown-up world ran on kid's tricks! And I watched Uncle Fun dive into his pie. And to tell the truth, I felt sick about the lie we'd told; but pushed the whole thing into a dark corner of my mind. I'd straighten it all out later; but right now, Uncle Fun wanted me to play cards!

The next day, after school, Uncle Fun took me to the bowling alley. We sat in the snack area listening to the high metallic ring of strikes and spares. I could feel their vibrations enter the soles of my shoes and then travel through my butt to my waist!

"I got it all figured," Uncle Fun tapped a cigarette from its pack, "--about how we can clean up! First, we put on a squeeze play by betting high to drive up the other bets. I saw that one in Vegas and Monte Carlo a million times. And nobody'd expect it from a kid." And you might think his words would make me happy or proud, but--and all the bowling pins in the five alleys seeming to crash down at once, I pushed myself away from the table shaking my head.

"Hey, count me out of that! Pa's gonna' kill me if he finds out we lied last night. And now I'm supposed to cheat on top of it?"

Uncle Fun cocked his head. "You don't get it, do you, kid? Cards are *about* cheating. People expect it; and that's half the fun! Well, and the money, of course. EVERYBODYwants the *moo-lah*, eh? Yesterday, people were cheating here all the time!"

"Not me! And I never cheated those times before when I beat you. I never cheated yesterday; and even so, we won a hundred-five dollars!" I felt my chest puff out. "I don't have to cheat!"

Uncle Fun lit his cigarette, then blew the flame out with a long leisurely stream of air. "You're telling me your Pa never cheated on anything? He never made up one little lie, say, on his Income Tax?"

I shook my head. "No. My Pa doesn't do that!"

"Well your Ma was a little liar when she was a kid. Used to lie about doing my chores for me. Did it all the time. Never thought a thing of it."

I crossed my arms over my chest. I shook my head again. "That's not the same thing," I said, but didn't know why it wasn't.

Then slowly, Uncle Fun stubbed out his cigarette, and never taking his eyes from my face.

"Well, I guess I made a mistake," he said, then. "Because you're so smart, I thought you were older." He fixed them upon me a long minute, then shrugged. "Well, no one ever said you have to help your Ma. And your Ma, she never asked you."

Oh, but I *wanted* to do something for Ma! And I wanted to see the look on Pa's face when I handed over to him a wad of twenty dollar bills; and the look on my brother Eddie's face, too. I wanted to hang around with grown ups!

I stirred the ice in my coke, looked out over the twelve bowling lanes bouncing light. Well, if everyone else was cheating; if my own uncle said it was all right—. And I let myself slide over the line. "But just for a little while!"

"*Okaay!*" Uncle Fun slapped his open palm on the face of the table. "*Okaay!* And I've got me a signal here that these farmers in Rocky-ford never clamped their peepers on! Oh, and it's gonna be *bee-ootiful*, little man." And his eyes glittered like just-washed stones.

From out of his pocket, then, Uncle Fun pulled some change and a playing card. He placed a coin on the card's upper right-hand corner. "Kings." He moved it, then, to the opposite corner: "Queens." He moved it to another corner: "Jacks"; then to the center of the card: "Aces." Next, he doubled the chips, each new combination in play meaning something different. "'You show me your hand, I'll show you mine." Hey, a real love tune, eh beaneroo? Picked this one up in 'Carlo--only you need to find something besides a coin to use. Use a coin all the time and somebody'll catch on. And don't do it every hand, either. I'll show you. And we'll split the take sixty-forty 'cause I'm the one's got to find the games.'"

I nodded, swallowed, high up there on the roof now against the sky and walking the slick edge, careful not to look down to where Ma and Pa and Eddie were so small and far away.

Two days a week, now, after school, Uncle Fun and I would go to a poker game. Two days a week I'd go to the library and do double-time on homework. I also joined the Science Club after school in case I might need more "time" cover. And Uncle Fun and I saw to it we were never late for dinner. And any smoke smell on me, my Ma and Pa'd think it came from Uncle Fun's smoking. So, it was easy, really--and "just until we got enough money" Uncle Funt told me.

Deep down, though, it scared me that my parents didn't pick up on anything. And nights, I'd dream really weird stuff that set my heart to pounding; and made me glad to wake up.

Well, and we were bringing in sixty to a hundred a game, now! And the fifth week, Uncle Fun sent six hundred-forty dollars to a guy in Chicago to invest for us—in Uncle Fun's name, of course, me being underage. And really, the hardest thing was not telling. After dinner, sometimes, I'd see Ma paging through a catalogue or reading ads in the newspaper. "Oh, just get it," I'd want to yell out. "Go ahead, Ma. Get whatever you want!'"

And Uncle Fun started having Ma iron him a shirt for the next day. "Got a hot prospect," he'd tell her. After a week, he came home saying he had something at Grundel and Grundel, an insurance office downtown. They would train him. He was waiting to see if it would work out, if he liked it. And he started giving Ma twenty-five dollars a week room and board. And Ma switched around the house with this smug look. And Pa's face began to relax a little.

Job or no job, Uncle Fun would be there at the schoolyard fence every Tuesday and Thursday after school. And I was really surprised that his boss had let him off like that. I even asked him once, "Don't they want a note from your doctor or something?"

Well, and Uncle Fun made it our business to stay on the sprawling slum side of town, going apartment to store front to garage. Once in a while, I'd see someone from Fresno's; but mostly, each group of dedicated card players seemed to stick to themselves. Uncle Fun and I'd play one group until they didn't look too glad to see us; then we'd move on. And while Uncle Fun got "shit" (as he called it) regular as rain, he'd be the one to drive up the bets. And me? Well, I'd haul in the cash, the winnings. And, like Uncle Fun would say, we two were "slick as ice"!

Well, and while the cheating was nerve-wracking, it was exciting, too. I tried not to let myself think too much, either, about Ma and Pa because I wanted to be with Uncle Fun. I wanted to be with grown-ups. Oh, and I really wanted the money!

Now, the men we played didn't seem to work, to have jobs. And I asked Uncle Fun once where they got the cash to play; and my uncle made a gesture like fanning out playing cards. Once we took home two hundred eighty-five dollars. And Uncle Fun clapped me on the back. "Hey, baby boy, you're the Mother Lode," he crowed. "You're the whole ball of wax!"

"'Man! and did I feel like a king!

After dinner, then, one night, I went with Ma to the A&P to help her carry to the car a couple of twelvers for Pa, a case of canned chili, tubes of cookie dough and some smaller stuff Ma liked to keep on hand. So, we're standing in the checkout line and this black guy in dreads and overalls looks over and gives me the high sign. And my stomach drops because the black guy is Lotto! And I nod back a little, and then look away. But Lotto, he steps right up to Ma, anyway.

"Evenin' m'am," he tips his ball cap. "A real smart boy yuh got there, m'am," he says; "-- a real banker. He shore does yuh proud." And then, Lotto smiles and steps back into the other line.

"Why, now who was that?" Ma asks me, digging in her purse for her checkbook.

"Um--I met him with Uncle Fun, Ma. Someone he works with."

And Ma gave me a funny look. "He works with your uncle?"

Later, I told Uncle Fun about it. "But what if I'm with Pa some day and something like that happens?" my stomach still in knots.

"Same deal. Just don't say we work together." We were sitting on my bedroom floor; and Uncle Fun had started shuffling the cards. "I got something new I want to show you, kid," he told me.

"But if Pa finds out, he'll kill me--money or no money."

"Naw! Not when he sees those stocks we're piling up."

Well, I let myself relax against the bed, then. "About how much by now, you figure?"

Uncle Fun let his eyeballs roll upward; then he shrugged. "Two, three thousand and something." He started dealing.

"With or without stocks?"

"Hey, it's all stocks now. I took care of that. Pick up your hand."

But I sat up straight, instead. "No. we've got enough, then. And I want to quit."

And at that, Uncle Fun screwed up his face. "Naw. This is peanuts! You're just getting the jitters from that bozo in the store. And hey, we've got room to do better now---a whole lot better!" he said; but his eyes turned shadowy; and in a way I didn't like.

"Well, hey," he went on again after a moment, "and you don't want to quit now; not while we're getting ahead! We're partners, you and me, remember? And we quit now, then what happens to me? I got plans, responsabilities! Listen, two months more at the outside, o.k.? And we'll double what we've got now!"

"But everyday I'm afraid I'm going to blow it! I want to quit now, before Pa and Ma catch on."

Uncle Fun let out a long slow smile that froze his face, then.

"Hey, you're not going to welch on your partner now, are you?" he said. "Hey, who got all this going for you? I got needs too, you know. And I need more games! Hey, it's payback time, kiddo. And your ma and pa, when they see all the *do-re-m* we pile up, why, they're going to be thanking me--us--for this!"

Well, and I got so I didnt like his voice any more, *not at all!* And I didn't like his smile, either! In fact, it was getting so I didn't like Uncle Fun very much at all, anymore! But "O.k., o.k.!" I told myself and turned to him, "Two months!"

We went deeper for games, now--went into those outskirt neighborhoods with languages different from English. And Uncle Fun took to renting Fresno's car to get me home on time for dinner. Well, and I was surprised such hard-up people would be interested in what *we* had to offer.

"Naw," Uncle Fun would cackle over the roar of the engine, "that jig'll do anything for a dime." And his wasn't much of a car, either: the windows wouldn't roll up; and we had to keep the heater blasting all the time, it was that cold for April!

And by then, too, I'd look at Pa and feel the lies piling up like jagged rocks in my gut. And sometimes I'd want to grab Pa's arm and tell him everything--and ask him to make Uncle Fun stop. At night, I'd lie on my back and go over the list of what I was going to buy for everyone in the family as soon as I got more money.

Then one afternoon after school, Uncle Fun took me for a Tasty-Freeze. "Hey, it's about time we played Fresno's again," he said, and with his tongue plowed grooves into his ice cream. "After that, I want to move on to a new game I heard about in Mexi-town." he licked his lips clean.

"But can't we just stop now?' the words burst out of me. "And I'll be having finals in four weeks. I need to study." I crossed my arms over my chest and drew a deep breath. "I can't play this anymore--at least for a while--not until school's over," I stretched the boundary.

"HEY, BUDDY!" Uncle Fun threw his hands out. "Hey, I thought you wanted this as much as me!" We were sitting in a little booth in a fast food place. Uncle Fun put his feet up, then, to lean his head against the wall and look at me for what felt like a long, long time. "You know," he said finally, and smiling a little smile, "you've been great--just great, Kidderoo! And you are one talented dude.!"

"I don't care!" to my surprise, I came right back at him." I can't do this anymore!" I said and shut my mouth hard, afraid I was going to cry.

Uncle Fun reached over and socked me on the arm. "Hey, listen now, kiddo! We'll quit soon. I promise! And we'll talk it over soon, real soon." H peeled off bills for the check. "But hey, right now," he dropped his feet to the floor, "you and I got business!"

And too soon, we were picking our way up the familiar dark, sagging stairs to knock at Number six; and me hoping Uncle Fun didn't have anything in his pockets but *real* money this time!

The Chinese guy, Starch, opened the door, looking me over as I stepped into the room. "Baby Booda no dwarf now!" he announced. And it was true. I had turned thirteen and now was tall as Uncle Fun.

"You come take our groceries 'gain, Baby Booda?" Shotgun, leaned back in his chair and looking up from cleaning his long fingernails with the corner of a playing card. Behind him, the kitchen faucet dripped and Lotto came from the fridge with bottles of beer and an RC for me. "Thanks," I told him. And really, I was glad to see them all; and wished that *just this once* we could play it straight!

Uncle Fun bought our chips, then took a chair across from me, shook a cigarette from his pack and lit up. The smoke rose overhead, a moving gray ribbon among moving gray ribbons.

Fresno came from the bedroom carrying a bottle of Jim Beam and adjusting and his eye-patch. The game today was a version of Seven Card Stud. And lifting the corners of their already-dealt face-downs were Fresno, Road Hog (big gut, diamond pinkie ring and warm smile), Shotgun (thin secretive face), Uncle Fun and me.

Oh, and my cards right away were hot; so I kept sliding chips on and off the signal card; but then noticed Fresno watching me. And starting the fourth round, Fresno leaned across the table to Uncle Fun. "My, my, but ain't yo' boy learned some mighty fine tricks since we seen him las'." Then he took a swig from his bottle of beer.

And in response, Uncle Fun reached into his pocket, and out it came again wearing a big rubber thumb he held up, then, his hands next to one another and fingers spread. "Hey, dude," he said, "we're clean! We're a polished floor!"

And everybody guffawed, except for Fresno.

"So, I see someone bringed his toys along to keep hisself 'mused. Now, his nefew here, he don' need no toys. But I likes this one 'cause I can view his hans real clear. In fac'," and Fresno leaned over so far I could see his bald spot, "I'd 'preciate yuh sitting next ta one 'nother so's I can see the both of yus at onect. Shotgun here swap yuh seats."

Shotgun looked up, surprised.

"Hey, no problem to us!" Uncle Fun's voice was like light bouncing off a windshield. He came around to sit next to me, then. And you'd better believe my heart was pounding into my ears!

So, Fresno pulled his eyes back to his own hand, then; but it was as if those eyes of his were on a rubber band. And Uncle Fun looked down at his cards and then started drumming something military on the table and then, still holding his cards, let his fingers spread out so that the index finger was pointing to the corner of the card nearest his thumb; and signaling me the squeeze was still on.

Idle talk slowed until there was only silence and the up/down of throw-aways, the chink of chips and rattle of the refrigerator bringing ing itself awake as play went on, strings tightening across my stomach. And for the life of me, I couldn't bring myself to signal back to Uncle Fun even though I could feel his anger piling up like mortar.

Lotto took the next pot; took the one after that.

"Fresno," Uncle Fun said suddenly, "why don't you throw that old junk heap of yours in, too?" And he leaned back to pull a cigarette from behind his ear; then lit it real casual; and Lotto whopped, "Hey man, nobody here want Fresno old tuna can. Monkeys runnin' it from uner'neath. An, plus gas, you got 'ta feed them monkeys twice 'a day, too!"

"Fresno car?" Shotgun scratched his chin with his long fingernails. "Hundret year old dog move faster'n that car!"

Everyone laughed at this, Uncle Fun's cackle riding the crest.

"Hey, there's a rich dude I know 'ud love ta park that bucket o' rust front uv his bank fer a joke. 'An I could sell that pile rust t'morrer—if'n it's still runnin' then," Fresno put in, stacking and unstacking his chips, his face still as a board.

Then it was Shotgun's deal. First Street: two cards down, one up. High card bets. Fold, call or raise clockwise.

I had one king of Diamonds and one queen of Hearts down, a four of Diamonds up. Uncle Fun pushed a chip onto the upper right corner of his second facedown; and staring deeply into his hand, then, he tapped it as if absently, with his forefinger.

"Hey now, an' you think ah'm some kin'na fool, White Man?" Fresno bellowed. "You think ah be blin' an' cain't see nothin' nohow?" Temples bulging, Fresno leaned towards Uncle Fun.

"Nix it!" I screamed in my mind, then, at Uncle Fun. "Just drop the whole deal!"

But instead, Uncle Fun threw a wide grin at Fresno, then raised his hands, fake thumb and all. "Okay, okay; you got me!" he crowed and put the chip back in his stack.

Then Lotto started in whistling some slow kind of tune; and I swallowed and pushed twenty dollars of chips out to ante up. By now, Fresno's visible eye looked bloodshot; and something told me to get out of there--to just get up and walk away! Yes, but then I'd have to face Uncle

Fun at home! And Uncle Fun had all the money I'd won tied up now in Chicago "--to *triple it*," he'd told me, nodding.

Second Street. One card, face up. I showed a Jack of Hearts.

Third Street. Shotgun dealt me a nine of hearts, face up. Uncle Fun raised on whatever he had. Lotto folded saying, "Rag pickins, rag pickins", then spit tobacco juice into a glass, crossed his arms and sat back to watch while Starch, next to him, folded.

Fourth Street I got a ten of hearts as my last card; and I can tell you that the sight of it made me so sick that I started prayers in my mind that there was another straight flush out there, ace high.

"Double dip." Uncle Fun pushed four twenty-dollar chips out, the cigarette between his fingers spinning smoke. "And a cherry." He added four more, riding on my hand, now because I *always* got the cards.

Road Hog arced his empty beer can into the trash with, "*Jesus y Maria!* I am one dead duck! My ole lady's gonna' kill me." He wiped a beefy hand across his face, the stone of his pinky ring flashing first blue and then deep rose.

And now it was just Uncle Fun, Fresno, and me.

Fresno studied what he had in the hole while, with his other hand, he covered his little pile of chips as if to keep anyone from seeing his treasure chest.

"How 'bout that broken down oil can, black man?" Uncle Fun drawled, then. "Why not throw it in? That is, if it's all right with the Squirt here!"

"*Will you please shut your mouth?!*" I wanted to scream at Uncle Fun, then, my heart at the base of my throat all jagged edges while Fresno sat up stiff as a board and staring at his cards. He took a swig of liquor.

"Well, and I can see why you wouldn't want to let that old pile of crap go," Uncle Fun carried on, his voice high and light. "--'cause I guess it's just about the finest thing you're ever gonna own. And if I was you, I'd never give it up either, knowing I'd probably never get anything better again." And with that, Uncle Fun stubbed his cigarette out, keeping his eyes on Fresno's face. "Naw, we're just gonna' take the money you got in this pot and the other pots we won today; and we're gonna' buy us a *real* car," Uncle Fun smiled broadly, carrying on. "Why, Lady Fortune's been smiling on me and the Squirt here--." He dragged on his cigarette, exhaled, squinted through the smoke. "--but she don't seem to care much for nigg—."

And thank God, Shotgun hustled in, then, calling for the discard. At the same time, Fresno reared up, his face covered with tiny beads of sweat. I saw him raise his arm and heard Lotto yell "Hey m' man--!" And Fresno's belly hit the table with a grunt. And I smelled whiskey like squeezed from a sponge amd turned away and feel a thin hot flame dig itself into my left side;and hear myself go "Uhhh!" And I dropped my eyes to see what looked like the handle of Uncle Fun's joke knife standing up at the top of my belly--and with a bright bubble of blood that grew and popped,; and then little droplets of blood flew to dot and soak the brown of my pants.

And immediately, Fresno shouted into Uncle Fun's face, "Why you move, devil? That were for *you*, not the boy! *WHY YOU MOVE?*"

Yet somehow, my heart pounding, I didn't feel pain; but couldn't catch my breath for anything. It was like trying to pull air through a real thin straw while the room turned so wobbly; and I kept thinking "If I could just get my breath--!" And then I thought maybe outdoors' air would be easier to take in, so I tried to get up; but right away fell like a sack of grain against my uncle who said, "Hey, easy, kid! Take it easy--." though his face was white.

He propped an arm around my back and reached for a knife.

"NO! Don't touch!" Starch yelled then, and reaching to stop Uncle Fun's hand. *"Too much blood! Let doctor!"*

"Gotta get the car." Lotto's voice.

The door banged. I felt its breeze like a mercy while in my mind I kept hearing Starch saying "Too much blood!" and wondered what would happen to me.

Then Fresno's big arm was under my knees; and the painted tin ceiling above me cartwheeled while a thick musty smell slipped over my face as we moved into the hallway, and then lurched down the stairs. And my hands felt so far away, and like rags jumping up and down while the air around me boiled with fear while the low ceiling leaned and followed us.

"You're gonna be all right, kid," Uncle Fun kept telling me.

Oh, and how I wished now that it was my Pa's voice I heard as my head bounced against Fresno's shoulder and I struggled to breath--wished that it was my Pa holding me, carrying me. And then there came a gigantic blaze of light to slice through the gloom of the stairway and we passed into the honk and clatter of Albany Street.

The next thing I saw was Ma's tight face and puffy eyes. And I heard her crying out, "Oh Tony, I'm so sorry, so sorry!" And then I didn't see or hear anything for a long time; but I wasn't so scared anymore.

When I woke next, I had a tube in my side, a bottle for fluid on the floor and a white-haired doctor telling me that I was a mighty lucky young man. Starch had been right about not touching the knife. The blade had entered my lung. Even now, when I shower, I still see the scar like a thick piece of string plastered between my ribs.

Pa sat in a chair in the corner, locking and unlocking his fingers; and when he saw Ma give me water, he got up to shoo her out of the room.

And that's when I started to cry. "It was my fault, Pa; it was all my fault!" And my voice echoed in my ears as if it came through a metal tube. "I shouldn't have gone there. I knew it was wrong." Prying the words out was like digging rocks; and I had to stop and pant and be knifed in the side while I drew a breath and the tears trickled into my mouth. "I lied to you and Ma," I bawled; "but it was going to be just until I got enough money."

"We know all about it." I felt the weight of Pa's big hand like a warm animal upon my forehead; and it made me feel safe, made my eyelids want to droop.

"You sleep, now," Pa"s voice to me came strong. "Don't worry. We can work everything out." And I had never seen his face like that before, the way Ma's looks sometimes, soft and with nothing held back; and I wanted to stay there forever with Pa looking at me that way. I wanted to tell him there were stocks, *lots of stocks*; but my eyelids rolled down like heavy doors. And the next day, it was doctors and nurses and Ma and Eddie and sleep and more sleep. And then, about eight-thirty that night, Ma shrugged into her raincoat and gave me a kiss.

"They might give you real food tomorrow," she told me softly.

But I wrinkled my nose because my mouth tasted like a pencil eraser. And I kept drifting off as if my bed were a boat in a dream. Over and over, I kept seeing Uncle Fun's frozen smile; and then a diamond flash of light. One time my eyes flew open, and there Uncle Fun stood at the foot of my bed, soaking wet and with his own eyes swollen nearly shut. He stepped nearer my hospital bed; and I smelled the Chicago rain that clung to his coat.

Uncle Fun's lower lip was all puffed out; and he moved his words carefully around the cracks and splits there.

"How'r you doing, kiddo?"

I wobbled my hand: So-so.

He dug into his pocket and tossed three crumpled bills onto the nightstand. "Here. Put 'em in the bank for later, for something you really want." Then he looked at me a long moment. "The doc says you're going to be o.k." He turned to leave, then; and as he passed my foot sticking up under the sheet, he gave it a light squeeze; and I could feel how small the bones of his hand were--like chicken bones.

"THE MONEY!!" I called out over a terrible stab of pain in my side. "Where-are-the-stocks?"

Uncle Fun turned at the door. He raised his shoulders high and then let them drop. "I had my expenses, kidderoo. It costs to find games. The rest went to the dog races. Thought, with any luck, we could make a killing there!" He shrugged again. "Three hundred's all that's left, now." And with that, he passed through the hospital room's doorway to dissolve like jello into the lowered lights of the hallway.

The next day Eddie told me that when Pa got to the emergency room and saw me, he dragged Uncle Fun outside behind a hedge and started pounding him--pounding him and crying. Everyone was busy with me; and Eddie said that Uncle Fun took it without a sound; and that Pa did a good job on him, too, before a hospital guard could put a stop to it.

"Did Ma know? Didn't she try to stop him?" I shoved aside my tray of chicken broth and Jell-O to stare at my brother.

Eddie nodded; he had a big square face like Pa's. "She knew; but she just stayed out of it; and crying. Then Eddie looked sheepish, "I even cried," he said in a low voice." But then he threw his head. "Naw, are you kidding? Me crying over a bug in the road?"

I stuck my spoon into the Jell-O and catapulted a green cube at his head. It arched high and wide of its mark, bouncing off the wall, then landing in the little sink while Eddie called out, "Three points!" And we high-fived.

The hospital informed the police, because it was a stabbing. Uncle Fun told everything, but made up names and the street address, saying it was a bunch of men that he'd never met before, maybe around Evergreen or

Maple, naming some streets farther north. So I was grateful and relieved that Fresno, Lotto and the others got away o.k.

The police asked Pa and Ma if they wanted to press charges—something about "a minor." Pa looked at Ma; she shook her head, "no" back to Uncle Fun.

"And Ma never once looked at Uncle Fun?" I don't know why, but I felt happy about that, like she'd chosen me over Uncle Fun; like she'd chosen all of us over Uncle Fun. And the way she just let Pa do what he felt. I was happy about that too.

Pa turned to the cop, "But don't let me see him again!" he warned.

"Uncle Fun, when he saw that you didn't die, he looked at Ma's back," Eddie said, "and he was crying. Then he looked at me; then at Pa. And then he looked at you again. And that was it."

"No!" I broke in. "He came back to see me. He left me three hundred dollars!" I could still feel the chicken bones of his hand rest for a moment on my ankle, then give my foot a little squeeze.

Eddie snorted. "What was that, payment for your lung?"

Pa and Ma came over again that evening--and real quiet toward each other. Pa slipped his arm around Ma's shoulder; and when he looked at me and at Eddie, his face didn't close up.

After the numbness wore off of my feelings, well I couldn't help hating Uncle Fun for losing my money I won--and just for being who he was, a weasel.

Well, it felt like quite awhile before it didn't hurt any more to breathe--and before I could run again. And I couldn't help but think that I could have died! But later, after time rubbed the sharp edges off my fear and anger, and I could touch what happened to me a little with my mind--well, I had to see that. Yes, though I was just thirteen, I knew better than to lie! And I knew Uncle Fun was taking me to scummy places--and that I'd wanted to see scummy places, to be with grown-ups! And Uncle Fun never forced me to do anything!

Now I'm forty years plus, a computer programming geek raking it in here in Chicago. Ma's still in Rockford; and I can get her nice things whenever I feel like it. Pa died five years ago from the mills. Eddie's in the Air Force in California making a name for himself. So when they sent Uncle Fun's remains back from Saudi-Arabia in a pine box and with a roped-up suitcase and twelve American dollars in his pocket, I was the one to go and help Ma.

Ma wanted me to take something of Uncle Fun's. We were in this hot little room at Halston's Funeral Parlor; and Uncle Fun's suitcase was open on the floor with nothing to look at but khaki shorts, tired grey underpants, a tattered copy of a girlie magazine in French I hated to have Ma see, his worn straw sandals, three T shirts, a pair of blue jeans, a worn white shirt, beach pants, crumpled pajamas and a Chicago Cubs baseball hat.

Ma held out this little tray with a watch, a ring, two Chinese coins, an arrowhead, two small ivory dice and a key to our back door. Well really, I didn't want to touch any of it; and couldn't look at Ma.

"Take something," she nudged the tray against my stomach. "He was your uncle, honey."

So I took the ring and held it by two fingers wondering "Why that?" because it had no sheen, but just a battered oval stone of a color like darkened blood. I dropped it into my pocket; figured I'd get rid of it after Ma passed. And then the funeral director ushered us--Ma and Pa, my brother and me--into the parlor to view the corpse.

All Uncle Fun had needed was a jacket and shirt, but Ma wanted me to get him new clothers--"the works". And, to tell the truth, it really rankled me to buy anything for him!

Well--and then, to tell the truth again, except for the white hair, he looked like a twelve year-old boy dressed up in his dad's suit. And my stomach lurched at the familiar contours of his face so eroded now by age and the parasites that killed him. Again, I saw him hang on the fence at my grammar school, fake knife in his chest; saw him at the table at Fresno's picking up his cards, the hazy blue smoke from his cigarette spiraling upward, wider and wider.

Ma crumpled at the little prayer stand in front of the casket, her face pure pain. And I saw that I wasn't the only one who took a knife. There in the funeral parlor, I found out what family meant to her, how it was as if we all were knit into her--into her very body--and that she could never come apart from us, nor even want to.

We followed the hearse with the yellow and white roses Ma had wanted. And I couldn't help but think about the guy in the coffin: a bad news dude; a real sick, separated guy; my uncle. I thought how he had a love like Ma's right in his lap and couldn't take it in or give it back--he was that far away.

Then, something besides repulsion and anger toward him stirred in me a little,. Maybe there was a special kind of feeling of grief that what we did together and had together couldn't have been --or meant--something different, something better.

The seamy side of Rockford where we gambled all those years ago is townhouses and dress shops and specialty grocery stores now. And I wonder at times whatever became of Fresno and Lotto and the Chinese guy--I forget his name. But I taste again the rich feeling of being all together around that poker table in that sinking room with the smoke lying low over our heads.

We pulled up to an intersection, nosed onto the expressway to Queen of Angels Church and Cemetary, day of the burial. And I reached across to take Ma's hand. Seeing what she was made of (and Dad passed over three years ago, now!)!-- pride in my Ma, how she took her suffering and didn't lay it on anyone else-- that was something really good I got from all this! And playing cards with Fresno, Lotto and the Chinese guy-- Starch, was it? That was good--and fun too, except the last game. Hmm. Stroch? Stradch? No, no. Starch. Yeah, that was his name! *STARCH!* The guy who kept Uncle Fun from pulling out the knife so that I didn't bleed to death!

Figlia Mia
The Passion of Mother Adelli

1. There Will Be No Problem, Dr. Rhenehan

The floors had just been waxed that brilliant September afternoon in 1948 when Michael Rhenehan brought his ten year-old daughter Helene to the Convent of the Holy Angels for school.

Before dawn, and down upon their hands and knees, six religious Sisters spun out thick amber paste until a golden ice shone everywhere.

Standing at the front door, the prominent young heart surgeon saw sagging grey stones, crawling green ivy and milky windows. Michael Rhenehan took a deep breath and shot his right index finger forward to jab the doorbell twice. "Oh God," he thought, "I hope to hell this is going to be all right!"

It was exactly three o'clock. And at the sound of the buzzer, he passed through the narrow vestibule and inner door with its pale etched glass to mount the dark worn wooden steps worn and strode into the foyer.

Immediately, his heavy physician's sole sailed out from under him; and in a rush of air, the fluted wall lamps, European side tables and antique vases sprang out while from the ceiling, the ornate ceiling fixture of shining glass balls reeled downward toward the freshly waxed floor had risen immediately to strike a hammering blow into his left rump, and to empty his lungs.

And for a moment, the doctor just sat, staring.

Ahead loomed the chapel doors with the carved oversized hearts pictured on the front of the Order's brochure; while everywhere else there stretched the shimmering self-expressive pond of wax. And why in hell would anyone bring floors to such a high shine that no one could stand on them! he thought in a rage while his hangover gonged, gonged, gonged behind his eyes. Next there came the urgent tippytap of portress feet.

"No, no. 'm-fine-thank-you-Mothe. No-problem!" the doctor found his knees, his feet, then, smoothed his hair, his injured throbbing ham while his redheaded daughter, dawdling up the stairs behind, night bag banging at her knees, froze just in the doorway while her father raised himself to lean upon one elbow to stave off the clucking nun.

The portress steered them into the parlor where tall French windows let dollops of sunlight splatter over the antique furnishings; and while the lace curtains breathed in air from the changling window outside, only to release it with a sigh--and as the portress murmured something in French and disappeared. And why is it that *she* never slips on these floors? Michael Rhenehan wondered sourly, nursing his shins.

Father and daughter escaped onto the settee near the windows.

Michael Rhenehan, massaging his elbow, took in small rugs floating like exotic postage stamps upon the polished parlor floor. Oh, but he saw solvency! Why, were his wife Helen still alive, this is exactly the school she would have wanted for their daughter: One of the best Catholic girls' schools in the country—(everybody said so)—and with teaching nuns drawn from some of the most prominent of Catholic families! (Who must surely be royalty; the place was costing enough!) Why, his own Catholic grammar school had been bare bones by comparison! He looked around.

Portraits of past Superiors bossed the walls. And in each face he read disapproval of a father who would bring his only and motherless daughter here like a dog to a kennel so that he could gallivant around Europe lecturing on surgical procedure! Well, but in his own defense, wasn't that a charitable act--and tax deductible as well?

He shook the thought away to breathe in the floor's spicy wax as it collided with the smell of his own alcohol-driven sweat. Oh, if he could just unzip his skin! And had that nun gone for someone, or were he and his girl just supposed to sit all day guessing what to do next? He stole a glance at the figure beside him to see the motherless daughter rummaging in her nose with a stubby finger. He let an elbow fly.

"Use your handkerchief," he hissed.

The girl frosted him with her blue eyes--a startling robin's-egg blue, they were from under the wild copper of her dead mother's hair. The girl was tall for ten and thick; and carrying square shoulders and a flat, pan-shaped face of freckles.

"If 've told you once, I've told you a thousand times, *'Always bring a handkerchief!'* Your father is a physician, for God's sake! Here!" He rolled onto one ham and held out a white square.

The girl slid the finger in and out of her mouth. "I don't need it, now," she grinned. and oh, how his blood simmered!

They had argued the thirty miles north from Chicago. She had wanted a school in Italy while he was away; or else to live with her grandmother in New York. Well, but she didn't speak Italian; and he would be traveling God knows where all the time. Also, her grandmother was not as well as she pretended to be. And in any case, it would only be for six months--and maybe only for four!

And the daughter had turned her nose into the wind, then, for the rest of the drive while, from out her car window, Lake Michigan flashed brilliant and sapphire through its screen of rangy woods and partially hidden wealthy homes.

As he stuffed the handkerchief back into his breast pocket, the father noticed now that her socks did not look clean. Jesus Christ, these nuns were going to think she's lived in an alley! "And straighten up, will you? You're like laundry just off the line."

"Well, I wonder who I learned that from," the daughter came right back.

"Well, I'm just hoping, with all that sitting on the plane tomorrow, I don't throw my back out. But hey, and what a beautiful day it is out there!" he cranked the talk a new direction by reaching to pull aside the drape on the parlor window and let in a stabbing blare of light. Helene threw her arm across her eyes.

Out the window, if you looked high, columns of clouds marched east to west, above the trees. The father dropped the curtain. "Well, the school looks really fine!" he went on; "--even better than what the brochure shows.

And I'll bet your Nana wouldn't find any dust here!" He ran his index finger over the coffee table. "I could do surgery!"

"*Please*. And you can put me into any school you want in Rome." And he could see the tiny muscles that control tears tighten around her eyes. "I can pack in a jiffy! And I won't be any trouble!"

"Well, what will I tell them here, then?" As if they could just throw everything over now! Children always think things happen like in their storybooks. "Besides, there's your uniforms. They were made to order. We can't send them back."

"I'll wear them. I'll wear them out. Please, Dad. Look at the windows."

He had noticed the elegantly curved wrought-iron bars; and for the hundredth time, forced himself to picture Helene scuffling along behind him through the streets of Rome, her lower lip in a characteristic pout. No. *No* for the hundredth time. It would be hell!

"Why, you'll be going to Nana's in New York for Thanksgiving, then to Rome for Christmas, remember. Really, you're making too much of this Helene. It's not for that long. And lots of kids do this." And where in God's name was that nun?

"I don't care. *It's too long*. Besides, you promised you'd *never* leave me." And she turned upon him her eyes of righteousness.

They'd had their little ritual down the years that he would never leave. "Not even if Chicago falls into Lake Michigan?" she'd cocked her head, the little grin beginning. "Not even if a hurricane blows the United States off the face of the earth? Not even if there's World War III?" she'd repeat for the hundredth time. "NO!" He'd always bellow, or "*NEVER!*" and reel her into his big bear hug and carefully tightening the hug until she squealed.

But now he met her eyes and then looked away. Well, what could he say, "Some promises can't be kept"?

Just then, a short wide square of black boomed through the parlor door; and Michael Rhenehan jumped to his feet as Reverend Mother Gregory, in perfect command of the waxed floor, crossed with an outstretched hand, her black veil flaring. "Dr. Rhenehan! A pleasure to meet you after our telephone conversations."

Well the woman had a handshake like a sea captain!

He judged her to be about sixty-two or three, thirty pounds plus overweight and built like a naval destroyer, all chest and stomach under her mannish head and unnervingly wide mouth jammed into the white curlequed bonnet, its black veil falling about her shoulders and to the waist.

Helene climbed slowly to her feet.

"And is this our new 'student'?" the Superior swiveled toward the girl-—"Miss Rhenehan--*Helene*, isn't it?" She swiveled back to the father. "Well, I know this will be a *wonderful* association!" and she clasped her hands as if she'd caught a moth. Then, a swivel to the girl again. "And YOU are going to learn and learn here young lady!"

Helene's face darkened; she climbed back onto the settee.

"Please have a seat, doctor," the Superior waved.

Michael Rhenehan bowed, waited courteously for the Superior to select a chair noticing the bunion on the woman's left foot bulging in the front left of her black tie-up shoe.

Now here was an unusually attractive man; and well turned- out! the Superior decided arranging her floor-length black skirts. Here was a man with the supreme self-assurance and impatience of highly-driven professionals. Glancing quickly, she could see no damage from the reported fall. And the daughter? Well, a bear cub slightly overweight dressed in a fly-away shirttail, and with an insolent slouch that, in time, would be trained out of her!

Outdside, birds quarreled amongst the junipers while a north wind began to draw long dark fingers of cloud across the sun so that the light through the windows sobered and played hide-and-seek. In the parlor, the Superior stiffened her back, opened her gunwales and began firing: The mission of the Order even for modern times; for the young, the necessity of integrating spiritual, social, physical and intellectualand life; the philosophy of Madeleine Sophie Barat, their founder; needed especially now that World War II was finally won!

The father counted the Persian rugs: six, including the one in front of the small Victorian fireplace. And with his eyes, he traced the luminous ring of the frame of the antique magnifying glass on the coffee table. Hey, lots of kids went to boarding school! Boarding school was an advantage. But what if Helene got really sick? Well, he, Helene's father, overseas or not, could always be reached!

The father picked at invisible lint on his left sleeve. There were questions he should ask, he knew; but what were they? He locked his neck to hold his head up as it steadily filled with the older nun's voice, very dry but weighty, like sand. Oh, how long did this dismal affair have to take?

"—and so for safety, discipline must come first, here, Dr. Rhenehan." Reverend Mother Gregory jabbed at her temples. 'Spare the mind/Spoil the child' is our--and indeed society's--experience."

Helene chewed a thumbnail and, from under half-lidded eyes, shot a glance at The Jailer in black; saw her father now as if a puppet on the slippery brocade couch cover, and sweating and weaering that phony smile he had used with the other nun. And she felt the trap closing, closing; then bolted. She shifted her eyes to a far corner, and the piano -dark and hung with a silk throw.

"I noticed from your application, Dr. Rhenehan, that your daughter has not made her Frst Confession or Holy Communion. But she is Catholic? She has been baptized?"

"Her mother had her baptized."

"And you have kept her in Catholic schools?"

"Oh yes. I know the best education," he said, and watched pleasure flare in the woman's face.

"But you prefer that she not—"

"I am a man of science, Reverend Mother Gregory. I am not strong on religion. I want Helene to make up her own mind in that regard. She is not to be initiated into anything further just now. For the present, the atmosphere in a Catholic school is good for someone like my daughter who lost her mother so young, at four years old, and who has a father too busy, I'm afraid, most of the time to give the careful attention she deserves and requires."

"Well, but saving lives, Dr. Rhenehan! And yes, you choose wisely. The Church is the mother of Western civilization, old and new--and so rescues us from ignorance and godlessness."

The Superior beamed across the coffee table while she told herself that here was another child overblown by privilege and in a futile power struggle with those responsible for her. Well, they would make something of her for this worthy doctor! And if she, the Superior, judged the matter correctly, the girl would be with them through the fourth academic, the last year of high school. So, all the way around, it was just as well because a handsome, ambitious father wants and *needs* his freedom to accomplish his works of mercy!

"*C'est bon!* I've asked Mother Adelli, the Mistress of the *Third Cours* (from the French, translated as "Middle School") to join us. She is most anxious to meet you, Dr. Rhenehan. And you, of course, Helene!"

Helene let her only smile of the afternoon, actually a sneer, move momentarily across her lips.

"Now, your new Mistress, *Mere* Adelli —" Reverend Mother Gregory began to the girl but deferred immediately to the father. "You notice we use the French. We were founded in France." Back to the girl. "You will learn to speak French with us! I'm sure you'll like that."

"And when you are free for Christmas, you and I will have a little trip to Paris. You can help me to order in the restaurants, then," the father, beaming, made a menu of his hands.

"We are so pleased to have your daughter, Dr. Rhenehan. The other students are barely unpacked, themselves. Mother Adelli will see that your daughter makes up her work."

"I am an American; I speak English!" Helene raised her voice, her blue eyes sparking under her pinched copper eyebrows.

"Come, come." Reverend Mother Gregory patted her dimpled hands upon her lap. "A second language is a great advantage *pour tout le monde, n'est-ce pas?* And once you've had a good run on the hockey field, you'll feel as though you—why, our Mother Adelli is really new here herself," the Superior interrupted herself again to defer to the father. "--and stepped in for us from Omaha when Mother Boreman took ill last March. You might be interested: a rupture in the left ventricle."

"Oh?" Michael Rhenehan nodded, pulling himself back to the woman to purse his lips professionally while he strained not to look at his watch and in his mind, his convertible with its grey leather seats and top thrown back gleamed quietly under the portico. "Well--"

"And here is Mother Adelli now!" Reverend Mother broke in.

She came to them across the shining floor, a young woman not much taller than the girl and dressed in the black top cape and long whispering skirt of the Order, her rosary chattering, hanging from her waist and chattering lightly. The way she held herself, shoulders perfectly level, spine supple and straight as a young tree, made Michael Rhenehan think of a dancer. He rose to his feet to acknowledge the woman.

Reverend Mother Gregory did the honors while Mother Adelli slipped into the chair across from her Superior. Michael Rhenehan watched Helene survey the young nun to a cold count of five.

"We expect that our Mother Adelli here will be going to Rome, herself, this summer, Dr. Rhenehan, to make her Final Vows." And the Superior bestowed a broad smile, then, upon all, as if that last fact gave both nun and doctor a personal link.

"Oh?" Michael Rhenehan, nodded and forced his eyes to open further. Well, what was he supposed to say? Wasn't that what she was in here for? But the way the young nun sat, hand meditative upon the arm of her chair, her eyes modestly in her lap, made him remember one of Giotto's teenage virgins.

"Oh, but you must be sure to stop at the Trinita, our Convent in Rome, to see the miraculous fresco of *Mater Admirabilis*," the Superior went on, as if reading his mind. "Why, the color comes and goes in the Virgin's cheeks. I've seen it myself. And each Sacred Heart school keeps a replica of that painting. You'll see ours-- a stunning life-size statute!-- during our tour of the building and the grounds."

But Michael Rhenehan's eyes remained upon the young nun. If it hadn't been for the slight underbite, she would have been attractive, even pretty. The dark fringed eyes now softly taking in his daughter, though set a bit wide, were wonderfully bright beneath the delicate black brows shaped like birds' wings or twigs in a Japanese print. And that chocolate mole on the lower crest of the right cheek was out and out seductive. Really, he never could understand forcing the soft rounds of the female body into these odd-looking and harsh clothing constraints. Support, of course, was right; but this get-up with the tightly fluted bonnet and black wrapping over the forehead --. And those long black wool sleeves, day in, day out, must be like living in a sarcophagus. Odd the neck is left bare.

"I've mentioned to your classmates that they will have a new member now," Mother Adelli was bending to the girl. And the father wondered why the woman kept her voice so soft. Didn't she need more volume to handle girls his daughter's age? "--and everyone is excited to meet you. They're downstairs having *goûter* right now--"

"Another French word here," Reverend Mother Gregory bounded in. "This one comes from the verb 'to taste'. I've ordered *goûter* for you here in the parlor. I was sure you both would appreciate some refreshment after your long trip. And what a lovely way to spend your last hours together—driving along Lake Michigan, then tea with us," she added, as if father and daughter were sweethearts. "Have the uniforms arrived, Mother Adelli?"

"I don't have to wear those things all the time, do I?" Helene rippled her lip at her father. "I saw them in the catalogue. *Ugh*." And she turned a look upon him as if he owed her money.

Michael Rhenehan stirred. "Well, but you wore a uniform at Cathedral, Pumpkin."

"Well I'm not wearing that funeral-looking thing they have here!"

The Superior did not look amused. "White uniform is for feast days" she went right on. "And everyday uniforms keep us from being distracted by externals. You'll have no need for your outside clothes unless you are going to Chicago. We have sports uniforms for athletics. We wear white socks only, with brown oxfords. So, no saddle shoes. White gloves are for important ceremonies. Black veil for chapel."

"I've put everything in your alcove, Helene," Mother Adelli, watching the girl's face darken, waited respectfully, but then hurried in. "'Alcove' is what we call your sleeping place in the dormitory."

"Oh, your own room!" Michael Rhenehan rebounded.

"Not exactly a room," Mother Adelli intervened, respectfully; "-- more of a single bed, a small dresser, single chair, then curtains all around. Everyone has the same."

"We find that too much attention to physical things makes the mind sluggish," the Superior hefted forward; the chair gave out a soft crackle, then a shudder. "Don't you agree, Dr. Rhenehan?"

Michael Rhenehan smiled weakly and managed a small circular yes/no movement with his head. The woman was a brick wall; and whenever she spoke, everything in the room seemed to tumble toward her. He worried again about the other one, the young one--about her small frame. He had seen his daughter wrestle with her friends. Could this woman handle girls like that? Well, but hey, this Reverend Mother was experienced; and the younger woman must be competent or she wouldn't be trusted with children--and certainly not childen of the "better off"! considering legal suits, so on.

Then the surprise of *goûter* arrived chirping on a silver tray.

Michael Rhenehan balanced the china plate to cut away with a fork a small corner of brownie and then to chew dryly. The Superior explained that cloistered nuns take food only in private. Helene refused brownie and lemonade alike in favor of gnawing her fingernails. When her father hissed for her to "sit on her hands if she couldn't stop fidgeting," she drove air hard through her nose and jammed her closed fists under her thighs.

Meanwhile, Mother Adelli searched amongst the folds of her skirt for her rosary beads. Oh, and if only the father could ease back against the settee; if only the girl could take a lighter attitude. But of course, the father was anxious that his daughter's behavior not prejudice others against her. And of course the daughter felt she was drowning, like always, in a sea of adult bossiness and unfairness. Oh, if only the girl could just meet her classmates now and be gathered into a game! But there she went again with her "if onlys".

In August she, Mother Adelli, had received her new "chapter of faults."

Twice a year, this honing spiritual practice came around. Each religious would have her visible character defects compiled by two other religious whose names were drawn from a cardboard box. And then, the Community would gather in a circle of chairs three rows deep in the convent lounge; and Reverend Mother Gregory would call each penitent forward to kneel in the center of the circle and receive, for the good of her soul, correction of areas needing "work" from her superiors and the religiouss community.

"Seeing too many sides of an issue" was one fault Mother Adellia had acknowledged. And "not being able to make up her mind," being "too much of a loner," combined with "not seeking advice frequently enough" were areas needing "work". To these failings, the young nun herself had silently added her "short temper" and "covert vainity when her students showed friendliness or spontanous obedince to her."

And now, in the parlor, Reverend Mother Gregory's arm disappeared deep into the pocket of her religious garb; and then reading spectacles flashed in her hand as she looked from doctor to daughter. "While you are enjoying yourselves in our beautiful parlor, I'll explain our Rules of

Conduct". The Superior took a printed sheet from a folder she had carried into this meeting.

"*'1) A student is never, under any circumstances, to leave school grounds unless accompanied by an adult and/or with written permission of parent or guardian and/or the religious in charge.'*

"*'2) Proper decorum includes standing whenever an adult enters the room, speaking only when spoken to, and giving a curtsy to open and close any exchange with a religious, priest, parent and/or visitor.'*

"*'3) Courteous behavior and self-restraint are expected at all times.'*

"*'4) 'Students' alcoves, desks, and lockers will be inspected for cleanliness as necessary. All packages will be opened. No pets are allowed.'*

"*'5) No talking except at meals, goûter, going to and from physical education, during classes when appropriate and one half hour before and/or after bed time. Exceptions are feast days and special periods when the Mistress in charge or her superior shall decide to relax the rule.'"*

Michael Rhenehan felt the heavy presence of "no" while his daughter made complicated knots of her fingers. For the Superior, the unexpected sight of the girl's puffy teeth-marked fingernail ridges caused her to blink and looked away as she continued speaking.

"You will hear the phrase *nolo me tangere!* It says, "Do not touch me!" Students are NOT ever to touch one another except to give requested help or by accident. Students NEVER touch a religious!"

At his daughter's other school, the doctor father had seen the students silent in the corridors and at their desks while the nun in charge moved among them looking to be helpful and keeping an eye on things. But also, he had seen the same girls, their bodies wired now for play, a happy hilarity expanding like a balloon among them. And at three o'clock, he learned, the "day students" were allowed to take one another's arms in fun and friendship as they left to go home. Ah, but Helene would not be going home! And then the brownie bite caught in this throat; and he set down his plate, fingers stealing off to his pocket where he kept his tobacco and pipe.

"Ashtray, doctor?" Reverend Mother asked then, an oily tone to her voice as though she had caught him in an indecent act she was chosing to ignore.

He shook his head "no" and fetched his hand back sharply, his hang overdrilling his forehead.

"How many girls will Helene have in her class, Mother Adelli?" Reverend Mother turned to the younger nun.

"Well, it's twelve now, Reverend Mother!"

And Mother Adelli beamed upon the new prospect. "Helene, you are badly needed for the field hockey team. You may even get your choice of positions, for the Reds are short a player!" And at this, the knowing grownups passed around a soft chuckle.

Then Michael Rhenehan stirred a little. "There's rarely provision in the city for sports for girls, Reverend Mother; so I was very happy to see field hockey listed in your brochure. Helene will be good it--and she will be quite the runner if she ever gets the practice."

The Superior eyed the bubble of baby fat poking from under the girl's unhitched blouse: Indeed, parents' penchant for fictionalizing their children must be one of the wonders of the world!

"Field hockey, basketball, tennis, softball, cricket —" Mother Adelli leaned forward to lay out the program.

"Cricket! And for girls!" the father cried out, then.

"Which sport are you best at Helene?" Mother Adelli tried to draw the girl to invest in her own future.

But Helene only shrugged; and would not turn her head again until her father nudged her sharply. "Well, I'm not any good at sports," she replied, then; and the father's neck reddened.

"And you will make new friends here, Helene!" Mother Adelli waded in again.

"All my friends live in Chicago," Helene threw her shoulders about; "but I won't have any after six months here!" And she turned and glowered at her father.

"Oh, but of course you will write to your friends; and your friends will write to you!" Mother Adelli persisted, surprised at herself barging in that way.

"Oh! your own post office box!" the father hallooed. The Reverend Mother pressed her lips together, nodding.

"And our school has *its own* Post Mistress!" Mother Adelli, encouraged, bragged on. "And the students like to call her 'Mother Mailbox'!" the young nun added; but then with a look from her superior, quickly dropped the subject.

"And I'll be letting you know all about all the places I see. And you'll be telling me everything that you're doing—" Michael Rhenehan started in again; but faded at his daughter's look.

"Why, you'll be writing your father about our *congés* —" Mother Adelli beamed and spread her hands.

"'--holidays'," the Superior translated.

"—and when you see your friends again, you can teach them the games you learned here! For instance, have you ever played a game where a whole team hides and the other team has to find them?"

"THE WHOLE TEAM HIDES!" the father wagged his head. "Did you hear that, honey?"

And Helene turned upon him with flattened eyes while the window's drape billowed a rivulet of chilly air reaching necks, uncovered upper arms, backs and ankles with the sky turning grey.

"Oh, for heaven's sake, now!" the Superior motioned toward the window. "Why I believe it was nearly seventy degrees out there by noon yesterday."

Helene's father reached over to pull down the old wooden sash.

"This game our students love to play is called *câche-câche*," Mother Adelli went on and spelling the name in the air with her finger. "The name comes from a French word meaning 'to hide'. Last year, the Red team hid in the tool shed near the grotto. The year before, the White team hid in the circular fire escape."

"Wow," the father exclaimed, too enthusiastic, "I would have liked to have seen *that* myself!" The daughter rolled her eyes; and Mother Adelli saw the girl's lips silently form the syllables "stu - pid". Nevertheless, the young nun plunged ahead to say that on special occasions--and weather permitting--there was time of all the students running in the ravines, Mother Adelli snaked her hand. "But a team has to be *pretty quick* to keep up with my team!"

"Our activities are all perfectly safe," Reverend Mother Gregory intervened to the father, but with a cool gaze fixed upon Mother Adelli.

"Well, and what am I supposed to do with games like that when I get home?" Helene's voice exploded. "*We* live in *apartments*!" Then she turned a look of disgust upon Mother Adelli. "And I'm *not* wasting *my time* on games that *my* friends would—"

"You'll watch your tongue, young lady," the father clipped her off, then. "And you'll do what you're told!"

"Oh, but you can—" Mother Adelli's eyebrows flew upward.

"OF COURSE," Reverend Mother Gregory stepped in briskly, "our new student will learn *EVERYTHING* the other girls learn! And you have my word that there will be NO problem, Doctor Rhenehan! Mother Adelli and I will see to it. Every student goes through a period of adjustment. We understand this. Helene will have a good time. She will learn. She will be happy. The days will pass quickly."

But Helene's face had turned to wood; and Mother Adelli thought she saw a diamond chip of defiance wink in the girl's eye as she stared straight ahead; and the atmosphere of the room descended into an uneasy silence.

Then the buzzer from the front door punctuated the air followed by the unlatching of the door. Footfalls sounded outside the parlor followed by sentences in French. Then, a low, "Thank you!" and the sound of shoes again, but now passing the parlor; and then the song again of the front door's hinges; then the footsteps gradually dissolving.

And Michael Rhenehan felt his nerves like fiery worms begin to crawl to the surface of his skin; and he pictured himself escaping through the tall parlor door. He cleared his throat. "I noticed the ravines as we drove up. Magnificent! How far do they extend?"

"We have ten acres, the gift of a French count. The ravines run through most of it," the Reverend Mother nodded proudly.

The spired building and grounds with its convent, boarding school and womens' college sat within the equivalent of a wide shovel's swipe of forest that for centuries belonged to Native American tribes before there ever was an America.

The Superior paused. "You might be interested in the history of some of the gifts from friends of the Order, Doctor Rhenehan. For instance, our altarpiece is—"

And the nun drew her chair in to close the space between them and exhaling something sour and old. Quickly, Michael Rhenehan turned away to see his daughter's forefinger buried deep in her nose. Quickly, he turned back and there was the Superior's wide mouth again, and the single grey hair vibrating upon her chin. And the woman's voice ran over him like small hard rubber tires.

And it was then that he felt his head bobbing and saw his daughter next to him on the settee but already remote. And he realized with a stab of guilt that he was bone dry and had nothing more to say to his girl while the parlor released from the brilliant wax of its floor a perfume, funereal and spicy. And sweat rushed to his forehead. and suddenly he couldn't draw a breath. And his hangover hammered, hammered, hammered behind his eyes!

So he stretched out his arm, then; and the ruby chip emerged at his sleeved wrist to flash a long blue signal upon the watch's face, it's narrow hands pointing to ten minutes past four while the stiff blood-red line of the second hand swept everything before it. And he heard his voice crack, then, "Why, ten past four! Oh, I'm afraid I must be going." And he watched the red line sweep away his words, his daughter's widened eyes, sweep away the Superior's large opening mouth, the other one's sprung eyebrows and rising body, sweep from the walls the rectangles of old Superiors, the heavily-framed portraits, from the floor the prancing furniture and premeditating rugs, sweep away even the preening arch of the ceiling, the high-toned posture of the windows and then the floor's shining and malevolent trickery.

Next, he saw his leg lift its trouser and the ox-blood shoe follow to take the long first step away from the settee now slowly blowing its dimple out. And he felt his hair hoist, then saw as if from across the room, his hands swat his jacket into place and his head swivel as his daughter collected her body

"But Dad—"

and her voice passed through his ears and eyes and then through his heart to catch painfully at his stomach while her face rising toward him made the panic in his stomach boil so that he turned quickly to the Reverend Mother and the other one--.

"Oh, and I'm afraid that I have patients I still must examine at the hospital; and then my plane leaves tomorrow morning at six a.m. And tho' I would love to see everything, there's the packing yet --", the sounds of his words like pebbles scrubbing to scour away the daughter's bulging pain-fille eyes, her bitten finger ends. "Perhaps another time. Reverend Mother, Mother Amelli--. And Pumpkin," he turned to his daughter, "you understand", he pleaded. "You know dad has to—" his heart pounding in his throat while his girl's freckles lurched gigantically, her lower lip violently alive and—Oh, don't let her face--

"Goodbye for now, Tootsie-pie. Write your old dad now!"

shatter, his towering surgeon's hands grasping the square of her shoulders while the smell of fear steams from her arm pit and he watches himself kiss just over her eyes where the pimple there is huge and furious

"And don't forget me with all your studies and new friends."

and the silk of a curl of her red hair springs against his lips. But she refuses to clear the way; and her pale blue eyes ulcerate his cheek so that he reaches past her, jiggling her small rises of breast, so new now; and horrified to have touched her there, turns to shake the pudgy Reverend Mother's hand with "Thank you for everything. I believe I left all the numbers with you—"

"Of course, if you must. We understand perfect—"

"But Doctor Rhenehan--" from the smaller young nun and the stunned nun voices reel backwards while the deliberate floor exhales again its odor of sepulchers to stir the mess in his stomach and the furniture unsheathes its claws while he watches his long lean figure in the hound'stooth suit bounce against the dense grey clouds at the tall arched parlor window, his polished face, professional eyes with the hangover gong gonging behind them and under the darling boy curls, feels the fierce hooks yank his lips sideways, the broken crockery smile rip through the threadbare sack between his ribs, the playdoll nun blinking as if struck as his throat lets out the words "Mother Amelli Take care of my little girl now" and the nun blinking as if struck while one kiss for his daughter with her young-skin bouquet, the quick smacking sound, then low warning growl of chair legs as the shards jammed into his throat, the bumpy ornate knob beneath his sweaty hand, benediction from the cool foyer and pale rivering of incense, then out-turned palm holding off the hurrying portress while his long shoe searches out a rubbery step away from the robin's-egg blue eyes floating toward him through the parlor door with the hollow "Wait! Dad!" as he lifts his thousand pound legs, triple-stitched jacket tail flap-flapping, his shoulder against the door and Helen's baby's bawling sawing through his bones as he passes through the great door and to his car, the shaking key finding the dark slit of the ignition, *the Go back for God's sake and do it right,* the building's hoary beard and cataracted eyes and motor come alive like a cannon Go back before it's too late the little stones ping pinging the mouth at the front of the school sealing in the fury of Helen's fine baby's hair and frantic awkward body the screaming tires the grey stone bull's eye of the towering gates slamming his cells shut the motor on free rein, the long pluming tail of darkness.

2. Hide and Seek

Waking *congé* morning, almost immediately the thought came of the duck; and then the vicious plunge of pain that Popcorn was gone! And the *Third Cours*--ranks and ribbons and rules--drifted off to their place of brilliant images and nonsense stories again until a sweet, gentle voice, like an oar dipping, parted them from their dreams until

> *"Don-nez, don-nez nous un bon jour,*
> *don-nez, don-nez nous un bon jour,*
> *don-nez, don-nez nous UN BON JOUR!"*

Mother Adelli sang to call her girls, again to morning, to a good day. And she came to each bedside, then, parting curtains with the holy water fount, looking pale and tired but nodding and smiling into their eyes. And they would bless themselves down the front over the pajama frogs and buttons in the name of the Father and of the Son and of the Holy Spirit.

At Mass, forty minutes later, the priest wore vestments (white for holy days); and a large embroidered cross gleamed upon Father's back as he faced the altar. The same gold cross glanced into their eyes when he turned to hold the Host --the living Body and Blood of Jesus, small and pure white between his fingers above the chalice and murmured, *"Agnus Dei, qui tollis pecata mundi, misere nobis"* three times, then carried the very God Himself to where they (nuns at their private Mass, students at theirs) knelt at the communion rail with its long cold marble step to press the sacred pure white disk against their tongues, thus giving them the very Author of Life to take unto themselves; and the priest's blushing fingers always smelling of oranges.

Holiday French toast waited piled in great pyramids in the kitchen. And Soeur Josephine filled silver syrups at the student tables, and handed over dishes of hot pared apple slices dotted with cinnamon, and along with jugs of steaming chocolate.

Next it was Red Rover, and then playing theater where Mother Adelli, improvised by GeeGee with notebook paper fluted around her face, taught French to Sylvia, a fictionally slow student. The hilarious audience joined in at the end, *"nous oublierons, vous oublierez, ils oublierant: We forget, you forget, they forget."*

And Helene sat to the side, quiet, but not, Mother Adelli noted, staring from a black hole as she had seen the girl do ever since the pet duck's death. The sight, again, of the little body in the cat's jowls wrenched her mind and she drew a sharp agonized breath. Well, and it would be that way today for Helene, for the other students as well: for the memory of that pet duck would move like a shudder through this one, then that in a replaying choreography of grief. Outside, the blue of the sky gradually had withdrawn under a blanket of grey.

Well, and everyone was waiting for *Cache-cache*, the group game of hide-and-seek Mother Adelli had told Helene about nine weeks earlier in the Visitor's Parlor--a game played only on *congés*--holidays--in every Sacred Heart school. And students loved to think of their counterparts half a world away also searching for places large enough to hide "the whole team".

Well, they had to wait for ithe game through lunch and through an hour of pleasure reading under the overhead globes Mother Adelli snapped on because clouds outside had become dense while and the activated radiators clanked and hissed.

The students just hoped, peeking over their books, that it wouldn't rain. And they also had to suffer through the making of articles of clothing out of paper sacks; and then through the "fashion show" which followed. And then, after *goûter* (chocolate chip ccookies and lemonade) *finally* Mother Adelli called them from their snack to come to Study Hall to be divided into teams.

"We'll stay inside, today, because it may rain."" she told them. "And only the cloister and chapel will be off limits. Our dear Mother Ling here has offered to lead one of the teams while I lead the other. Mother Ling is on her way down now. Meanwhile, we'll count off: one, two; one, two." Mother Ling was always late!

"Aw *Mother*, can't we go out, *please*???" they slumped under the disappointment, flapping their arms and turkey-bobbing their heads, "*PLE-E-EASE?* We're not afraid of a little water. We'll wear our jackets. We'll wear our hats. Can't we, *pleeease?*"

All day they had been thinking of outdoor places to hide—hunched under thick shrubbery in the ravines, clinging to the backside of the grotto, flat on their stomachs under the North Shore train platform, jammed into the far corner of the visitor's shelter--but, no. It was much too raw out, Mother Adelli shook her head. Why, it could rain any minute!

So one, two, one, two they pared themselves off. And now every student was thankful for any Day student sick at home today, as well as for the two cold-infected boarders counting roses on the wallpaper of the infirmary. Still, the teams were not small: fifteen on one side, sixteen on the other; and add a nun to each team.

Mother Ling arrived squinting her Asian eyes, smiling and nodding. "Mother Mailroom", the girls knew, never said much; the team that drew her could pretty much do as it liked. But Mother Adelli was feeling intense about rules again; and so both teams prayed to get Mother Mailroom.

And if it had not been for a distinct moment during lunch, Mother Adelli would have tossed a blackboard eraser, as usual, to see which team got which nun as monitor. But passing behind Jennifer's chair in the refectory, her eyes were drawn up suddenly to meet those of Helene's, intensely blue and cold,; and which the girl had locked in a stare of absolute abhorrence upon her from across the table. So Mother Ling, she decided, would take the team standing near her desk, Helene at its edge. And she, Mother Adelli, would take the other.

The moment both nuns moved their glance from her direction, Helene, leaning at the window, slid to the floor and into a pocket of shadow behind Mother Adelli's desk where she sat during the eraser toss to determine which team would hide first. Mother Adelli's team won. And gathering into a bunch and whispering, the hiders planned quickly, banging the Study Hall doors behind them, then bolting to the second floor and down the length of the hall, Mother Adelli in the lead and her veil rising off her shoulders. Just opposite the seated lifesize statue of *Mater,* Mother Adelli held up her hand, then began tiptoeing down the wide center stairway that opened to the foyer on the first floor. Behind her, and in an agony of quiet, her team tapped their fingers at their lips to the nodding portress as they tiptoed past her table there. They planned to make fools of their opponents by threading their way back to the basement and into the laundry room from which they would triumph as a mound of sweating sheets; and breathing only the tiniest slips of air, while the coldness of the rough cement floor burned their skin and they pinched their lips shut with their fingertips.

"Two hundred!" the searching team bellowed ending their counting. They rushed through the Study Hall doors, up the stairs to the second floor corridor where they stopped, ready to run in all directions while Mother Ling, spinning in their midst, an index finger to her lips, began the hasty recount: Fourteen heads.

Well, it was no problem for Helene to slip quietly out the Minim's door. *Turn, open* then *pull, shut* and her breath bloomed upon the cold air. Then she crouched, freezing, to give her classmates time to pass beyond the landing and possible sight of her through the door's window-glass; and finally she sprinted up the two cement steps and into the cold--actually knowing exactly where she wanted to go!

It was toward the ravine she ran. And once over its lip, she could travel to her destination, grabbing slender tree trunks and shrubs for support until she was out of sight of the school.

Well, she had not counted on the rising wind, on the freezing mist almost a rain which turned her wrists red and socks to ice around her ankles. She buttoned her jacket, visualizing the large concrete drainage pipe from weeks back when they had all run snaking and sliding behind Mother Adelli.

It was lying awake the night before Popcorn's funeral that she had decided to hide in the old pipe first chance she got; and to stay there until Dilly-dally, Rancid Murmur and all the holy-holys--and maybe even her father--gave up looking for her.

Well, for once, let them be the ones to feel bad, thinking something terrible had happened to her! *And let it be them, for once, to be scared 'til their stomachs hurt, like hers had for her lost duck!*

And the idea warmed her while the rapt ravine hung silent in the cold silver mist. Spent leaves sank and split under her feet releasing a secret perfume. *And let it be them* to get into trouble with her father if they couldn't find her! Hey, they'd have to call him all the way in Italy. And wouldn't old Dilly and Adelli sweat then! Yes, wouldn't they, though.

But now her feet began to burn with cold while cold silver beads stood all over her uniform jacket.

A shiver of loneliness slipped through her, then, while she searched over her shoulder for the cupola, floating now at a distance small and fairy-like above the trees, above the nuns, the classrooms and dormitories and her own schoolmates hiding and searching. *Oh, ha, ha,* soon enough they'd be searching for her! And that old fat Rancid, her knees would be shaking under her big belly and long black skirts telling the Important Famous Heart Surgeon doctor over the telephone they somehow had managed to lose his little girl! And she snickered aloud at the thought, clutching a tree limb to keep her wet oxfords from skating out from under her as she, tripping every ten seconds, trudged up the sloping sides of the ravine.

Well, the storm came on, but as rain. And Helene, wet hair hanging in her eyes, came striding to find the drainage pipe where it jutted from the side of the ravine, its curved bottom perhaps a foot off the ground. Then as quickly as the rain came, it stopped. But now the wind turned maniac, quiet one minute, shrieking and thrashing the next. And Helene had to fight both its tearing at her skirt and the ground's downward pull while she uprooted small bushes to drag into the opening of the pipe to seal it. And beneath the pipe, she uncovered leaves still dry enough to make a mattress. Oh, this was a perfect hiding place!

Well, she could sit up in the pipe only if she bent her head and hunched her shoulders; but then her breath was cut off. And lying on her side, dirt from the hillside forced her feet and knees into a fetal position. But that was fine, fun like sleeping--andnd the scent of the old leaves comforted her.

Once, pulling herself out of the pipe, she grabbed onto its upper lip and heard it crack; and concrete bits rained over her knees. She tested the jagged place. No, it would be all right; she wouldn't pull on it anymore but put her hands on the sides, instead. Now if it just didn't start raining again!

So she cushioned her head upon her arm while a rivulet of cold air teased through the top's fissure to snake down her neck. Otherwise, the pipe was snug. And hey, it was way better than her stupid alcove. Why, she could stay here long as it took, and until the stupid nuns called her father!

She peered out through the twiggy screen. Why this felt just like being a squirrel, a mole or fox watching the bushes bow and dance before the fury of the weather, smelling the wetness and seeing everything shine. She remembered when she was little, how she and Gimme, her cat, used to hide under the dining room table to watch the housekeeper's thick ankles go back and forth. And a moment of sharp longing pierced her.

Now the rain came on in earnest, straight down and tramping around and above her like many boots. But good! This would make Dilly even more frantic! And Dilly's candy wrapper ruffle around her face would melt and droop. Oh, and Mother Adelli!--her wimple drooping over her eyes and plastered against her cheeks. Her feet would be wet and freezing, too, just like Popcorn's had been and like hers, Helene's, were now!

But now she wished she didn't have to think about Popcorn. And she wished she hadn't seen into that handkerchief carrying his small body. Why, if Mother Adelli had let her, she could have found Popcorn outside with her flashlight so Popcorn would still be alive. And then everyone would still be happy. But, no, that Dilly wouldn't even let her go out. And so Dilly deserved whatever she got!

Water ribboned along the crack overhead to slip inside. The one trouble, she thought, inching back to let a drop fall clear of her body, was that she couldn't watch the fear creep across the grownups' eyes when they discovered that she was missing. And she couldn't laugh *Ha-Ha* in their faces. Right now her job was to keep still until she heard voices or footsteps; and then pull her dark jacket over her head so that her hair wouldn't show. And they would be missing her a long time, thinking maybe even that she was dead before she walked, serene and superior, into Study Hall to stun them out of their wits. She lay shivering, playing these scenes over and over and feeding upon vengeance as the light of day slowly dissolved over the ravine.

Muddy water began to trickle along the bottom of the pipe. A large clump of earth loosened and fell over her feet, the cold of it turning her stomach. She kicked it off. Maybe she should find some other place to hide. No, it was too late, now; this was the best place. And they would never find her in this old pipe. And this was much better than *câche-câche* because she would have both teams AND Dilly AND Rancid looking for her! Mother Mail Room. Sister Kitchen. Maybe the police, too. And next *congé,* the girls'd all want to hide with her! They'd say, "--where Helene hid and nobody could find her!" Well, and she'd be gone by then and back with Dad.

The icy stream widened along the floor, soaking her skirt and then fingering her stomach. And every time she drew a breath, she smelled wet clay and the pale ghost of her breath would hover before her. Then her small white bed at home would fill her mind with its bulky flowered comforter, then; and from nowhere the piquant edge of her father's cigar smoke and the feeling of his arm pulling her tight against his chest materialized. And she would grit her teeth. And, soaked and freeing, everything in her wanted to bolt. And lightening would wink its great eye; then, while thunder boomed and things rattled overhead.

Then the hail started in.

And she watched ice the size of mothballs bounce and roll down the steep slope toward the ravine's floor. And the scene beyond the pipe, through these pellets, turned pastel, pointillistic. She heard drumming on the pipe like a crowd running while above her a hairline sprinted sideways out of the jagged split in the pipe, then across its top and down the side. And the hail stopped.

Thick mud oozed beneath her thighs where her skirt bunched into a knot. Mother Adelli would have to order a new uniform skirt. She pushed up onto her elbow to pull the skirt material out, but it was tangled too tight; so she jacked herself even higher, her fingers stumbling in the soaked cloth, then rammed her shoulder with a searing pain against the top of the pipe where the concrete broke free, balancing for a moment on the small point of her shoulder. When her shoulder crumbled beneath the terrible weight as if a giant had stepped on her, bright sent lights exploded behind her eyes; and along with stabbing pain in her neck and collarbone. At the same time, the breath was forced from her lungs while the left side of her face was thrust deep into the mud while her cheek and jaw were jammed against the stone-littered concrete of the pipe's bottom.

Well, she had no time nor way to cry out. And her first breath drew such a clog of mud into one nostril that her mouth popped open to let mud ooze over her lower lip with a thick taste of iron while a terrible pain throbbed where concrete leaned against her jaw and ear and warm liquid ran down her neck, her arms and twisted behind her to ride the channel of her backbone. And by then, mud had worked its way over her left eye and one nostril. And she lay still, careful with her breathing and trying not to swallow while the hail faltered, then ceased. And for a long while, then, she heard no sound but that of the random dripping of water.

And the sight of Mother Adelli and Big John reeling through the trees would cross her mind: that they would be coming any time now and calling out her name while an acute longing to see her father unexpectedly captured her body. Oh, and to feel him lift her from this pipe! But no! She mustn't cry and draw more mud in.

But after a bit, the pitty pitty of fresh rain started up; and then the downpour began afresh. So Mother Adelli would wait to look for her until the rain stopped. And how could they *ever* find her in this old pipe? And why had she hidden so far away? Well, she just must hold on, listen for footsteps and call out! But try as she might, she could not move; and a grunting sound was all she could get from her throat. A heavy blanket of mud toppled forward over her legs and feet, then; and water began to course in the pipe; and the worst of possibilities passed through her mind so that her stomach clenched in terror reflecting on her own small size and the huge will of the weather! Oh, and she wished, then--and with all her heart--that there really was a God Who would help her, a Sacred Heart burning with love for her, a Blessed Mother to sheild her, guardian angels to carry her from this terrible pipe!

At last, she closed her one free eye to shut out the writhing black water; and now there was nothing but to swallow and swallow and feel her stomach fill. And to wait. But then a cold line, like the edge of a sheet, eased over her nose. And through the small opening left at one corner of her mouth, her face reaching upward, she felt her lungs pull in a long ribbon of air. But then the edge of the cold water crawled over her mouth and up her cheek while her lungs clung to the last small stream of air carried into her body, and she seemed, now, to be a separate person observing her body flail and fight and stiffen in defiance although it could no longer move. Then she thought perhaps she heard faint footsteps; and so "hold on, hold on, hold on" until (and trembling violently) she felt her lungs seem, as it were, to burst apart so cold at first was it that her stunned body flinched sharply in response; but then pulled itself back into something like a stiff shield; but then let go, again, next to turn soft and pliable. And in the dark (but still, some how luminous) gloom, the pounding rain diminished, then dissolved into drifting notes like flower petals while a soft breeze seemed to take up to climb through her body to buffet her cheeks, fill her forhead, then playfully tickle her scalp. And it was that moment she felt an astonishing light fill and wrap itself around her to cradle her. And a singing movement the equivalent of a voice, but not physically heard, filled her and at the same time opened a place like spiral stairs both within and before her. And then, she wanted more than anything in the world to climb those stairs. And it was from this unfolding that she heard a clear sweet voice from very long ago (and one she recognized right away without knowing its name) calling to her, "Come on! Come on, Helene! Come on, my honey!"

And it was when Mother Adelli wheeled from the laughing triumph of her own team reporting smugger than smug back to Study Hall from their successful hiding place in their recreation game, that she, their teacher and supervisor, noticed Helene missing.

And Mother Adelli, a little zipper of fear running through her, caught Mother Ling's eye.

"Is the Rhenehan girl in the bathroom?" she mouthed across bobbing heads and the chatter of her students.

Mother Ling, surrounded by her glowing winning team, responded, leaning on one foot, her hand to her ear: "Eh?"

Mother Adelli mouthed the question again. And it was then that, in a strike of lightening like the firing off of an enormous flash bulb, the bushes outside the windows and, by a short count of three, thunder crackled following the lightening while Mother Ling, her team barreling past and through the Study Hall's door and taking their turn to hide, smiled, nodding back. And by the time the students had squeezed into the cleaning closet on the third floor, the downpour had begun again.

Team Two squeezed behind a carefully stacked wall of toilet paper and cleaning supplies cartons.

"Phew!' Deborah pinched her nose, then, and added, "Well, how are we expected to _breathe_, here?" And indeed, the air in that tiny space reeked of soap, cleaning ammonia and floor wax.

An hour later, having seen her victors through the dining hall door for supper, Mother Ling started down the corridor to her own dinner in the cloister when Mother Adelli ran after her.

"Mother Ling! The Rhenehan girl; I didn't see her go into dinner, Mother!"

"Rhenehan girl?" Mother Ling repeated, her forehead puckering.

"Yes, Helene Rhenehan. She was on your team."

Mother Ling shook her head. "No, she must have been on your team, Mother Adelli. She was never on my team."

"But you told me she was in the bathroom after the first round." Mother Adelli's dark eyes searched the other nun's face.

"Did I say she was in the bathroom?" Mother Ling began to rattle her rosary in the folds of her skirt.

"Yes, Mother. I asked you twice from across the room if the Rhenehan girl was in the bathroom. The first time you couldn't understand me. I asked again. The second time you nodded 'yes.'"

"Oh," Mother Ling laughed, her very white teeth gleaming, "I thought it was something about 'laundry room' or 'brooms'. Actually you gave me the idea of the broom closet on the third floor. *Merci!*" And she nodded deeply and turned to go.

"Oh, but she never was on my team, Mother! I deliberately didn't put her on my team."

Mother Ling's eyes shifted back and forth, then. She'd had fourteen at the top of the stairs; she brought fourteen back; had taken fourteen out again for hiding. And never once had one of them been the Rhenehan girl!

"I'm sorry Mother Adelli; if she was supposed to be on my team, I didn't understand. I didn't take any notice of her. I don't know what to say." And young Mother Lind looked about the dim corridor as if for a clue; meanwhile, the rain clattered at the windows with a sound like loose coins thrown.

"But you must realize the girl is in a bad way! Why didn't you think?" Mother Adelli wanted to snap at the other nun. But instead, she forced a shallow laugh. "Well, she's somewhere. Thank you, Mother—and for all your help today. We couldn't have played *câche-câche* without you. It's the high point of the *congé!*"

And Mother Ling, moving off through the gloom of the corridor, kept searching her pockets as if she might somehow find the girl there; and while Mother Adelli called Madeline away from her noon-day dinner to take a look for the new student in the dormitory.

Helene's alcove was empty. She was not reading in the library. She was not in any Third Cours classrooms nor praying in chapel or in the choir loft. She had not gone sick to the infirmary. No relative nor neighbor had called her to Visitor's parlor. She was not on the telephone with her grandmother in New York, her father in Italy. She was not in the furnace room, in the chapel or gym.

Perhaps the new student, Helene, was having her own game of *câche-câche* Mother Adelli suggested after noon dinner. So the Third Cours boarders fanned out for "extra team points"! For the finder, in addition, there was a small gold medal of the Sacred Heart Mother Adelli had been saving for something special.

Well, after a while, everyone grew tired of Helene's bad joke! And they watched Mother Adelli's face, oval inside her coif, turn sick-looking; and the chocolate mole on her cheek stand out starkly while their favorite nun's eyes grew wild and the hands of the clock crept towards dormitory-time, rain pounding their darkened bedtime windows.

The Third Cours boarders trooped upstairs after dinner and last Study Hall finally, to end their *congè* feeling cheated in a way they could not name--angered and uneasy at the sight of the far alcove on the leftand no boarder to fill it. A fourth academic ribbon saw them into "lights out" and sat hunched under the small desk lamp, her long hair falling over her French book.

Mother Adelli threw her shawl over her head and ducked out into the teeming rain. No Helene at the railway platform! No Helene hiding in the grotto or among the trees, nor stricken and fallen among the bushes on the grounds, nor visible over the institution's ravine's edges.

And then Mother Adelli went directly to Mother Crewelman, her superior.

"And why do you *always* wait and wait before you act?" Mother Crewelman pounded her desk. "The girl is gone! It is dark out now! *Do you understand, Mother Adelli?*"

Yes. Mother Adelli understood.

Probably call the train again, Reverend Mother agreed with herself, then, and lifting the telephone to talk with the operator who connected her directly (and since it was an emergency) with the North Shore stationmaster in Chicago. As the instrument was making the connection, she let her eyes drift to Mother Adelli gripping the sides of her chair's cushion, then to the large and angular Mother Crewelman who sat upright in the Louis XV replica like a dangerous collection of rocks. This matter was, the Superior knew, the very sort of event in which Mother Crewelman (Mother Adelli's immediate superior), reveled.

Of course, the Stationmaster told the relgious Superior, they would alert all train conductors ffor the ten year-old redheaded girl, about five foot—

"—four," Mother Adelli supplied, leaning forward anxiously.

—five foot four, one hundred and—?

"—three"

—about one hundred-three pounds; and wearing—?

Well, and it all became too real! The saliva in Mother Adelli's mouth thickened; her mind had turned arthritic. But of course it would be the uniform, wouldn't it; and perhaps, with her outdoors' jacket—navy blue, waist length, quilted with buttons, was it?—no, zipper up the front; and then grey fur at the edge of the hood, wasn't it? And it would be a stocky red-headed girl, perhaps looking a little rumpled, the Superior had put in--one with many freckles on her face and hands. Also, she would be in uniform; would have little or no money. And the school would send a car for her immediately, *wherever* she was found! And the Superior replaced the receiver slowly.

"Call the police," the Stationmaster had suggested. "If she's a runaway, she might be hitchhiking. "These things happen even in the nicest schools."

A runaway!!!

"Well, we must call the police immediately," she told the two religious, then. But first she must call the Mistress General of the Order, her Superior in Manhattan.

Mother Crewelman swiveled in her chair, leveling her eyes. "But this is an outrage, Mother Adelli, do you understand? An outrage! A scandal! The girl was your responsibility, your charge; and you, with your starry-eyed disregard for all rules designed to keep students safe, let her slip through your fingers!" Spittle leapt from the woman's mouth. "And just what do you think our rules are for, Mother--to put in a handbook or prattle to parents?"

And Mother Adelli shrank under the lashing.

"Yes, yes!" she told herself, then. And Mother Crewelman was right. It was *HER* fault. *SHE,* Mother Adelli, had handled everything wrong, poorly. And oh, Helene! Where *was* she? Out somewhere in the darkness and with no money, in danger and no one to help her! *Oh, God help her!* she prayed, then; and waited humbly for the verbal beating--*fully* deserved, she felt-- to come now from her Superior.

But, no. Reverend Mother Gregory said nothing to either nun. A strange calm filled the superior's face. What they must do now, the Superior told them, was to keep their heads so they could think!

Reverend Mother Gregory sent Mother Crewelman to dig out the girl's papers, for she wanted privacy with Mother Adelli who appeared bent on dissolving with guilt at just the wrong moment. And obviously, with Mother Crewelman firing off every thirty seconds, Mother Adelli, already pale as a bedsheet, would be more than useless by the time police arrived.

Together, then, the Superior and younger nun picked over the day for what it could tell them while the wind, now having spent its rage, whined softly past the office window like a dark river spotted with snowflakes. And then the house phone on the desk rang. "Yes. Show the officers to the Visitor's Parlor," the Superior told the online portress. "Tell them that we will be right down."

The police officers jumped to their feet as the Superior entered the room, good Irish boys with big shoes polished, hats in their hands and melted snow glistening upon the shoulders of their black leather jackets. The larger older one, a Sergeant Mooney, produced his yellow tablet as they sat again, Reverend Mother Gregory to their left, Mother Adelli, licking her lips and white as a sheet to their right. It was 5:15 p.m.

"We have a missing student." Reverend Mother swept a wide circle in the air before her immediately.

"Yes m'am." The Sergeant jotted several words upon his tablet.

"The father is in Italy," the Superior bulled on. And the girl has been, let us say, 'disturbed" at being separated from him. She ran off once before, several months ago—a short jaunt on the train to Lake Forest— and nothing we needed to report. We took it for a 'new student' prank. But this time, Mother Adelli," the Superior nodded to the younger nun, "in charge of the girl, searched the school portion of the building with her students, searched the grounds with our staff as best she could in this weather and has turned up nothing. I called the North Shore authorities, but they have no reports of unattended children on their trains. They will keep and eye out for her."

Sergeant Mooney nodded again, his face carefully blank so far. "Do you have a picture of the girl?"

Reverend Mother Gregory sent for Mother Crewelman whose tall figure hurrying through the door caused the two police officers to jolt from the settee.

"This is our Mistress General; she will be available later if you need her," Reverend Mother told the officers, taking the folders and nodding a 'thank you' as dismissal to Mother Crewelman who hastened back across the room to pull the parlor door shut again.

And looking from over his brown tuft of mustache, attemding young officer Halloran saw in the photograph a girl's pan-shaped face covered with freckles and framed by wavy shoulder-length hair, her chin thrust out and confrontive eyes staring from over a Peter Pan collar.

"This portrait was taken last year," the Superior explained, "at Holy Spirit School in Chicago. The girl was in fifth grade, then."

"Well," Sergeant Mooney stood up, leather jacket creaking, "we should start with a look around. Is there a telephone? I'll call in some extra men, if you don't mind, M'am. Fresh eyes, you know. Could be the girl's playing games and is right here on the premises. And then there'll be no need to disturb the father in Europe."

Half an hour or so, and six additional officers arrived.

The careful tread of their feet and white-gold beams of their flashlights glanced off of every surface, even in the cloister where the religious were roused, then hustled down to the lounge in their white muslin gowns and caps to stand huddled together, obedient and silent while male hands and feet explored their emptied sacred and committed space. And the nuns, somehow, mad the officers feel compelled somehow to speak in whispers as they wove their way through the dormitories, lavatories and tubs, nuns' cots and dressers, linen closets, the tiny infirmary, private chapel and cloister dining room and lounge.

The men quit the building at 1:30a.m., Officer Halloran asking Mother Adelli for an article of Helene's clothing who led him, then, to the girl's locker and there to discover the outdoor jacket she had described to the police dangling by its hood. The officer folded it under his arm and when everthing was done that could for the time being be done, slipped with it out the Minim's door and into the deep night where small dense snowflakes had begun again to sift.

But she was out there, had been out there, in this cold and rain and hail—and now *snow*—and with nothing to protect her from the weather but her uniform, Mother Adelli worried as she closed the door.

And then, a longing to help the girl so fierce that she thought it would burst her asunder passed through the nun's body; and Mother Adelli let her arms fall helplessly to her sides while her body collapsed onto the lowest step of the staircase where she buried her face in her hands and wept; and then prayed.

Mother Adelli sat there a long time before she could, with a leaden will, draw together the disparate parts of herself to carry up the stairs and there dismiss Mother Palmer who had come, on an emergency basis at nine p.m., to release the overseeing fourth academic student to her own dormitory and watch over Mother Adelli's Third Cours "sleeping" boarding students.

On her cot somewhat later in the darkness, there rose up for Mother Adelli her new student's brilliant smile along the words the girl had thrown over her shoulder as she had turned toward the school that late afternoon on the hockey field--words she, Mother Adelli, had failed to share withher Superior. But now they rose up like savage scorn, and a retribution. "I would get away from here if I could," Helene had said.

And Mother Adelli repeated them now, and over and over recalling them into the endless hours of the night; filling the small alcove where they left no space for Mother Adelli to turn, to breathe.

3. What The Daughter Owed

For an instant Mother Adelli, answering the unexpected call to the parlor, saw an immigrant man and woman in tired clothing and peering from tired eyes into the polish and gilt of the place.

Then suddenly the familiar landmarks emerged: The woman's small proud bones, delicate head, darting eyes; the man's square-cut peasant body, open face, slow thick hands. There was a painful knock in her chest and she quickened her step to her parents. It was 2:30 p.m., and the Friday after Thanksgiving.

"But you told me you wouldn't be coming. Oh, what a good surprise."

When the first mention of her student's death had appeared in the *Chicago Daily Tribune* three days previous, Reverend Mother Gregory had told Mother Adelli to phone her family. It had been wise counsel, for friends had already seen the story. A second article appeared in the *Daily Herald* and a third in the *Chicago Sun.* Alarmed, the parents had ridden the North Shore train from Chicago the two hours north.

At the sight of her dark haunted eyes, Lorenzo and Angelica Adelli felt the artificial bridge of dutiful letters they had built to their daughter collapse. After ten years away, first in New York and then in Omaha, she had been back in Illinois since last March, except for the summer. And why hadn't they, the parents, been to see her? Well, she hadn't asked them, really.

Their daughter showed them the chapel, the life-size statue of *Mater Admirabilis,* the high school library. But the worried parents' eyes lingered more than anywhere upon their daughter's face.

In the Study Hall, they wandered slowly down the narrow aisles, touching with their fingertips the smooth worn surfaces of the desktops and chairs and lightly tracing the interiors of the stained old-fashioned inkwells and pen cradles.

"Everything looks just like the Holy Heart School on Fifty-first Street, where I went," her mother sniffed. "And why is it all of the hallways feel the same, and with the same statues everywhere," she hitched her handbag over on her arm.

"Oh, schools are schools," the father waved his wife off. "In Chicago, the Archdiocese orders all its stuff every year from McNulty & McNulty, with warehouses of ceiling lamps, desks, chairs, bookshelves, journals, notebooks, pens, pencils, rulers and you-name-it. But then a cough deep in his chest orchestrated suddenly, bending him head to knees while the alarming clatter from his lungs rang upon the air to strike the walls, the desks and chairs and the daughter's eyes widened while the mother looked away.

"Sit down Dad, both of you. Please. I'll get some water." To hear "Dad" aloud, and in her own voice and after so long was like a bell rung in a tunnel and that drew thundering back the shape, weight and consistency of the young nun's childhood. She motioned her parents to the desks where the father slumped on a student chair, his face ashen, and let his head fall into his hands as he waited for the next spasm.

The kitchen, down the corridor on the right, stood deserted. Mother Adelli, breathing in its tail ends of rich scents from lunch, filled the tumblers too full at the sink and dribbled the water along the floor all the way back. And crossing the threshold, then, with the cups, the sunlight through the bars at the windows illuminated the folds of her parents' faces, coats, the skin of their necks, hands. They were nearing the end of their lives, now, she realized with a jolt--the mother unwrapping a lozenge ordered by the doctor, passing the tan-colored bit to her husband, the smell of eucalyptus on the air.

"Here we are. *Salud.*" Mother Adelli pressed the water glasses into their hands.

And the parents turned their eyes of dreamers upon their daughter whose tiny bottom and legs they had seen disappear around doors when she was two; whose perfect pirouette on the blazing stage of a darkened theater had left them stunned when she was nine, was twelve, was sixteen--and now dressed in a floating veil--protected from anxiety and hurry--a teacher of the children of the rich; and studying to become a saint. And in all those ten years, they had never gotten used to it.

"That cough, Dad. How is your health?" Mothr Adelli bent toward her father.

"Well, *you* look worn out and half starved," the mother came right back at that. "And the idea of cooking here is probably boil, boil, boil; and then a teaspoon of everything."

"*Dio mio.* She's been through a nightmare, Angelica. Give her a break!" the father cried, seeing the the stress in his daughter's haggard face. "And *salud*!" he raised his water glass, then, all around.

Father and mother sipped ceremonially, glancing about as if in a museum; careful to keep their wet tumblers off the wood. The cloistered daughter did not join in, while a floor below on the inner wall above the Study Hall door, a bronze Jesus stretched his crucifixion over the small family.

Well, the Corellis' son had gotten a vocation (God's will be done) and gone off to Quigley Seminary. Mr. Longuri's heart finally quit--God rest his soul--lugging a box of potting soil from the basement. The man never would listen to his doctor! Their new cocker spaniel Arabella caught a piece of glass in her paw and went into a fit of barking when the doctor tried to take it out. Now she was limping but would be all right.

Mother Adelli privtely clenching and unclenching her fingers while she shifted forward and then back again on her elbows and an icy anxiety raked her innards.

"I must tell you both something. Since we talked on the telephone last, our Mistress General has ordered some changes here. Reverend Mother Gregory has already been replaced by Mother Crewelman."

Well, the names meant nothing to them. "Oh?" her mother nodded. But her father's eyes narrowed. "Because of—?"

They all knew he meant "the girl's death".

"I phoned a lawyer, Mary Agnes." He never could, like some parents, call his own daughter by her religous prefix "Mother". "According to the newspapers, where they found her was off of school property. And the lawyer says the school is clear of her— ", he didn't want to voice that word, "death"; but instead, waved his hand. "And he asked about a negligence charge against anyone, though."

Mother Adelli shook her head. "No. Dr. Rhenehan has not pressed charges." But her stomach began collapsing as she spoke. "Why, *animals* take better care of their young!" the doctor-on-call who had come to the school infirmary, siren sounding, had shouted at her, the teacher, then, his eyes bulging and wild.

Well, and her father and mother visibly relaxed, then, as if they'd let go over-held air, stripping off winter coats, laying them aside. And it was just about then she, Mary Ann Adelli--MOTHER Adelli, had felt the middle school's Study Hall exhale its deep and lonely comfort of old wood.

"--and I am to be replaced in my position here." she told them.

"Oh!" her mother sat down hard, then on her chair. "Oh!" again, and then fell deeply silent, turning her back, floundering in her purse until she found a handkerchief she pressed against her mouth.

"Then he—*they*—DO blame you!" the father boiled. "But there were others involved! And wasn't there another nun?" Beneath the skin softened by drink, his rough-hewn face drew itself up tight and hard as it could. "*Gesu, Giuseppe, e Maria!* That girl snuck right off on you and—.

"But *I* was the one in charge of her, Dad!"

"Well, she climbed into that drainpipe herself. You didn't put her there, for God's sake! And nobody likes to see a child drown, but now you're supposed to take the blame for what she brought on herself? Good God--"

"Lorenzo!"

"Well, I've heard people say worse, Angelica. And how many of these rich kids can you police? Then they want you to be a mind reader too? And what about the father? He left her in the first place, didn't he, the fancy doctor going to--?"

"He thought we would take care of her, Dad," Mother Adelli flared; then immediately was sorry: After all, her parents were only trying to help! She took out her handkerchief and wiped the palms of her hands.

"My replacement, along with Reverend Mother Gregory's, was one of Dr. Rhenehan's conditions for not going to the press and the state," she told them in a lowered and more controlled voice.

"Well it didn't happen at the school, and you can't keep someone from drowning who's hiding where no one would find them in a million years!" Lorenzo Adelli barked, looking as if he wanted to take a swing at somebody. "And what was she doing off of school property in the first place?"

Mother Adelli slumped at the small desk, her hand capping her mouth until color could climb back into her face. "I *am* supposed to be a mind reader," she said finally, wearily, patiently. "And it was my responsibility she was off school property without my knowing it. She was probably trying to punish me. Children--people!--do that sort of thing. I responsible for her while she was with us. Her parents *have a right* to blame me!"

And she saw pain leap into her father's eyes, then, by claiming the blame against his defense of her. And she hadn't the energy to cover up; nor stay any blow, now, that must fall upon her or them.

"*Dio Mio!* But that's crazy," her father batted the air. "You're too hard on yourself. I know you. You could't be responsible for harm to anyone, to a beetle, Pretty Feet, *figlia mia.*"

But his use of his old and forgotten terms of endearment riled her, now; and made her desperate. No! She must *not* let her father's need for pretense draw her in so as to excuse herself! And, oh dear God, though she kill him with her truth; though she kill them both!

"But I *could* hurt others, Dad. You just don't know." She held him with her eyes." I've done a lot of praying since Helene died—and a lot of remembering."

And Angelica Adelli lifted her proud head at her daughter's reply. Why, this was the one for whom they had sacrificed so much, whose dance shoes, tights and tutu she had put away with a terrible struggle, bowing to the will of Heaven that their daughter pour all of her mortal life into the four walls of the cloister––one of the most prestigious religious orders in the world, yes; they'd had that cold comfort. But now, this horror!

Mother Adelli pushed herself from her desk and stepped to the window. For a moment she stared deeply into the puzzle of the lilac branches outside. Well, she must put herself on trial, then, with her parents. Didn't she owe that much to them?

She faced them with the story: The girl's father leaving her so abruptly; the girl's continual misbehaviors and little thefts; the awful desecrations (which made the mother gasp and father's eyes light up); unrelenting and open hostility and turning the other students against their own Mistress-- and all this despite her, Mother Adelli's, own efforts at kindness, patience and understanding. "I even broke the 'No Pets' rule to let her keep a duck downstairs near the backdoor to visit. Her grandmother had sent it from New York a few dys before she came. But the duck got out, there, and was mauled by a stray cat. Then Helene blamed me because I wouldn't let her look for it outside at night in the rain. We combed the property for it; and when we had to give up, the students and I put together a kind of little funeral for it at at the grotto. At student dinner that night, she told some classmates she knew how she would get back at me; and I would be sorry we didn't stop everything and find the duck." Mother Adelli's voice wobbled. "Well, she was right about that!"

"But why didn't you go to your superiors immediately when the girl became a problem?" the mother leaned forward, one eyebrow raised; and immediately the daughter felt the knife of appraisal enter her ribcage in the old familiar place just below her left breast.

"Oh, but I did. And several times," she pleaded. "But Reverend Mother Gregory told me I must handle things by moving on; and that I couldn't keep the other studend from their education because of a duck. And Mother Crewelman told me to discipline the girl. And I tried; but I wasn't—*couldn't* be-- strong enough or know how to stop her taking matters into herown hands." And her eyes flew from one parent to the other, then. "I couldn't stand to make things worse for her." She heard herself telling it now. And it sounded so lame; but it was the truth!

"Well, we just gave any *farabutti* at my school who wanted to be a troublemaker a good crack over the head," father whacked at the air with satisfaction and an open palm. "Then that was that!"

"It's against our Rule to be physical, Dad. *Nolo me tangere*, 'Do not touch me'. Both students and rel—"

"That's where you made your mistake, Mary Agnes, being so kind; and, following your feelings instead of your Superiors." The mother snapped the opened mouth of her purse shut. "And the duck thing, of course. Deliberately going against the ru—"

"Her father left her; she hated being here." Mother Adelli cried out. "To see the child suffer more hurt was too much. I might as well have asked myself to breathe under water."

"When you children were at home, you did as I said.," the mother drew her head up, then. She had decided to speak her mind. Mary Agnes was still her daughter! And she had gotten herself into this trouble, now. And so, ao as her daughter's mother, she, Angelica, had held her tongue too long!

"Your superiors knew what was necessary to keep that girl safe. If you want my opinion, you should have done exactly as they told you, and nothing else! The rule would have protected the girl *and* you, Mary Agnes. Disobedience nev—"

"*Dio mio.* You don't know anything about what its like in a classroom, Angelica. It's just not that simple. Things always look easy enough from the kitchen sink." It was at the sight of his daughter's collapsing face that the father had burst in. "And those Higher Ups don't always know everything either. Sometimes they make bad mistakes and then lay it on the guy under their thumb, *mascalzoni!* Why, I've had students like this girl, walking the thin edge just for the fun of it; and too slippery to get ahold of, too smart for their own good! And there are a few necks I would gladly wring today if the Church didn't stand against it. Such things. are necessary some times." And the father twisted clenched hands. "Sono *tutti diavoli* --devils--at heart, students like that."

"Oh you've always been ready to take things out on someone else," the mother turned on him, then; "then bring your petty school violence home to the dinner table."

"Please!!!" Mother Adelli clapped her hands over her ears; and the parents stopped abruptly "I have been over and over this with myself an hundred times. And I couldn't or wouldn't or didn't discipline her properly." She wrung her hands, then and began walking in a figure eight, her face white as a sheet. "Helene saw through me to my weak spots; and thn played them like a musical instrument. Oh! I wish I were a stronger person. This wouldn't have happened. I try, but--" her voice caved in.

And in the midst of her painful confession, it struck her then that the life she lived in the Order with its complex elegant filigrees, its refined spiritual goals and precise rules of development was meretricious, and a bauble set next to the uncut gemstone of the life of a student--and this one now seemingly and hopelessly lost, now. She laid her head upon her arms, her arms upon the windowsill and knew she must leave the Order. And the father looking on suddenly glimpsed an awful gulch yawn about his daughter. And it froze him in his seat.

Beyond the windows, the sun's last orange rays skipped and jumped and ran West under the grey blanket of nightime drawing itself over the landscape. Purposeful footsteps came and went. Beyond the doors, the parents sat blinking into the gloomy silence.

Finally, the father shook his head. "No one is safe from trouble. It searches you out behind the highest of walls. How can things—each so small, innocent and unimportant in itself—lead to such a terrible—?" And he pulled his eyebrows and lips together to shake his head again.

The radiators came awake to clank and hiss about the room, then. And from down the corridor, soft sounds of pots and pans intruded; and from that faint musical clang-clang, student knew that Soeur Josephine was back in her kitchen.

"This—thing—incident won't effect you— your—progress—I mean in the Order, will it?" The mother straightened herself at last, her words wrapped in cotton.

The daughter raised her head, surprised. "I'm sure everything—Final Vows, the trip to Rome—everything is in question now—probably beyond question. I--" the daughter turned, wanting to say something, then, about leaving the Order; but when she tried, her twisting thoughts slithered nervously apart.

The mother dug her handkerchief from her purse. "We tried to do the right things--" she buried her face in it." The work, the hopes, the disappointment--God forgive her--of the call. Then accepting it as best she could. At least, she had quieted herself, her daughter could be distinguished in this Order; and then they would have one child, *someone* in the family, who had got somewhere! And now this—this shame--" and she threw her arms out, "--this crucifixion. And why?" she cried to through the ceiling to God. "First my Julian, killed! Now this for my Mary Agnes? And for what? Haven't I served You well with my life? You know I have tried!" And the mother raised her hands, then, her fingers clenched; but then let them drop to sit amidst the small choking sounds of her tears.

"*Per Bacco.* And you're the only one who's suffered, as usual!" the father's hand came down, then, with a loud slap upon the desk. Well, he had seen his wife crucified before. "You.You just never got over wanting her to go to New York so you could be the mother of a diva."

"*And what was so wrong with that?*" Angelica Adelli blazed back, jerking herself upright. "She had the talent, everyone said so, everyone could see it--Madame Vargas, the newspapers. She stopped the breath in their lungs. Why, she could easily have been another—"

"*Prima ballerina. Alicia Markova.* And owed it all to you!!!" The words curled over his lips; and Mother Adelli pictured his body shifting into its familiar fighting posture. "I told you and told you, 'Stop pushing her. Stop pushing! You'll ruin it for her.'" He hacked at the air with the side of his hand. "She was just a kid! She needed time."

"*Dio Mio.* That's just what you never understood. *TIME* in that business is just what you *don't* have. You're thirty and it's all over!"

It had always been at night that the knives flew back and forth, her mother's giant shadow raving against the cabinets; or on a dreadful Sunday afternoon when her father's endless cigarette smoke hung above the green couch while her mother wore out the carpet and their shouting rattled heirloom teacups upon the shelf above the upright piano. She, Mary Agnes, the usual trophy in these wars, would creep away with her school books to close her bedroom door.

"And I suppose it was all my fault," Angelica Adelli shouted now. "You just wanted her to grow up with thick braids and thick hips in a kitchen full of steaming pots and squalling brats like all of your friends' daughters did? It seems to me I remember more than a few conversations late into the night and you figuring more courses you could teach. Or were they really just another excuse to stay up late and get sloppy drunk and blame everything on your daughter's career?" She raised her head, eyes flashing.

And Mother Adelli's old familiar template of guilt snapped into place: She was the reason her parents smote one other down, the reason her brother felt pushed away; the reason there was never enough money; and that everyone's free time was gobbled up by recitals.

"Stop it," Mother Adelli turned on them. "Will you stop it? Please! You always do this; and it never solves anything." And they ceased abruptly, baffled as if someone had clicked off the knob on the radio. "Haven't you learned anything, either of you? Don't you realize you took it all away from me—all the pleasure—and that I actually came to hate having to dance?"

At this, Angelica Adelli's mouth fell open. "*Maria*. I don't believe that!"

The daughter, her veil flaring and features down sewn tight, wheeled toward her mother.

"What do you think it would do to me, that look you would get on your face—as if you owned something extravagant—when the audience would applaud, or someone, a reporter, would come back stage to talk to me? It scared and disgusted me. I don't think you ever saw *me*. You saw something that could carry you away from—", her hands floundered in the air, "I don't know what—from your kitchen, from our life, from yourself."

And at this, she watched her mother's eyes grow round, her breasts sag backwards below her wiry neck and opening mouth; then heard the vacuum-like suck as she drew in horrified breath. But she went on, nevertheless, merciless and beyond prayer of stopping.

"I never told you what it did to me, your greed for my dancing. I never told you how it made me lonely, a foreigner in my own body, in my own house. Actually, I stopped giving dance my best effort when I was about nine. Why, I could have been much better than I ever got to--." And she laughed a high painful laugh to see—like some complex and elegant filigree—a pull in both her parents' eyes. "You too, Dad." She couldn't stop--as if she were running downhill, though the dread washing into her father's face wounded her. "It wasn't your drinking that was the real problem. Oh, it made me feel guilty, yes—but it was how you treated me, as if I were a porcelain doll, that was so hard. You loved me as the perfect little dancer. How could I dare to disappoint you by being anything else? And Julian. I lost my brother Julian because of dance. He had died to me by the time I was ten, hating me for the attention you gave me, you and mother—which I took, of course. Oh, I took it," she cried out, "but looking for something else. You made me a ghost, the two of you. You walked right through me."

And she saw their paled faces, at this; and her own body was shaking violently, feeling such eruptions rage and grief and wounded love all at the same time.

On trembling legs she stepped toward the door of the Study Hall and found the light switch. The overhead globes flooded the room. The mother flinched and covered her red eyes with her hand. The father dug into his trouser pockets for a handkerchief, turning away from wife and daughter. Mother Adelli stood against the blackboard and gripped the chalk tray.

Her father stared at his daughter from over his worn wool jacket as if she were a stranger; and that awful clawing started up in his blood for a drink while her voice trudged on.

"I have come to see that when I entered the convent, I did it to get away from you and mother. To get away from being a dancer, to keep dance from eating up everything I—"

"*Santa Anna e Maria.* I've listened to just about all I care to from you!" the mother threw an arm into the air, the fingers of the hand closed togetherinto a fist. And anger blazed from her eyes.

"Unless the laws of nature have changed, we are still your parents no matter what age you are, and you owe us some respect! Or perhaps the fourth commandment doesn't apply to someone in a habit." Angelica Adelli unfurled slowly from the student desk and stood, bracing herself against its top. "Now let me make sure I have heard you correctly: You let us give up every extra cent we could ever get our hands around, our Saturdays, Sundays, evenings, to sew, to iron, to ride the train and watch you rehearse in those freezing auditoriums, to pander to your teachers--"

"Mother, I never asked! You--"

"And you let your father take on night courses, year after year—on top of his fulltime job at that terrible junior high school—and then sit up until two and three in the morning grading papers while we never got our trip to Italy-- never even got to Wisconsin in the summer, except for two miserable weekends in cabins that rats shouldn't live in. We never saw any theater but yours. Your father got a new sports jacket once—once!—in fifteen years!"

"I didn't ask for that, Mother."

"You're telling me that you went into the convent and you didn't have a vocation? All that hard work, all that saving and saving and saving, all that money; and you didn't have a vocation?! (The convent isn't free, if you remember; we paid for that too.) But you just wanted to get away from dance—and from us?!

"I didn't know then, I thoug--"

"And I am to believe that all of my efforts on your behalf gave you nothing but misery? Greedy, was I? If I wanted a new dress, I made it. I wore shoes from thrift shops. And you never actually wanted to dance, yourself? Perhaps dance was more work than you cared for. Perhaps you were lazy. Madame Vargas suggested as much to me many times. That's why I had to stay on you day and night. Your body had to be trained; without that you could never get *anywhere*. And don't make your brother Julian a hammer on us! If you thought you were getting too much attention, why didn't you do something about it?

"I *told* you, it wasn't laziness that kept me—"

"The child is mad," Angelica Adelli bellowed at her husband who sat with one hand over his eyes. "I don't understand a word she is saying. Who oiled her feet every night as if she were the king's own pig? What is the girl talking about, Lorenzo? Ten years in the convent and she still needs a rope around her waist to keep her from wandering over a cliff."

"There. That's just exactly what I mean," Mother Adelli pointed a trembling finger to the empty space in which the mother's words still vibrated. "The way you did that just now—talked about me to Dad as if I weren't here, when I *am* here! Well, that's what you always did—treated me as if I weren't there, talked about me, about my leg extensions, my *gran jette*, my arabesque--as if I weren't even connected to it." She could hear how it sounded, so infantile, so full of self-pity. Well, now she couldn't stop. "Do you understand that made me invisible? I wanted you to see *me*, *Mary Agnes*. I didn't want to be a dancer if it meant not having a mother, or family for that matter."

Angelica Adelli threw her head back grandly and rolled her eyes. "*Madonna Mia,*. Mary Agnes! You've had a mother every day of your life! And you make me into a monster! I was simply doing my best to help you develop. I never had such a luxury, nor such a friend, myself. As soon as I was able to change my brothers' and sisters' diapers, my life was laid out for me. People told me I could have been a movie star! Fine. Where's the money for that when you have seven brothers and sisters, a sickly mother who barely speaks English, a father who barely speaks English and is always washing other people's floors? *No. I did my duty.* And I didn't even finish high school. 'For what,' my father wanted to know, 'you just gon' to make babies and meat balls.' That was in 1916; and there were plenty of jobs because of the war; and *everyone* needed money!

"When I met your father, I thought, 'Now there's a man going somewhere!' His family was poorer than mine, poor as mice. You remember Grandma and Grandpa Adelli's idea of Christmas—a nickel, a scrap of lace; and those Sunday dinners with the meat sliced thin as that veil you're wearing. But your father put himself through college; he got himself a job teaching. Your father could have been a professor at a university one day—— he was so smart, always at the head of his class—" she turned slowly; "but he decided he'd rather drink." And she paused to scar her husband long and wickedly with her eyes. "So then you—and Julian—had to be our hope. But Julian didn't stay home--and his head always in the clouds. Like father like son!" And she shrugged disgustedly to let her hands slap her thighs.

"--And there was nothing at home for Julian; because home was all about me!" Mother Adelli couldn't leave it alone. Why couldn't her mother see it?

"Don't drag me into this fairy tale now!" Lorenzo Adelli twisted in his seat to face his wife. "Just remember, it's my salary we're living on now, from the job I've held onto, Depression or no Depression, war or no war. Julian went to Loyola; Mary Agnes went to Sheridan Road! We didn't have *our* children in the public schools!"

"They were in Catholic schools because you were teaching in a Catholic school. And what will we be living on when you retire in seven years—the royalties from the books you were going to write, or the fees from the grand lectures you were going to deliver, and then present me afterwards as your wife? And remember the great return to Italy to show the relatives what we have become? Whose fairy tale was that?" The wife spat the words back at him, her chin jutted out.

And Mother Adelli felt herself jammed again into the small kitchen on Granville Avenue, anger pummeling the air. ""PLEASE don't fight." Don't you see that dance cost us every ounce of good feeling we had?"

"Oho-ho, don't be so self-centered Mary Agnes. We fought about plenty besides you, didn't we Lorenzo?" Angelica Adelli smiled grimly at her husband; and then turned on her daughter. "But if we made dance such a misery to you, why didn't you stop? You danced for twelve years." The mother was nearly shouting now while the early darkness pressed at the closed windows where the daughter stood shivering. (?)

"Well?!"

And it was over. Now they knew everything. And Mother Adelli shook her head slowly, her face layered despair.

"I don't know, Mother. God knows I wish I could be clear, myself!" And she flung her hands silently into the air. "I didn't think I had a right to say anything! *You* were my *parents*. *You* wanted me to do it. *You* seemed to be counting on it so much! And *I* was afraid to lose all that attention!" It sounded so foolish now as it came out--so lame, so childish. Still, it was true. "And I *did* love it! My body was SO happy when I danced! But then, always reaching further, it would get out of control; and I couldn't imagine what would happen to us if I got better and better! We—I-- would have no life at all but dance, then." She pleaded with them to understand; but the mother sat like a block of wood staring straight ahead while the father glanced between his daughter and the thick joints of his hands which he turned back and forth.

"Then the feeling came of God calling me to Himself," Mother Adelli went on, "-- so unexpected and compellingly. And it was such a relief to think I knew at last which way to go; although now it seems that may have been a mistake." And she buried her face in her hands so that her voice came muffled through her fingers. "And how can I ever, ever make up for all of this?"

And silence froze the room.

Then, suddenly, there came the near inaudible rumbling; then the father's cough exploded, the awful rattle raking over the empty desks. "Damned cigarettes!" he gasped between spasms, then glanced apologetically at his daughter.

"Is that all you can do?" Angelica Adelli glared at her husband. "Have you heard what your daughter has been telling us?"

Lorenzo Adelli lifted his head from where it now hung between his knees., his face grey. Wordlessly, he waved his hand. And after a moment, he raised his eyes to his daughter.

"I can't believe you could have danced better than you did, Pretty Feet; or that you were holding back, the way that power seemed to take you!" He touched her face gingerly with his eyes; and the old reverence filled his voice. He could see now she had had no place to go, that when the door to the Convent had opened to her—Still, the awful waste of effort, of the years made his stomach turn!

The mother slammed to her feet, jamming her arms into her coat, her purse swinging in crazy arcs.

"We're getting nowhere here, Lorenzo," she announced.

The father continued to sit; but then rose, also.

"Please." Mother Adelli rushed toward them, "Mother, Dad. Oh, *please* don't leave like this!"

"I don't see that there's anything more to say, Mary Agnes. You've made fools of your own parents. The least we could have expected was a little gratitude. A stray dog would have given us that."

"But I *am* grateful!"

Nevertheless, her mother's back disappeared stiffly through the Study Hall door. But her father turned on the threshold.

"I didn't know," he whispered sadly; "I tried to do the right thing, honey."

And she stood staring at the empty doorway, heard their feet on the corridor, then slowly climbing the stairs, then on the corridor above. Oh, how could she have made the mistake of telling them these things? But didn't she owe them that much?

She raced up the stairs, down the hallway, then coming even with them in the hall where it opened into the foyer.

She followed them past the elegant tables, the Chinese vases, the Italian lamps, begging them to wait. The petite portress at her station outside the parlor dropped her eyes discretely and rummaged noisily in the desk drawer.

Her mother halted suddenly where the short flight of stairs descended to the front entrance way and turned to her daughter.

"Was all of that true?" she asked coldly; "Is that how you've really felt all these years?"

"Yes," Mother Adelli admitted it sorrowfully.

Then down the stairs the girl's mother marched to the etched inner door, and then out the front. while the father hesitated, then followed his wife; and the cumbersome door of heavy wood and stained glass whooshed air behind him then clasped shut with a throaty click.

Mother Adelli stood frozen at the top of the stairs. She was losing her parents, her family. Oh, but it must not end like this!

She took the stairs two at a time, struggled with the heavy door and sprang out into the air calling "Wait! Please!" But neither of the disappearing backs turned in response in the snow-flecked gloom.

Running alongside her mother, the young nun recounted again the anguish, the fear, the love—and saw also for once the pitiful confusion that had to this day been her life.

"--and it has come clear only these past few days, since my student's death. Please, I so want to make it up somehow!"

Too soon, they were at the commuter platform; and the North Shore train already rattling and blowing and sighing to a stop.

The conductor swung off, a flashlight in his fist. "Boaarrrdd!" he fixed the yellow beam on the throbbing threshold.

Angelica Adelli looked at her daughter. This one could have been diva, a GREAT diva! And her own feelings wrenching dumbly, she raised her hand in a stopping motion, then stepped up onto the train.

But it iwas the father's turn next. "When it's darkest, Pretty Feet, *figlia mia* it's then God is not far off," he whispered through her veil in a choked voice.

Oh, and she clung to him, then--and long as she dared, before she spoke. "I'm going to have to leave the Order, Dad; and soon as I can." She just blurted it out; it was the best she could do.

Her father pulled back, his confounded eyes searching her face while the conductor stamped the platform. *"Boaarrrdd!"*

Still stunned, he sat opposite his wife. *Leave the Order!* He leaned at the scarred window to hold, as *To do what?*

And long as he could, through the window he held his only child in his eye, the crisp fluted mark of her Order ovaling her face, and waving her delicate white-fingered flag of a hand.

With a jerk, the train pulled away; and his daughter, waving her hand after the train, shrank and shrank while the rocking car rounded the bend. He knew one thing, nothing on earth compared to the value of his daughter. He rummaged in his pocket for a cigarette, wishing to God it was a drink. His wife's face, set in stone, jolted over the rail bed in the darkened train window.

Mother Adelli dropped her hand. The disappearing train drew open between her breasts a trench of deep aching. New flakes drifting through the air, still she could feel her father's arms!

But somehow, he had understood something--though what she did not know since she understood so little herself! And she felt sure that, in his feelings, he did not--would not!-- abandon her.

And on that slim thread--and balancing itself lightly as a dancer, as she turned to retrace her steps to the grey fortress of the school--there rose up a small flame of hope burning bright in the face of the oncoming storm.

William Cullen Bryant Day

It's 7:54 am, October 5, 1997;

It's William Cullen Bryant day; and I pick my way across the parking lot to pull on the only handle I can find. A weather-beaten Our Children Our Future emblem swings outward; and on the blast of over-heated air, I smell boiled hot dogs. Most students will eat out of the vending machines today. Oh, my name is Isa Fitzgerald.

I step inside to a metal detector. The guard takes in my trench coat, sensible shoes and briefcase, waves me on.

"Good morning!" I chirp, carefully cheerful in the foreign culture of the high school—that's what they call it in edu-speak, a "culture." The students are a "population" with an "ethnic profile"; the school has "demographics," a "poverty index", a "drop-out rate" and a "table of negative academic achievement".

A river of bodies boils by, up stairwells, down hallways and into classrooms on three floors. The open smell of autumn on hair, jackets and book bags evaporates in the heat of the building. Dress code requires white on top, black on the bottom; earrings on males and certain colors of shoelaces are forbidden. A fat boy in a yellowed shirt raises a hand at the stairs.

"Hi, Miz Fiz-gerul."

This boy, in fifth period English, is one who sleeps, nose burrowed into his arm, until the teacher, Mr. Jannis, raps him with a rolled-up newspaper or the bell rings. I take in the heavy face, hands loose and lost. His classmates tent their heads with their arms when I give a demonstration lesson in writing, as if I were sighting them in crosshairs desk to desk; and the teacher for whom I'm present, disappears into a file drawer or class attendance book or the *SunTimes*.

"See you fifth period," I say. "We're going to have fun." I hoist a cassette player.

In this far South Side public high school, I am seen as "The Enemy" and sent by the Chicago Board of Ed to spy, then clap people into leg irons. If academic scores don't go up this second year of school reform, staff could lose their jobs. There have been principals' heads on the parapets of City Hall since June, and teachers rattling tin cups in the streets.

I am not sent by the Board of Ed. I am as much under scrutiny as anyone, since I am held responsible for raising test scores by March. I am the EOP (Educational Outreach Program) of Elliott College, a formerly religious and now non-sectarian institution on the West Side, and now in a shotgun marriage with Bryant. Less than fifteen percent of Bryant's students meet state norms. This fact puts the high school on academic probation; and the Board requires it to have an educational partner or be reconstituted (read: Everybody gets fired).

I am white, forty-three, with a Master's in Writing I got to stay afloat after my husband died. Now, due to my success with low-scoring freshmen, and Elliott's hunger for a piece of City Hall's School Reform pie, I am a foot soldier in the war against sixty years of crumbling, dismal, decrepit, and defunct public education in Chicago.

Up the stairs. Young bodies blind as the blades of a revolving door knock me one way then another as they tower, elbow, bellow, dog whistle, leap-frog and torrent past. I notice the starburst of blood now three weeks old on the first landing. Two more flights. A clutch of kids barnacle the doorjamb of Ms. Trevor's first period English class. Most will not go in until they absolutely have to. The bell chews along my nerves. Excuse me, excuse me. I shoulder my way to the threshold.

It's 8:01 and in one corner of the room I see three limber brothers eye the girls, snap fingers and croon dirty lyrics; they flash white teeth at the University lady. Seated near the windows are four sports experts. "Man, Pippin jes' los' it, tha's awl," a boy throws himself back in his chair. "No, man," his friend hikes forward, cuts a chunk out of the air. "It Jorden, man. He an ol' man, man. He need give Scotty some room. Give the man a chance for onct." A girl submerged under corkscrew curls, eye make-up and headphones stares at me from a desk in the doorless coat closet. No teacher is present. I find a chair.

8:06. I look these embryonic adults over, wonder how they feel going to school in a failing building (even the building is failing, yuk, yuk), wonder how they feel seeing the month-old blood spot on the landing, person-size hunks of plaster torn from the walls or ceilings, and cockroach trails along the framing boards.

Last week was my first time in this room. That day it took Ms. Trevor, the teacher, nearly twenty minutes to complete roll. Then I read aloud to the class from the opening of *Black Boy* and held two loner students up front. The rest of the class acted as if I were silent oldies projected onto the chalkboard--and smack dab in the middle of their personal business to boot. The teacher bawled and threatened, then gave up trying to improve things and buried her nose in desk drawers and the supply closet until the bell sounded. If I were looking for a reform trophy for the principal, I could tuck Ms. Trevor right under my arm; but I'm the last one interested in costing anybody her job. I'm just here to try to show teachers new possibilities, new ways to do things; and my oblique connection with the Board of Ed is a liability. Today I'm bringing music, every teenager's basic food. There will be no wandering attention today.

8:12. The national anthem crackles over the intercom. I stand. These kids don't; they raise their voices to overcome the loudspeaker while a beautician applies polish to her client's nails, two boys play gin rummy and a girl flips through a video catalogue. The intercom clicks off. I take my hand from my patriotic heart and sit again.

8:14. The sports club moves on to baseball. One boy escapes out the door. Two girls in billowing jackets shuffle in, followed by a kid stuffing his face with popcorn. Someone blows a dog whistle in the hall as feet pound past and the floor trembles. "You ahr sub?" a sleepy-eyed girl leaning on a capsizing arm asks. I shake my head no. "You from the Board?" She can hardly hold her eyes open. "I'm a writing teacher. I was here last week," I tell her. She yawns. "Oh," she sniffs and her arm and head flop to the desk. I go back to my lesson plan.

8:18. Ms. Trevor, slip hanging a full inch and a half below her dress, bangs a paper sack against the door frame as she crosses the room, shoes flapping, wig favoring one ear. In her sixties, Ms. Trevor sets the burden of her textbooks and papers on the floor by her desk. The singers heighten their falsetto, two catalogue readers consult and fill out order blanks. Ms. Trevor is of no more moment than the October breeze through the window. I check the clock, unhitch part three of my lesson and let it float off into next week.

Bosoms sag under her navy dress with its large purple and green flowers; Ms. Trevor rights herself, frowns. "There shouldn't be no talkin', young people. You-all know the rules. If I am detained, you are to go over your homework. You-all owe me your word lists from Monday. This the third day I be askin' for them.'"

"Oh," one of the singers, a red t-shirt under his white uniform shirt, lifts the eyebrows of his long face; his hands, delicate as a violinist's, escape toward the ceiling. "Oh," he swivels from one face to another, voice as high as his hands, "Ms. Trebor say we need be doing our hom-work. Where y'all hom-work at? C'mon now, git it out, git it out." He frowns around, moving his arm and hand like a scythe. "Missus Treevor, she want the hom-wark," another male, dark hair slickered back, legs stretched out, Adidas flopped apart, calls. "Geeve up the hom-wark. Missus Treevor, you can see she ees waitin'"

Boys shrug; girls raise slim shoulders along with their palms and, smiling widely, shake their heads as if bewildered. Homework? Why would they have homework? Another student strolls into the room. The clutch of singers picks up the thread of lyric still suspended in the air. "Do me some mo-re; do me on the flo-or"; their torsos slip around to the beat.

"All right," Ms. Trevor straightens her belt and flips open a black spiral book. "I'm taking names, starting with you, Darren, an' then you, Victor."

"Oooo, y'all," Darren plucks at his red shirt, gives a little scream; "Look out now. Ms. Trebor takin' names. You know what that mean—." He beats time with his feet. "Mi-ster Jones, Mi-ster Jones." The class takes it up, pounding on their desks, tromping on the floor. Mi-ster Jones, Mi-ster Jones.

"Aw right, Darren," Ms. Trevor bawls; "Aw right class, ah'm gettin' the guard. Ah'm calling the guard." She spanks the floor toward the door, index finger aiming for the buzzer on the intercom. The ruckus dribbles away.

Sniffing, coughing, shuffling of chairs.

"And she got her hair done today." Darren's voice warbles bright and high out of the constraint of silence. "What kine hair you got, Ms. Trebor? Look like that long fur offen them monkey arms."

His boys howl and high-five. The rest of the class whoops, laughter honed for humiliation, parting the sculptures of their lips, letting the brilliance of their tongues leap onto the teacher's desk where she sits with her grade book.

I am appalled. This is an older woman.

"Naw," another boy wearing an earring some teacher later will tell him to remove breaks in, slapping his knee, "that a dog I seen runned over front 'a school yesteday. Miz Tebor done ripped that fur right offen his back 'fore he even got colt."

Ha, ha, ha, they turn on her the jewels of their eyes, glittering with the will to cut.

Laughter in the classroom ricochets off the stained ceiling, rebounds from the scarred floor. Ms. Trevor seems impervious to the insults. I am assigned to four teachers at Bryant, and only one so far has had complete control of her classroom. At my West Side Tuesday school, no teacher black, white, yellow or green has complete control of the classroom.

"Now y'all stop." A slender girl with big eyes and marcelled hair throws an arm into the air; her long red fingernails are like petals of a jungle flower and brilliant against the dun of the walls. "Y'all gone hurt Miz Trebor's fillins. An' here she come today in her pretty dress from Am-Vets, an nobody say nothin' nice to her." She leans forward in her chair, gold loops gleaming at her ears, a crease down the front of her jeans, her freshly ironed blouse, its top button undone, glowing against her skin. "You look real nice today Miz Trebor. Tha's my fav'rit dress you got on. Ah don' care how many times you wear it, Ah always be glad to see it." Around her, the wave of mockery rises like a wall of water. "An' yo' slip look real pretty too."

She shrieks the last line out doubling over in her chair, then falls sideways into the arms of the boy next to her; and the wave crashes over the room, filling it up with the dirty oil-slick of the joke, with the howling voices, boys high-fiving and falling out, girls sliding onto their tailbones as if they were drunk, weak with the fun of it, while the partly submerged debris of their lives bobs and collides and submerges again.

Color climbs the drapery of Ms. Trevor's jawline. "Put them chairs right," she points and barks. "An' stop that singin'. Tha's no kine words for young folks to be sayin'. It got no place in mah classroom. Y'all know mah rules."

"Oooo. Do me he-re, baby. Don't you have no fe-ar," boys and girls turn the volume up, lean against one another like barroom buddies.

Ms. Trevor is at my elbow.

"Ah spec' you can go 'head wif yo' lesson." She waves a hand crumpled by arthritis toward the chalkboard. "Thiz lady from Elliot College," she tells the class. "She here las' week, those you here. She gon' teach today." Mrs. Trevor retreats to her desk.

I feel the shore pull away. I look over at her. I won't be helping you, her body says. I'm gone until the bell rings. It's all yours, University lady.

"Carramba, thees ees boring," the girl in the closet pronounces from under her headphones as I walk to the front of the room to face the class. Student eyes already glazed look through me, through the chalkboard, through the wall, across the corridor, through the opposing classroom's far wall to the street, across to some far-off fountain that spouts that magical potion of the future they need to slake their thirst; and which draws them to itself without mercy.

Showtime.

From my briefcase I take two tapes. Talk volume increases again. Nevertheless, the cassette player gets looks. I hold up the plug. "I need a technician," I say. A boy in front of me—ironed shirt and pants, new gyms—raises his hand. His friend with a ring through his eyebrow yells, "Hey, you no *tecnico*, *bobo*. You don't even able to get yore car door to open." Easy laughter eddies about the room. I am elated; my trick has worked and I don't have to stick my rear into the face of this fractious giant.

"You'll need paper and pen." I make light bounce off my voice.

The giant slides onto the end of its spine, buries its head in its arms. "Today you are going to be music vendors," I sparkle away. The giant groans as if this were the sixteenth time this week it has had to be a music vendor. "You're going to do what they do in the music business." I have no idea what goes on in the music business; but hey, some of what I'm asking them to do must go on sometime in the music business. "I am going to play two songs. You develop a fact sheet on each; next week you pick one song to write a sales pitch for, using your fact sheet."

I surmise Ms. Trevor, into her paper sack, has missed my brilliant ploy of getting expository and persuasive writing from the same pre-writing activity. Her inattention is a disappointment though, since this lesson is for her benefit.

"You'll need to note what instruments you hear, style of song, the story or meaning in the lyrics, the target audience you envision, and so on."

The giant stirs onto an elbow, follows the voice vibration, searches until it finds the middle-aged teacher at the front of the room in her black slacks, out-of-a-bottle brown hair, crows feet, J. C. Penney earrings, her eyes behind the drug store glasses too big and too bright, her mouth repeating they'll need to take notes. The giant shifts onto the other elbow, pulls a page of crumpled paper from a backpack, catches an end-over-end ballpoint mid-air.

"What song you gon' play?" This from the fold of musical young-bloods at the back of the room.

"You haf sumthin" mi ol' lady wou' hate?" ring-through-the-eyebrow rises up and snaps his fingers like a flamenco dancer. His buddies laugh, snap their fingers too.

"The first is Jim Croce doing "Bad, Bad Leroy Brown." I scan their faces for recognition of the lyric about their part of Chicago. Nary a ripple. In my West Side high school, Croce and folk singer Bob Gibson beat out Satchmo and got a grudging "moderately cool" from students who felt they could market Croce and Gibson to swingers in their thirties.

Hearing my selections, these boys release air like tires flattening, lay their heads on the desks.

"Ain't you got nothin good we heard of?" It's the kid who helped me.

In my briefcase I have a two-song promo of the popular young singer Usher. I glance at Ms. Trevor with her Bible Belt body. The song is heavily sexual. I got the artist from a sixth grader in my Wednesday school, went to Coconuts, listened to the tape on the way in. When I heard the repetition of "I'll f —you right, I will," I thought, forget it. However, the flip side is instrumental.

"Well yes, I do have something else." I let a swagger into my voice.

"Ah bet it Jingle Bell," a kid with a shaved head rises out of his seat, soaks up the laugh. On his lower lip is a purple scar shaped like a wedge of cheese.

"It's not Jingle Bells. And it's not the national anthem." I let my satisfaction glance off their faces, open for the moment.

The room becomes still.

"What it then?" the shaved head kid frowns and fingers his scar.

I let the pause lay there; let them feel the weight of it; feel for the life stirring in it. "Usher," I say, finally, and rake in the looks of disbelief, of reappraisal.

Darren leans back until his chair is on two legs, shakes his head, jabs his thumbs toward the floor. "Naw man, she ain't got no Usher."

I feel a surge of power, fish for the cassette, hold it up. On the front is a handsome bare-chested young man with glistening hair pulled into a pony-tail, arms crossed over bulging muscles and intense eyes looking out from the plastic box.

"Lemme see." The boy who helped me unfolds his body.

He comes on too fast. Instinctively I hide the tape behind my back, then feel guilty, argue with myself that I am too suspicious. "Jeremy," his dangling student i.d. says, is the boy who helped me out with the plug just a moment ago.

I hesitate, hand him the tape.

His eyes buck, eat the name, the image; his mouth gapes. He holds it high, rattles the case.

"She got Usher sho' enuf," he tells his friends who begin jumping for it. Lemme see it man. Gib it ober, Jer'me. Gib it here.

My stomach drops. What if he doesn't give it back, goes off with that sexual material to the sea of headphones in the lunchroom, tells everyone he got it from that teacher lady from the university?

"Give me the tape, Jeremy." I hold out my hand.

Jeremy stands like the Statue of Liberty, the cassette high over his head, his suddenly invigorated friends, the turbulent waters.

"Give me the tape," I repeat the command, keep my voice even, though my heart is pounding—walking the high wire without a net. I've met Jeremys before, white, black, brown—all will, nothing but will, the lords of the land.

Jeremy waggles the tape at my nose. "Play this one."

There are shouts of agreement, and a funny shift in the room that says they, the students, are possibly remotely prepared to consider something akin to perhaps even liking the University lady, especially if she gives them music the school and their parents don't approve of. But they are also a pot on a high flame, the excited water jumping at the rim.

"First we'll hear Jim Croce. Then we'll hear Bob Gibson. Then we'll hear Usher." I make my voice firm, step toward Jeremy.

He ducks the tape behind his back. "How we know you gon' play it?"

"Because I said so. If we start now, we'll have time to hear it before the bell rings; if we waste any more time, it'll be too late and you'll have to wait until next week." It is a masterstroke. Jeremy surrenders the tape.

I press the play button. Silence, hissing; then the stepping up, stepping down of the piano banging out the intro to "Leroy Brown." There are grimaces, blinking eyes, hands over ears. Someone waves in a circle: Turn it down.

I am stunned, dumbfounded. Who can't like Croce doing their Chicago, speaking their lingo? I think back to Usher playing in my car, and realize I was hearing Motown reborn—soft, mellow, and now explicitly sexual. That's what they're hungry for, not the jumping jack songs of the sixties. How could I have been so stupid?

Then, as if she ascended out of the floor, Ms. Trevor is there, dancing a slow dance in front of the cassette player. Donna Reed hair cocked to one side, a shy smile on her lips, arms pumping to the beat, her slip sways below her dress. In old-lady steps, she turns, raises her arms over her head. Tiny grey hairs sprout under her capped sleeves. Ms. Trevor steps to a melody of tenderness, of the past; she dances on a dance floor we cannot see to music we cannot hear.

Her students gape, roll their eyes, but hesitate, confused by this shocking unasked for display of her humanity. They read it as a betrayal and subversion of the unspoken game of school: They are to hate and torment Ms. Trevor until June to show their contempt for anything that is not their own; she is to berate and unjustly police them Fall to Summer and so crystallize their self-righteousness and will to resist.

"*Mama mia!*" the boy with slickered hair sets down his *People Magazine.*

"Git up an' dance wid her," Jeremy elbows his buddy.

"Aw, man, she too fas' fer som-body my age."

I am aghast, humbled, thinking perhaps Ms. Trevor has done this for me, to support my lesson. Now I have a visceral need to throw my body between Ms. Trevor and her class while Croce pounds on.

"Mm-muh! Now thas' sexy. Ain't tha' sexy?" Darren asks around, shaking his fingers hard and fast and eyeing Ms. Trevor's age-flattened hips under her skirt. "Wou'nt y'all call that hot?"

But the class lets it go. Ms. Trevor, eyes still half-closed, soft smile still on her lips, completes a circle and sways back to her desk.

"Take notes. What instruments do you hear? What story?" I'm in there without missing a beat.

The giant blinks, jots a word, a line. A few shoulders roll, a few fingers pop. The room quiets. Glee uncurls in my solar plexus. By God, I've got them. I stroll, smiling, peering over shoulders, feeling smug and powerful.

The weak light of a Chicago overcast struggles through the grime on the windows. Gum wrappers, cellophane bags, balls of crumpled loose-leaf sit on the floor like modern art. There is the clank and rattle of the dumpster outside, the buzz of the overheads, the scratch and tap and of pens and pencils, the melody breaking off as if cut with a scissors.

I whirl, see a wide grin floating near the cassette player, as a life-sized puppet on a stick, a striped shirt under a white shirt, leaps away from the player, then dances toward it with his male cronies around him, their leader, Jeremy, their grins breaking like light on water. As if in a dream where details glance off your mind, I see the odd thing in his eyes, the discrepancies among the grin, the dancing movement, and the wary way he looks at me, one hand high over his head like a dancer, the other down, partly concealed by his body. I see him bring the second hand up from behind his thigh, and with a movement fluid and flame-like, punch the door open, pull Croce from the player and drop in a different cassette. The little door shuts with a snap and Jeremy's index finger punches downward to release sounds of metal against metal, like trains on the loose. Jeremy dances away, long legs bending, head thrown back, eyes glittering as if waiting for a burst of something. Then the singer—if you could call him a singer—breaks through the music—if you could call it music—shouting the one word you never use in a classroom.

The 'f' word.

Over and over, the performer bellows it through the saucer-sized sound system of the player, pumps it into the classroom like sewage under pressure.

The kids go on a rampage, yelling and clapping, high-fiving and knocking chairs over. Like a wild sea they rise and fall, slapping into one another, hilarious, shouting the word, letting it knock them around, weak with the joy of it. All the Sunday afternoons in church; all the yammer, yammer, yammer of adults to which they have not responded so they wouldn't get hit; all the furious, frustrated wordless waiting for time, for nature, for God to make something good happen to them—they let it all into that one word, jettison it for the pure ecstasy of the release, the beautiful word bringing down all those barriers the grown-ups at home, in school, in churches, in stores, on the street, on television raise against them.

All I can think is where did he get a tape, and how did he drop it in so fast? And that I am responsible. I left the player unguarded, trusting them without a thought, rube that I am, easy mark, aging fool of a flower child who assumed there was a verbal contract. I stride past the riot of open mouths to the player, eject the tape and drop it into my pocket; then I raise my chin and give Jeremy my most triumphant look, though I am walking humiliation.

The students' relish of my discomfort is deep. I feel their wavering— whether or not to make something more out of this with this here University lady come in our classroom readin' her books, stick her nose in our business, tell us we stupid. She stupid. What she think she gon' do now, she so smart? I hear their minds go at it like knives mincing chives.

Jeremy teeters at his place, the corners of his mouth high, as if pulled by a cord. The smile has no depth. He bounces on the balls of his feet; the long fuzz on his head looks as if it is breathing. Jeremy loves the spotlight.

"Guess I got yo' tape now." He twirls it between his long fingers. His boys laugh.

I turn from him, force myself into a slow swagger, back and forth in front of the chalkboard. A standoff with a student is death; you never do it.

"I've got your tape." I pat the pocket of my jacket.

Jeremy shrugs. "S' fine with me. Ah'll keep this one uh yours, tho' Ah cain't git nuthin' fer it on the street."

His boys laugh. His girls glitter.

"Good," I nod deeply. "Then I'll have yours. Good." Back and forth.

He shrugs again.

I feel sweat in my armpits.

Jeremy folds himself back into his seat, tucking my tape into his shirtfront pocket, whistling off tune. Tittering sloshes around the room. Outside, someone leans on a car horn.

I see Ms.Trevor push herself up from her desk, her mouth opening. "You give that tape back to Miz Fizroy, Jeremey."

"Who Miz Fizroy?" a baby-faced boy yells and snaps his head to look around the room. "Who Miz Fizroy?" he asks his classmates.

"She Miz Fizroy," the kid next to him grins broadly and points at me; "only she Miz Fiz-gerul."

"Haw, haw," the girl in the coat closet calls out through her chewing gum; "Miz Trebor don' even know tha' woman name. And she our teacher."

"Tha' woman not our teacher," a girl with blue-black hair straight as rain drawls, picking at her cuticle with a nail that curves downward and is painted green. "Miz Trebor our teacher, only she don' know nothin'."

For a moment I don't care that the students, from all I've seen last week and today, are justified in their war with Ms. Trevor. I don't care that if Ms. Trevor takes over, the class will be excruciating in its dullness, its beside-the-pointness, small to a fault. I don't care that these students will have nervous systems jumping out of their skins as they watch the hands of the clock crawl from minute to minute until all fifty have eaten them alive. What I hope is that right now Ms. Trevor will stand all the way up and take back the class. But Ms. Trevor sits down instead and my hope flaps away, leaving me alone with this live bomb. I cast my eyes at the clock; there's still fifteen minutes to go.

"Of course," I say, all casualness, "we could make a trade, if you promise not to play that tape in here."

But Jeremy's not having any. He stands rooted, his back to me; I stroll, study the bulletin board. The class loves it.

"Geeve at the same time," a boy with unraveling cuffs and an infant mustache offers from over a dog-eared comic book; "like in moovies."

Jeremy looks over his shoulder at me. He wants his 'f's back.

"Get your tape up, Jeremy," I tell him and move forward. Jeremy turns. I hold out the tape. You can hear a pin drop.

We are within two feet of one another. If he should manage to get his tape and not give mine back, I will be Her Majesty Queen Fool. I feel all the eyes, but I keep mine on Jeremy's fingers, hold my tape level. Jeremy does the same. My face aches; I realize it's my smile, wonder if it looks like the letter slot in Jeremy's face. Jeremy's fingers come, come. I shunt the box forward. His fingertips dock on its end; I feel the coolness of Croce under my own fingers. Then each of us releases the other's, turns away, and the tension in the room evaporates. Jeremy pimp-walks to his chair, pants fashionably low, the crotch nearly to his knees. Students shift, turn to one another.

"Wha' she gon' do now?" a boy asks.

Never say die. I drop Croce into the cassette player.

Oh, the South Side of Chicago is the baddest part of—

"Ask yourself what instruments you hear. Take notes. You're going to need them."

I coach, the giant scratches on its paper, or scratches under its arm or picks its nose, or lays its head down on the desktop. The bass thumps up and down, the piano rattles along like a tray full of china, Croce croons out the words sweet and tart and chunky. I relax a bit, stroll, bend over a squatty girl in a Sox sweatshirt, look down the list of instruments she has going and absently notice dead air. Dead air. I spin around. The sound of metal clashing; the sound of the word you never use in school and Jeremy's grin floats above the player.

The room is up for grabs.

A tidal wall of anger slams against my eyeballs. I feel massive pressure on my vocal cords. My tongue swells with inarticulate speech, swear words, obscenities, profanity, racial slurs. I clamp my jaws, my body begins to shake. Before I can reach the player, Jeremy punches the stop/eject, drops the tape into his pants pocket, careens on his heel, plops like a straw man into his chair. The laughter is an open hydrant. They point at the University lady. Who stupid now? Ha, ha. Who stupid now?

All I can feel is rage, and how much I hate these teenagers.

I jerk the plug from the wall, the machinery of my mind smoking as if it's caught on a rag. From far far away I hear Ms. Trevor's voice, like a radio playing in another room: Now young people; now young people.

I collect the player and, as if watching from outside, see myself march to the front of the room, draw my body into a shaking column and then, past recall, ripple my lip and hurl at the blur of adolescent faces and open mouths the venom pumping through my nervous system.

"I came ready to work," I spit flaming match heads. "I put three hours into this lesson and spent my own money, but I guess you're not interested."

"You got that one right, sister," someone calls out.

"I was trying to prepare you for the IGAP. Maybe you don't care if your school goes down the tubes."

"Yes." Darren, red shirt blazing, raises the power sign. "Bryant, down the tubes." Everyone whoops and claps.

"That's fine. That's your business," I fume away. "But if this school goes down, you go down with it. People who don't know you will look at your scores. If they're low, where else can they put you but in the class for kids who seem slow? The slow class gets the worn-out teachers, the rooms in the basement, the textbooks from 1972. If you apply to college and they see the name of your high school, someone's going to remember: Oh, Bryant. On probation three times, then reconstituted. Deep six this kid."

Under the stained and peeling ceiling, the students listen, lean back on their elbows or forward on the palms of their hands as if sunning at the beach, like children of the rich who, when they are ready, will go to their grandfathers or uncles for the sports car, then the really good job—one not too demanding and with their own office in a skyscraper in the Loop. The job will pay lots of money for the designer clothes, pricey condos, sexy partners and European vacations they will require. Until that day, they have nothing better to do than watch this University lady whip herself into a high froth over something that doesn't have a thing in the world to do with them.

"We're trying to help you here," I splutter on, "and you don't have sense enough to know it." They stare at me, wide-eyed and placid. Then someone snickers and my rage erupts afresh. "You know," I inject enough fresh acid into my voice to eat holes in their ears, "when you get out there, a pretty face and good-looking clothes aren't going to be enough. You'll have to be able to *do* something."

My words slide over their grinning faces harmless as baby oil.

I jam the cassette player into my briefcase. Where does their arrogance come from anyway, I blister. These kids have nothing. What on earth is it they find to act so high and mighty about?

The buzzer shreds the air. Students clatter out of their chairs and swell toward the door. I have no problem stepping aside to let them pass.

It is while zipping my briefcase that the bolt of lightening strikes and I realize the fiction, the hallucination this whole thing of schooling is: That it is a dream we teachers dream and that we think it is real because we don't know we're dreaming. What is real is we are the past; and as the past, we are the poor. Whereas they, these students who sun on the beach waiting to collect their inheritance, are the future and therefore the rich. We don't know this because we grown-ups experience only our dream, a dream that only ends when we do.

But the play is too long, and they do not listen as they sit in the front row. They drum their fingers and wait for us to finish our lines, dreaming the play they will be in, rehearsing lines they know they will have. They will never enter our play even as walk-ons because their dream orders them to make an entirely new play. Already, in their bodies and minds, things light up, exert a pull, create a strong current, though they do not feel carried; they feel held in the unbroken calm of everything being just how it is supposed to be.

The new awareness grips me, holds me the way the alarm clock's buzzer holds you suspended between waking and sleeping. Why would I think I could have anything of interest to bring to players cast in a different script written in a different language?

White shirts and black pants jostle toward the door. I must serve them. We all must serve them. This is the law of nature, a law also encoded in their cells, in the growing of their bodies, in the galvanizing happening to them without their consent in the generation of a generation.

I search my jacket for a Kleenex, and Jeremy's head floats into my peripheral vision. "You have to have more than a pretty face," he advises his audience in a high falsetto, wagging his head like a woman. "You have to be able to doooo something," he repeats and passes in front of me as if I weren't there. I feel the mercy of whatever has already washed me out of his mind, though the insult of such a quick and easy death stings. "Doooo som-ting, *mi insectos!*" another voice bobs up. "Doooo something, *mi insectos!*" the students chant, punching out the door, only mildly interested in what may come to be in the next class. It's all the same to them, pressing up from the soil as they are—up and out.

I turn to escape down the hall; but there Ms. Trevor is, haunting my elbow, carrying her purse and paper sack. "My daddy wouldn't never 'low such low manners in our house," she says and shakes her head and turns on me a face like the earth abused. "My daddy beat me every day of my life," she tells me, tells me factually, the way a child tells a child, looking out at me from the punishing room of the crazed righteousness of parental law. I don't know how to reply, shocked at this unexpected intimacy, and touched by it. "He beat me every day of my life," Ms. Trevor repeats with pride and bitterness until we reach the stairs.

I swim the babble of the student cafeteria; feel soft drink cups, paper French fry baskets and sandwich papers crunching underfoot. I find the teachers' lunchroom where I stare at the TV with its Wall Street ticker tape stuttering along the bottom of the screen. Through the lunchroom's closed door I hear the giant winnowing fan of adolescence driving everything. My French fries resemble beached marine life. I have no appetite anyway. Two more classes wait for me.

At 2:35 p.m. I head for the haven of my car.

When I get home, I will call my chairman and tell him I cannot go back to that class; that he can fire me if he wants to.

He will say, "Why? What happened?"

I will tell the story.

He will say, "You're exaggerating, Isa. You're making too much of this. They won't even remember next week."

I will tell him he's wrong, that I have lost all credibility in that classroom.

"All you need is a good night's sleep. Besides, it will look worse if you don't go back. Then they really will have beaten you."

I will not tell him they have already beaten all of us; and also that it is an illusion to think there is anything to beat.

I'll hear him open and close a desk drawer. Then I'll hear him clear his throat and ask in a low careful voice, "Is it a thing with minorities?"

I will scrutinize myself while his chair squeaks. Finally, I will say no, not more than for anyone else, and probably less than with many. I will not add that this is bigger and deeper than anything to do with race, that it has to do with something like what Buddhists call the Turning of the Wheel.

There will be the relieved pause. "Then no problem going back," his voice will travel the line hearty.

I will not say there is every problem with going back because nobody sees the Wheel or knows we are all caught on its spokes. Instead I'll tell him I honestly don't know what to offer these students; that whatever it is they need, I don't have it, and that how to find it is a mystery to me. I'll tell him I'm not sure I ever was a teacher, anyway —just a would-be fiction writer trying to earn a living.

"There you go writing short stories again," he'll come back, booming. "You've done a great job at Elliott. Aren't you the one always telling me how smart these kids are and how much promise they have? Have you decided they don't have promise?"

No, I'll say.

"—that they aren't smart?"

No. They're smart, very smart.

I will not tell him I have sensed that mysterious authority that brims at the rim of their young skin, sensed it for the past year in every classroom past fifth grade, and this day recognize it for the dream forming of its own accord in and among them; and that in rooms with a weak teacher, this authority of theirs breaks over the top with no provocation other than the joy of its own will. John Murray will circulate with his index finger the number two pencils in his Michigan State beer mug, then straighten the backbone in his voice. "Oh, roll up your sleeves, Isa. You're topnotch. Tell them what to do, see that they do it and get those scores up."

I will run my fingertips over my cat's ear, feel the exquisite curve of the tip, trace with my eye its embroidery thread veins in the lighted tortoise shell and hear myself saying "um-hum" and "I guess so" as John Murray's voice keeps unrolling like the evening news. I will agree we are legally bound to fulfill this contract, and that next time the lesson should be simpler, something out of their textbooks. I won't bother to add almost nobody has textbooks, or they never bring them or have only dog-eared ancient editions. I won't bother to say that this class will stare at me over empty desks or Sears catalogues or the sports page of the *SunTimes*, laugh and chatter, shrug, mimic my voice and facial expression; and that every class I go to waits for this same opportunity.

I won't tell him the situation is hopeless unless someone wakes up to this reality that students and teachers are in different dreams. I will not point out that adolescents cannot be expected to understand this. I will not point out this leaves the responsibility to the teachers. Neither will I ask where we will find teachers who grasp that there are two dreams running like separate rivers in the same classroom, and who have the wisdom, patience, generosity and intuitive skill to tease from their students the dream they aren't aware they have and whose form neither teacher nor students know, and thereby to *ex ducere*, midwife, a world designed to leave the teacher behind.

I'll agree to go back, to try it again—because I need the job, because I want to be able to continue at Elliott when this year is over. I can't explain that nothing is the same, that I am not the same person, that now I know too much and too little to do this work. One thing will change though. Hereafter, I will understand the teachers I work with; and I will not sneer at them anymore.

A California Story

Perhaps it was the sudden awakening to the fact that her socks were soaked that told Virginia Curtain to turn around and start back. A February powder thin as window sheers hung in the air. She took in the silent authority of the Sierra Nevada, guessed the air temperature to be about twenty degrees, but didn't feel cold, tromping along in a ratty orange jacket, a little sweat glistening on her face, shaking her hair free, feeling fifteen years younger; no, more like a girl again in Illinois making her way home down cow trails through snow with flakes the size of your fist. This; you could hardly call this snow--so microscopic you could almost breathe it in. How did California make an industry of this? It fell down the backs of her E-Z Striders nevertheless and wormed its way into her socks; and she began to wish she had worn the damned boots after all.

She had been hiking along a flat stretch that looked like a birthday cake; the tall trees were candles. She breathed deep. Underneath all this frosting sat pure granite. This was a place her father would have loved: high, with thin air and plenty of signs of wild game: man's country.

But it was the silence all around that stole into the center of her bones and held her. She stopped, took a last long look ahead, then turned, breaking into the faint herringbone of tire tracks underfoot with the diamond pattern of her walking shoes. It made her feel like a kid, superimposing her diamonds on someone else's herringbone. If she'd had a hat, and with no one about to see, advanced in years as she was she would have lain down and carved out an angel with halo, skirt and wings. Lord but she hated to go back! Well, she would take her own sweet time. Really, she had not expected this scenery and its silence to move her so. It almost made up for having to baby-sit Carmella.

Around eleven, she and her sister Carmella turned off of Interstate 80 just beyond Auburn, and onto Route 30, heading for Pleasant Vista. Virginia watched in the side-view mirror as the valley's sprawl of oak with their knobby horizontal limbs surrendered the climbing terrain to the up and down of pine. It was then she became aware of her feet radiating like meat loaves in the oversized boots, Carmella's boots.

Carmella, in her Oreal #17 chestnut hair, her Max Factor eyebrows and mascaraed lashes, in her sixty-eight year-old dimples and double chins, wanted the visiting Virginia to meet her dearest friends at a cabin in the mountains. This was her idea of how to spend their one day together. Virginia Curtain gritted her teeth: A whole day with Carmella. When she unzipped the boots and flipped them onto the seat behind, Carmella wailed, "But it's all snow up there; it's nearly five thousand feet; and the temperature might only be in the teens. You'll freeze your feet off in those Striders." Carmella always wailed; otherwise she chattered. Why didn't Virginia move to Sacramento? It was a city just like Chicago, where Virginia spent her marriage. They could get a flat together. "Or you might meet a nice widower on a love prowl looking for a Cookie to marry," Carmella twinkled.

One marriage was enough for anyone. And if she did move, it won't be to Sacramento with all those old hotels, dinky stores and left over hippies. In Daytona Beach, at least people bathed and didn't tie-dye every living thing.

The crack shut her sister up for a blessed twenty miles. The road banked, rose, or gave way to startling precipices with only metal railings to protect them in the mindless speeding car. Beyond, rugged grey peaks emerged like royalty draped in ermine. Virginia squeezed her eyes shut to the gorges, but opened them to take in the trees.

These Sierra pines beckoned like some mysterious society that made her want to fling back the car door and, sinking to her knees in the soft powder, wade deep into the pool of their shadows. She found herself dreaming a story a child might tell in which the trees reached out their shaggy arms to enfold her, then drew her into some far-off secret place which, startled, she found to be a part of herself for which she had been longing. There they encircled her to breathe into her a message or a living seed. Having received it, she would stand among them changed, and begin to send forth the signal to another like herself, caught in a car's side-view mirror and struggling against the net of flesh.

Carmella was the older by three years. As the youngest, Virginia had to put up with Carmella's gabby idea of instruction, though it was Virginia finally who became the teacher and was married twenty-eight years, as opposed to Carmella's two one-year quickies; it was Virginia who completed a thirty-year career in elementary education, as opposed to Carmella's intermittent string of secretarial jobs; and Virginia who had a boy, Leonard, the father of two daughters, now in the hotel business in Daytona Beach; and another, Michael, finally finishing up in veterinary medicine at Davis, just west of Sacramento. Childless Carmella had four sets of cockatiels, and was fat. Virginia, by contrast, had a little "mature weight," and a farm-fresh face perfect for selling organic vegetables. Virginia was the realist. Carmella, too eager, friendly too soon, spent her life in Never-never land.

Preceded by her own breath, feeling the cold nip her cheeks pink, Virginia huffed upon a crossroads and looked in either direction. A patterned white ribbon wavered along an endless cloth; it would run up and down the mountains until it reached the Sacramento Valley on one side and the outskirts of Reno on the other. Where was it she turned left the second time? She peered at the pines; but they, who exuded such intimacy only a short time before, now straightened up and pulled apart, as if scrutinized by a stranger. Under the grey sky, amidst the all-encompassing whiteness, she hadn't noticed daylight begin to slide away, and darkness creep beneath the bushes.

To stifle an upsurge of fear, she went off, as usual, on her late husband Arthur. Hadn't it been perfectly typical of him to go dying just when things got really sticky financially? After forty-two years of boilermakers, the fact that he discovered a compromised liver, and so conveniently just before his dealership, the House That Buick Built, collapsed, still galled her. Publicly, she couldn't complain. There had been no overt drunkenness, no woman chasing, no abuse; just the steady ineptitude at business, like a dripping faucet wearing away the face of the bathroom bowl. While Arthur believed his own radio jingles and sold everything for a song, Virginia learned to harden herself to the dazzling Irish smile, the warm brown eyes and the soft feelings they stirred. Arthur was a business seed that never sprouted; and Virginia Curtain had not allowed herself to depend on him, nor anybody. Her father taught her that early.

She turned right, quickened her steps, figuring. About eleven-thirty, she and Carmella had pulled into Pleasant Vista; so it was twelve forty-five or one o'clock when she, Virginia, left to get away from the card-playing women. Throwing on her jacket, grabbing a five dollar bill and walking to the store took maybe ten minutes; buying the candy bar, another five. That would put her outdoors for her walk around, say, one-fifteen, one-thirty. It got dark early in the mountains, a fact she knew from sixth grade geography; so despite the decreasing light and all the glorious walking that made her release time as a totally unnecessary commodity, it still could be as early as three, three-fifteen.

But her body told her she had been walking longer than that. Her buttocks and hamstrings shuddered and flinched as if she'd trekked round-trip the length of the strip, Days Inn to the Daytona Sheraton, back in the Florida she'd called home the past six years. She felt chill air finger across her scalp, wished for a scarf or hat. But Hey, whoa! Come on, Virginia, she preached to herself; you remember cold. Having your nostrils stick together on the way to school when you try to breathe, that 's cold. This is nothing; this is God's country, and you have it all to yourself. Nevertheless, a delicate shiver dropped like a finely knit undergarment over her body.

"Leonard and Dora and the girls could move anytime," Carmella wailed that morning while the pines courted through the car window with quick seductive flashings of gold in the crevices of their trunks. "The hotel business is just like the army; you wake up one morning and everyone's left for Bangkok. I'm going to buy in at Pleasant Vista. All my friends are. We're going to dredge the lake, put in docks, a ski lift, a gambling casino. It's closer by an hour to the Bay area than Tahoe and Donner. We'll put up a huge sign that says "Little Tahoe: All the fun you could want!" You and I could go in together, have an all-weather and retire there. People on the ground floor will make a killing. It would be so nice, Ginny; just us sisters." Carmella cocked her head and laid on Virginia the puppy-dog eyes she used to beg. Virginia gritted her teeth.

Pleasant Vista's lake lay among the rocks like a callus. Virginia Curtain saw fir trees staggering out of sagging white sleeves, and the few buildings, signs and winter vegetation appeared lost in a giant bathrobe. The fixer-upper cabins and A-frames squatted and smoked, while jeeps and vans with empty ski carriers dozed in the driveways. "Oh for God sake, look around you. A miracle couldn't dig anything out of this god-forsaken hole. Nobody's going to make a cent here." She watched the words puncture the dream and collapse her sister's face like a party balloon.

Virginia Curtain stiffened her elbows and clapped her hands to keep the shiver off. Why, in Illinois she would run for hours in the pasture without mittens and then laugh when she couldn't bend her fingers to turn the back doorknob. All around her snow-covered trees rose up tall, and stretching away forever. She couldn't be lost; she'd kept strictly to right turns, except once to avoid a cabin, and once to follow a path that looked like a woman's arm lying along a bed sheet. She would recognize both those locations. Besides, she'd stayed in the tire tracks, which meant motorists, which meant a ride to a telephone. Of course, she would not take a ride from just anyone. She would look the person over carefully first.

She realized she didn't know Carmella's friend's last name or where her cabin was. Carmella's loud-mouthed buddies with their big secretaries' behinds and shrieks at anyone's pitiful joke would force a deaf mute outdoors at thirty-two below. These dearest friends of Carmella's turned out to be an entirely different set from those two years ago; and, as far as Virginia was concerned, came from the Goodwill where her sister also got her Fifties clothing. Carmella loved everyone, careened from man to man, from friend to friend, and from job to job like a dazed moth. Virginia, on the other hand, allowed herself few friends, and still corresponded with her sixth grade teacher, Mrs. Titch, now in her nineties and in a home in Milwaukee.

And what was the point of driving two hours to be trapped in a run-down rinky-dink A-frame with a fireplace like a blast furnace? Lunch had been salami sandwiches, green Jell-o and Oreo cookies; and beer, of course; beer and more beer; then watching the big behinds play bridge. But what it had taken to make Virginia Curtain bolt was the sight of the antlers nailed above the front window with the torn out scalp feathering between them. She grabbed the orange jacket and five dollars. "I'm going to talk to the trees." She threw the words at them as she slammed out the door, cutting off Carmella calling after her, "But Ginny, if--.

She would have a hike, have a little fun for herself for god's sake. How wet could she get in the snow just going to the store had been her reasoning. She shrewdly picked a back road, deserted at the moment but marked with tire treads under the thickening layer of powder. People were what she didn't want; she wanted those trees that seemed to call her and a message they might have. But, in the failing light and falling snow, her teeth against her wishes beginning to chatter, the trees took on an eerie look of wizards in drooping feathers, and snow spilled constantly over the tops of her shoes.

By now her ankles had caught fire, and doubts swarmed over her like gnats. No. Their dad always said she was as good as any boy out-of-doors. She had been the one to teach her sons to fish. Arthur got his thumb hung up on a lure, passed out at the sight of blood and had to be carted off to the hospital. And what about the time years ago she and Carmella visited cousins in Southern Illinois and got lost playing in the dense woods behind the farm? Carmella began to wail until Virginia yelled, "Stop it. I can't think when you do that." Carmella, thirteen then, stood sniffling while Virginia listened carefully, then tracked the faint sound of lowing back to the barn, her sister trailing behind, long ringlets bouncing, and soaking up her big tears with grandma's hand-knit scarf.

"Carmella's like her mother, a cry baby; but my Nate's a natural woodsman like me," her father bragged when the two girls came traipsing in an hour overdue. The father called Virginia "Nate" sometimes, after a childhood friend, later a pilot killed in World War II. "And if I had a son, you'd be it," he'd tell her sometimes, "because you're a realist, like me; and not like these from Never-never land." And he'd wave his farmer's paw at Carmella and their mother. "It's always the Brains rescues the Looks," he liked to say. "Nate here has brains." And Virginia had smirked meanly across the table at Carmella whose face got very pink and still, like a doll's. Carmella often got pink and still in her early teen years.

But Virginia had not liked it that their father called their mother a cry-baby. Their mother was not a cry-baby. Virginia watched her lots of times hang her head over the dishpan and, instead of crying, turn her body hard inch by inch, from the scuffed toes of her loafers to the tips of that long chestnut braid she wore. Then she'd pick up the paring knife or dishrag or potato brush and go to work again, sealed as if in that thick glass you use for baking. By the time Virginia was nine, their mother slept alone with the door closed in the sewing room off the kitchen; and when their father's farmer friends came to visit, he would laugh and tell over beer about saving their mother from a place called Easy Dan's, from a gulch in West Virginia. The mother would listen, her face puckered under the skin like someone had been sewing on it crazy; and Virginia would decide that nothing could be so terrible or shameful as to live in a gulch.

When their dad came in from the fields for dinner, he would lay his beat-up, oil-stained farmer's hat on the counter by the sink, right where mother was fixing food. Mother would work around the hat, slicing vegetables, opening and closing the oven door, handing off dishes to the girls for the table, her lips freshly glued. Dad would get himself a beer and turn on the radio in the front room until the news was over. By then dinner had better be on the table. Mother would hustle around the hat, picking bits of carrot or lettuce off the crown and bill as she went. After dinner, dad would pick his hat up, knock it against his leg and hang it on the peg by the back door.

Virginia trudged up to the next crossroad, her throat aching and body shaking; she hesitated. As dusk deepened, the sheer netting of snow, the clear call and response of birds, the sharp click-click of squirrel talk and every sound except for the light whistle of wind, picking through the boughs and the seams of her jacket, slowly diminished. Shouldn't she be seeing that cabin she passed before? Fear scorched her chest. What if she already passed it, daydreaming? What if these tracks were random and not roads after all? What if, instead of walking toward Pleasant Vista, she was headed into the heart of the Sierra? She recalled the members of the Donner Party in the 1860's falling into drifts up to their armpits. Don't be stupid, she told herself out loud, that's not going to happen to you; and set her chin square, like her father's, and turned right. But why, her mind started in on her, had she gone walking without a hat or gloves, without boots in the dead of winter with the temperature dropping, and in mountains she did not know? "Stop that," she ordered herself; "Push your legs."

She moved along the narrow corridor between the trees. If she lost this path, she had nothing. As she trudged on, the cold drove a nail through each of her great toes and forced her into walking on the sides of her feet. She listened for the thrum of a motor or thunk of an ax but heard only repetitive squeaking, as if someone were walking on popcorn.

She saw how the snow pack turned ghostly, felt an awful loneliness drift up to her heart. She could see her shoelaces below the cloud of her breath as her feet stepped into view, but the tire marks were so indistinct she took to reading the Braille of the sound and feeling of the their ridges underfoot.

She wondered vaguely if Arthur could see her, lost in the Sierra in the dark. He wouldn't anymore know how to help her now than he did all those years they were married. When she first began teaching in Chicago, she met a good-looking Irishman at a YMCA dance who, behind the independent stance, the flashing eyes and warm smile, was worn down, like her mother, by footprints Virginia didn't recognize for what they were until after she'd married him. And why was she wondering about what her deceased husband thought of her predicament anyway when she no longer believed in an afterlife?

With a leap of joy she remembered the Mars bar in the pocket of her slacks. She rummaged through floating dollar bills and loose change and tore at the wrapper. She hadn't realized how hungry she was until the chocolate released its bouquet under her nose. She wanted the sugar for her brain. She needed her brain. The bar was rigid and the chocolate shell broke under her teeth. She sucked the leather of caramel as she walked along, explaining once more to her sons how she got herself into this Mulligan stew, hearing how lame all her reasoning sounded. They would all get a good laugh out of it, later, lounging at the dinner table, probably next Christmas. Her ordeal would turn out to be worth it, if only for the story.

She ate half the bar, then put the rest away. She felt snow packing down inside her shoes. She looked up to face a tree. She had let herself stray, not noticed the more plunging steps she took, nor the sound of popcorn changing to the sound of a thin crust giving way. Her heart began to strike. She peered about in the near dark.

"Why can't you keep your mind on what you're doing, old woman?" she flapped her arms and raved. Her words bounced among the molecules of cold air. "Do you want to be out here until midnight?" Tears stung her lids and her logical mind elbowed forward. "What, are you a crybaby like your sister?" it sneered. "Find the holes. Feel for the holes you made." She ran her fingers over the snow until they stumbled into a shape like a shoe and in this way traced her way back to the tire tracks, seven paces away. "Listen," she continued through clenched chattering teeth, as if this were a bad day with her sixth graders at Volper Elementary in Chicago, "Dead heads get dead. Wake up. Use your brain. "

A froth of snow woke her to the unbearable pain of her ears, as if someone had trimmed away their rims with nail scissors and then left them unbandaged. She pulled at the rolled collar and hunched her shoulders, but the collar barely covered her neck. Damn Carmella anyway, for bringing her to this god-forsaken sinkhole, she tromped ahead. Another of her hair-brained ideas, like the health spa in Lovelock four years ago with no bottoms to the dresser drawers; or the mule-trip in Montana when she and her boys ended up in sleeping bags on the floor of a log cabin for five nights to the tune of one hundred dollars a night. Their father was right out, was a lard-o then too. "Gooey Gooey Chew Chew, whatcha gonna do do, eat until your eyes bulge, eat 'til you're a real tub." They'd stand around Carmella on the playground, eighth graders with greasy hair and pimples, taunting her about her jiggling lumps, lumps the younger Virginia found disgusting. When Carmella's tears would start, Virginia would rush away. Why did they have to have the same last name of MacRae, so everybody would know? And what could she do for the lard-o anyway?

Chew chew chew chew, her mind dittied as she tromped on. She began aloud on Campfire songs, then on to Christmas carols. But the first carol raised up images of their mother pressing raisins down the fronts of the gingerbread men, or staggering under a Christmas turkey to a table filled with relatives; and then of dad carving and handing the plates around as if he were God creating the world. Strangely, it was the memory of the delicate way her father held the carving knife and fork--a big man like that who slaughtered hogs--that made the song snarl in her throat.

She remembered one Christmas their mother gave him a railroader's watch. He had taken it out of its case to show his daughters the silent heart beating at the back, and then fitted the works back in again, so carefully the movement went on as if nothing had happened; but Virginia felt cold run up her arms, seeing him exercise power so deftly and totally over the delicate beating heart.

She was into the middle of the next crossroad before she realized it. Fatigue made the ground beneath her tilt and rock.

"Daydreaming again, ninny?" she staggered about; "Crying over dead people when you may be dead soon yourself?" The sound of her own voice saying the terrifying word set loose in her chest a pack of yelping dogs.

She noticed now how wooden her legs had become in her pantyhose and orlon slacks: the skin still burned, but now with each step her knees crinkled like grocery bags. Her bones seemed to have turned liquid. She would sit, would eat the rest of her candy bar and get her strength back. "Are you crazy? You'll freeze like Deborah Kerr. Use your brain for once," she scarified herself. Her body sat anyway, smack dab in the middle of the crossroad.

The chocolate and caramel melted together in her mouth and dribbled down her chin. Physical ecstasy brought a feeling of levitation, as though she might at any moment bounce above the treetops to look down on the blue-white expanse with its collection of grey-green spires; but at the same time, long flickering tongues of freezing air forced her to tuck her exposed feet and ankles as far under her legs as possible. What would Carmella think of the award-winning teacher now, on her behind in the dark, in the middle of the road, and sucking on a candy bar?

Her sister! Hope flared. Carmella, the worry wart, the wailer, the one who wasn't so bright would call the sheriff to search for her, the smart one, the woodsman and realist, dad's Nate; and they would surely come upon her any time now because she, Virginia, couldn't possibly have walked that far or for that long--why, she was sixty-four years old! But her heart and body knew she had been on her feet for hours.

Her hands in her jacket pockets now were discarded clumps of newspaper, and the down rag Carmella borrowed felt inconsequential as a shirt; but the violent shaking and teeth chattering had ceased. And the snow had stopped--that was something. The rising wind had shredded the clouds to bed sheets that could no longer hide their wealth of diamonds; however, the Big Dipper, the North Star, Orion's Belt were not visible for her to read.

Suddenly she filled up with a terrible longing to see Carmella, to crawl into her big bosom and breathe the Orange Blossom she wore too much of, to hear her wail her worry and relief, to be put to bed by her, to wake and be cooked for and fussed over. Why was it that she, Virginia, for almost as long as she could remember, had carried a hatred that her sister had done nothing to deserve? But even as she asked the question, Virginia felt the familiar wall of cold dislike rise in her chest. Her stomach lurched and roiled after food. With the tip of her tongue, Virginia searched the corners of her mouth.

But wasn't it a sad waste to push her only sister from her like that? The idea rose up a revelation. And what had she, Virginia, ever gotten other than sour satisfaction, from, for instance, the jokes she made about the gifts Carmella sent for birthdays and Christmas; from her scorn about the way Carmella dressed, decorated her series of run-down apartments, and the working people she drew around her? She felt her face burning. At least Carmella was generous. Who was it who hadn't a kind word to her name, was stubbornly living these six years in a place she hated, all her life trying to run the universe the way she saw her father and the other men take it on: without help and suiting it to themselves by banging doors shut over whatever they didn't like?

Her father didn't bang the door, but closed it carefully, as if he were fitting the watch works back into the case. She saw him turn and come down from hers and Carmella's bedroom at early afternoon, a rough-edged rectangle of black, as she, Virginia, climbed the stairs, home from school.

"Is Carmella all right, Dad? Is she still sick?"

The big farmer boots, the deep vertical creases in his face met her with their darkness; and the square finger ends settled under her collarbone and forced her to about-face.

"Let her sleep. Come to the barn, there's a new calf."

But there were birdhouses to paint or chicks hatching or a colt on a lead. Wasn' t that right?

It was the burning from the wind, as if someone held a Zippo lighter to her chin, that jerked her awake as she sat with her head pitched downward and thrust to the side, a blade of pain where her neck met her shoulder. As carefully as fitting the watch works back into the case. She couldn't feel her feet. She rolled onto her knees, crying. What did she think she was doing, sleeping? "God damn you, Virginia," she wailed. "Get up. Move your body. Do you want to die here? God damn you."

She crawled ahead ten paces, dragging her legs like a seal; then gave it up and rolled back onto her buttocks and saw she had cut her hand. "Let it bleed," she ordered herself, feeling down her legs for her feet. "Wake up, do you hear me? Wake up, wake up!" She banged one foot, then the other against the road, shouting at them until they slowly alchemized from stone to wood to leather. She shifted onto her knees and somehow staggered upright. It was like walking in cereal bowls. She turned jovial. Every step would put her that much closer to Pleasant Vista. She sucked at her cut hand and tasted iron; then, lunging about as if she were drunk, took a great breath and threw her head back to search once more for the North Star.

The unexpected splendor of the sky stole the breath from her body. How many people ever saw the heavens spilled out on a drape of indigo that pressed itself against the tips of the trees like this, each diamond chip the size of a giant thumb nail and suspended over the cloth of the snow in the profoundest of silences? Then the something the trees whispered about as she passed them in the car, the elusive something encased in and carried by their whispering, stole upon her, sifted down from the stars. Wait, didn't it seem the sky behind the stars, as well as the snow beneath them also strained to communicate to her that secret intimated earlier?

She stopped her breath and listened intently; but no feelings came nor words appeared in her mind as she turned and turned. Just when she thought to give up, all at once it arrived, streaking down, brilliant, urgent, flashing from everywhere simultaneously, as well as from within her own body. In a torrent it thrust aside all that had ever been of her, of her life, spilled from her eyes, forced open her mouth of a child, rushed through her but was of her, as if she were both fountain and fountainhead; yet the headwaters were outside her as well, in this snow, these trees and brilliant night sky, in the non-dissembling cold so clear it held everything transfixed as if in a mirror.

ONE.

The single word thundered from within and all around her, and she understood it to be the only language that was or had ever been. The sky reverberated: ONE. The stars, the trees, the snow, the ground gave it forth in grand harmonic. From the center of the earth the word rebounded, familiar as her bones, as the very core of her bones. She flung her arms to surrender herself to the heavens, rocking on her frozen feet, her mouth agape to let the swollen ecstasy escape. When at last the torrent diminished, she wiped away tears with the palm of her hand and dried it stinging on the inside of her pocket. With her body buzzing like a room just emptied, she stood blinking.

She wasn't sure which way she had been heading when she stopped to read the stars. On either side were meadows that could have been photo negatives of one another. Fear crowded her throat. Which way to Pleasant Vista? With all her turning, she had lost her direction. She flapped her arms in disbelief, in despair, and let out a long heart-broken sound that wobbled away toward the treetops. How could she have done this to herself? She bent over, her head nearly at her knees, sobbing convulsively. She didn't know which way to turn. What should she do now? The tears made her face freeze. She staggered forward and saw him close the door so carefully, like fitting the watch works back into the case.

Her glance snagged on a spikey patch five or six steps to her right. Was it better to crawl beneath a bush and risk not being seen, or to sit in the open and let the wind turn her to stone? Before she could think, her body moved sideways under the covering of the bush and hunkered down. Huddling there, she felt she had the luck of a woodland animal, and she might make it to morning after all. But when she counted the hours since she had left the A frame, it could be no later now than nine o'clock; and the temperature would continue to drop. She choked down the merciless fact.

She began bellowing her times tables toward the jagged mountains hidden in the darkness. At the same time she waved her arms back and forth or slapped her legs together or clenched and unclenched her toes, though it made her fall over. She went through the states, their capitols, the presidents, vice presidents, the continents and oceans. She tried the periodic table, recited Hiawatha, Hamlet's soliloquy, what she could remember of the Love Song of J. Alfred Prufrock. She sang the national anthem, Columbia the Gem of the Ocean, This Land is Your Land, Take Me Out To The Ball Game, Pour Me Another Tequila Sheila; Abilene, Abilene, prettiest town I've ever seen. The cold squeezed and squeezed. Her body gradually stopped shaking and her mind began to sneak away.

She saw Arthur, six months before he died, still talking and following the wedding guests out the door as if they were the last deserters of a town of which he was mayor; saw Leonard and Dora's friends and the dealership people wolfing down *coq au vin*, singing drunkenly after the waiters cleared the tableware; saw the women carry off three hundred dollars' worth of roses; knew they had teaspoons in their purses; watched the room empty, all that money run out the gold-painted double doors, down the red carpet, the hubbub receding like a tide, leaving the two of them beached with the bills. Dora had had no family to put on a wedding. Well, it was for Leonard, for her boy.

Her boys. She dandled them again upon her knees and felt her cells slowly pulled together as if by a great draw string; watched her sons' narrow shoulders rotate horizontally, heard the crack of the bat; the revving of their jalopy engines, smelled the gasoline, remembered the ring of their girl friends' voices; mused how her boys would miss her if she died, then admitted for the first time that really they had gravitated towards their father who gave them whatever they wanted and never thought of the consequences; admitted, also for the first time, that she had squandered her attention on other people's children and never even learned to map her own sons' insides; then realized suddenly and with astonishment that it was Carmella, really, who would be torn to shreds if she, Virginia, died. Carmella doted most especially on her little sister Ginny.

Something caved in and the tears came, tears hot enough to melt a glacier. About her, the tall dark trees sighed and swayed and brooded over the ghostly snow. She saw the square farmer's hand with its outcropping of black hairs scurrying over the wrist, climbing the love bulge between the thumb and forefinger and dropping into the cleft as he drew the door closed as carefully as putting the watch works back into the case. Carmella would have been thirteen or fourteen. Virginia's breath fled into her lungs. Now she remembered after school on the stairs the feeling as she and her father descended that if she so much as tapped the wall with her elbow, the plaster would shatter. She remembered how the farmer finger-ends beneath her collarbone, as he diverted her from the bedroom door, raised up licks of fire.

How many times had he intercepted her on the way to the bedroom after school while their mother volunteered at the library, or worked the cash register at the drug store? Her mother's sidewise looks, glued lips, the silences that gathered in her like rust as she ate alone in a cold she drew about her made new sense to Virginia in this darkness, in these mountains, curled in this womb of earth and of death, the stars above witness to her thoughts, the cold as pure and transparent as the angels in whom she did not believe.

Now she remembered their father in the front room, or on the side-porch in the summer; how he would stand behind Carmella where she sat, and let the silk of her ringlets slip around his fingers. He always wanted Carmella to keep her hair long. She, Virginia, had short straw-colored hair like her father's you could do nothing with; and it always put her into a silent rage to see him make a pet of her sister's hair. "Your mother's used to be like this," he would murmur.

Whatever it was the father brought to Carmella, she, Virginia, had wanted it too, was enraged that her sister drew it from him, as she seemed to draw everything, with her soft body and soft mind.

Huddled beneath the bush, she groped down a narrow hallway and into a deep closet, rummaged and sorted and picked through the jumbled paraphernalia of childhood until she came upon it, like one of those boxed sets of clay for children, far back in a corner, the seal on it unbroken. She had had the material in her possession but not made anything out of it. She had been ten or eleven. She had known and not known. It was like when you sense there's a gas leak before you're told about gas leaks, by the way that rabbit in your chest thumps, thumps, then freezes in place.

She saw now she should have hated him who made her higher than Carmella, higher than their mother; and after whom she modeled herself; would hate him now if she could feel her way through the shock of this awakening, could fathom and hold with her mind any part of what he had done and cost Carmella, cost their family. She should have hated him, and instead she hated her sister.

"Oh Carm," she whispered.

She reached from a long way off, and with an enormous effort flung the leaden baggage of her body onto its side, found her abstract arm with its wooden paddle of a hand and scooped up the bitter snow to scour her face, the back of her neck, to force it between her breasts where it ran to collect in her belly button then spill in freezing chains over her genitals with a series of electric shocks she felt in her eyeballs. A second handful she scrubbed deep into her scalp, behind her ears. On her eyes she held a third handful squeezed to ice hot enough to burn from her body and soul, from Carmella's body and soul the sprawling ragged scars of all the years of her, Virginia's, betrayals.

As the sense of her body steadily faded, she saw the appropriateness of the position she was in, the artfulness of it: freezing to death in the isolation she had sought all of her life. She thought of the stars, of the trees, of the whole multi-dimensional and masterful landscape; saw her place in it was no different nor important than that of a wren or nuthatch whose small body might this night turn to a lump of ice and tumble from a pine tree into the silence. She reached for that word that had flooded her before and raised her up in ecstasy, but met only her own frail insides, thin as dried egg white. A great truth had passed through her, left its trail within her; but she knew now (and yes, had known then) that its business was not to save anything from anything.

She said goodbye to her boys, asked their forgiveness for the foolishness of her death. Her mind flashed to her Florida apartment and she for a moment became obsessed with the thought of her son Leonard finding her old bra on the bathroom doorknob, the underpants for the wash folded next to the toilet, the magazine rack of unpaid bills, and, at the bottom of the bookcase, the old journals, in one of which was recorded her only infidelity to Arthur: a two night stand with a social studies teacher she met at a professional development series at the Chicago Board of Education.

Lost, facing the freezing night and death, she let go of all her foolish images as a perfect wife, perfect mother, perfect teacher—shook them out of her like scraps of paper. Carmella would come to Florida to help Leonard and Dora dispose of her things. She realized in her will she had left to her sister only the niggardly gesture of the grandmother's silver pitcher. Oh how she would redeem things now if she could! She had four dollars and twelve cents in her pocket. She hoped Carmella would find it.

All the children she ever taught came crowding around. She felt their love, of which before she was only vaguely aware, spread itself over her as a blanket of beautifully formed heads and arms. Good-bye Mrs. Curtain, she heard their voices, innocent of the meaning of endings. Michael came, smiling with his brown eyes; and Leonard and Dora and the children came. Carmella wept and blew a kiss. Virginia wanted to say thank you, to say goodbye; but somehow the whole crowd of them moved back and away, as if out of respect for some important event.

The chitter of night birds became lost in the harmonic moan of trees, which in turn unraveled to a single thread of sound so fine it dissolved into the night all around. Suddenly so sleepy, all she wanted was to lie down. She unlatched something inside and let herself sink into a sea of vague sensations like far-off heat lightening, let the plug pull loose and let the wayward island of her mind drift into a halt and dissolve in the darkness.

The darkness itself dissolved; was replaced by a sudden whiteness everywhere, vaster than the sea, than the sky--vast as the universe, deep and wide and high as the universe. Vaster than heaven. And she is part of the whiteness, belongs to it; is it, alive, alert and totally serene, totally peaceful, floating, floating, floating in whiteness for time without end.

Then without warning, a blade of fire runs her through; and as it does, it splinters into myriad swords. These shoot off, away until they are pinpoints, but then boomerang, and arching high, fly at her like a darkened canopy, piercing and slicing through her body and mind, turning and slicing three, four, five times until she is a collection of only the smallest of bits excruciatingly hanging together, helpless and exposed. "Oh please," she hears a voice cry out as a blade cuts into her a design complex and artful and exquisite with pain. "Oh, please, no."

"Yes m'am; don't you worry none." A barrage of rocks. "It come up fifteen degrees before midnight; held too. You must know the governor. And that orange jacket of yours; now what is that there under that bush, I thought."

She dragged her mind after the disappearing words. Then the cords of her eyelids shortened a fraction, and through the thicket of her lashes she saw a grey disk blow itself into a button, saw the letters J-E-E-P next to it, turned the rusted hulk of her head two degrees to the left, creaked her eyes around to find a boy the same age as her Michael, wearing a dark green ski cap with an orange stripe, gripping a steering wheel.

They had found her.

"Your sister's about gone crazy with worry," the boy went on over the engine. It was not the rocks, but the saw-toothed edge of his voice that snagged her mind and stayed it in its act of scuttling away.

"We'll be on 80 right quick now. I'm keeping the heater off so's you don't warm too fast; figure it's been fourteen hours. Good thing I had them snowshoes. Happy to feel your pulse, I'll tell you that. I'm taking you to Truckee; they got a special unit. Your sister'll be waitin'." The jeep jolted over the road like a boat smacked by waves.

Sister. Waiting. The words bobbed in her brain, and a ripple of warmth spread from them, spread to her solar plexus to become the harbor of her sister, her sister she loved and whose name she could not remember. And she, herself, whose name she could not remember either, she was the storm-tossed skiff.

She faded into a grey goop that sucked on her battered mind, drew it mercifully away through what seemed to be an opening at the back of her skull. She let it go, let everything go, heard only the trees as they reached out to her passing on the road, to feather their wings softly across her, mile after seamless mile.

Jophile's Story, In Short

Fall, winter and early spring, the sick come crowding to this small room, while the Brothers give me healings here at St. Bartholomew Abbey in Exeter, England. Beggars and cotters ("villein" to our Norman lords) squeeze onto its narrow benches, crowd the floor, fill the small doorway and spill into the courtyard. Last Fall, as a mercy against England's cold, the monks cut an opening into the wall of our healing room to give us heat from the kitchen's hearth.

Less than fifty years after the death of Jesus, the Romans, they tell, snatched this village then called Isca from the Saxons. Time passing, it took on whatever name suited its next invader until, in 352 Anno Domini, it became Exeter. And so remains to this day, with its river, cliffs, woodlands, and us, the poor and plain, persisting here like burrs.

I am Jophiel Balerais, an unconsecrated brother here at the Abbey; and upon this sixteenth day of November, Year of Our Lord 1182, sixty-four years upon God's green earth.

As you know, a time comes when you are overtaken by a fierce longing to tell your sons, daughters, nephews, nieces and grandchildren of who you have been. This for what good it may do them, and as preparation for the claim you will make upon what Eternity you sense may be.

Oh, I have kin would listen and gladly; but to give over to them all I have lived might indeed be a grave strike against charity. And so it must be in you, strangers kindly and curious, that I invest my tale as all I have to leave behind; and pray you may find therein something for your own well-being, and in payment, though modest, for your kindness to me.

And so I begin.

I am three years old, barefoot, and peering out the door of our hut open a crack into the dark murky air that raises goosebumps on my flesh. Men, long-armed and stoop-shouldered, lurch toward me, their heavy footfalls muffled in the dirt eternally encrusting our paths and hovels. Terrified, I suck in my breath as if to preserve myself.

In the early days, my Mamoon apprenticed me in remedies and healing.

Together, and always led by butterflies, we'd descend the hillock behind Rougemont Castle to the long brook announced by the calls of Blue Tit, fluting Thrush and the chirping voices of the creek waters.

My Mamoon always wore a vert about her neck, a wooden license with the owners' insignia of permission to enter the forest of our betters where she regularly gathered herbs for noble households, and so was free to mount the stile for our needs as well, and without worry of the Warden.

I remember her hands like butterflies touching the green growing things. I tell you I believed then and do to this day that the plants and rocks spoke with her, and she with them. And I remember she would school me then about the "Old Ways" of Nature spirits, of elves and fairies that unbelievers could no longer see.

And settling upon a log, she would pat a place for me beside her.

"When folk stopped taking their food from the wild and made farms, Jophiel, they cut the very threads that weave us into life. And 'twas then that we humans gave up our footprint as just bein' there equal with all the others, a wrongful thing and a sorrow canna be helped now." Her voice would come ancient as an oracle's; and listening, I would tremble inside fearing that I could neither grasp nor hold the great words she spoke. Mamoon would peer to see I was listening, then go on, her eyes solemn, her voice all shadows. And she would give a deep nod, and with a little grunting sound climbing to her feet, point out wild parsley or violets to pull.

Our cotter's hut, like many others outside Rougemont Castle, was mostly poverty and violence. My father tormented my mother; my sister and brother tormented me; and with no person but Mamoon to protect me. So small myself those days, Mamoon was to me big hips, big breasts, big bottom, big lap--oh, and everything to be trusted and to stand upon.

But even she had ways I could not grasp.

By the time I was fourteen, everything at home had changed: Father dead in a sword fight outside a tavern, my mother Ihelde perished from some street disease, my sister married, brother a teamster in Crediton; and myself living then with my Uncle Anthony who had brought me to a place far different from what I had known.

Mathilde, his wife, with brown tresses and a particular softness about her face, had laughing blue eyes and a steady manner very comforting to me. With four children, the house was already full, so a sleeping space was made for me upon a doorless cupboard where Aunt stored foodstuffs and herbs she wanted kept dry next the hearth. My pallet being short, I must sleep knees drawn up while the crackling wood below brought upon its rising warmth wonderful odors from the spices and foodstuffs stored below.

My Uncle Anthony was held to be extremely bright and was under the political protection of Lord Cornwall, and later of Lord Galton. And when a blacksmith in a neighboring village died, Uncle would buy up his shop and take on more apprentices. So after a time, he became a kind of overseer, managing smithies and customers in two or three villages besides Exeter where his own shop near South Gate was by far the biggest and busiest of all.

When I was eight and in my second year in the Common School in the old stable on Catherine Street, and learning to figure numbers, to write, sing psalms, and speak simple French, it was Uncle who opened to me the world of his blacksmith shop; where he paid me for fetching and sweeping so that I had money to take home. I believe he felt badly about how my father and his older brother treated my mother and us three children. And so Uncle Anthony became the person in the world, after Gran'mam passed, whom I could trust.

Extravagant-looking, and with a ruddy face, Uncle Anthony commanded attention wherever he went. His hair, a blondish red, very bristly and wild, was all over his body. And he looked for all God's kingdom, except for size, like one of those wood elves my Mamoon and the old women told stories about.

When I was small, the comfort of his presence made me bold with him. Gruff of speech and manner, yet he labored to catch himself in the midst of any curtness and turn it to something humorous or harmless. And

I had no experience of someone managing himself so artfully, for when my father was gruff, well you just had better get away, that was all! And while both came from the same rough home, my Uncle Anthony found ways to rise above it.

When not at my lessons or helping Mamoon, I would come down High Street to turn toward South Gate and the blacksmith shop. I liked the noise, the clatter, the testing, the raw display of human strength. I loved the fire turning the workspace into leaping light and shadow, and washing everything with red and gold. And how all the workmen there appeared to live in Hell, their bodies steaming from the flames and heavy lifting, and the anvil ringing like some great eerie Keeper of Time. I loved all that, and took on a taste for the smell of red-hot metal cooling in the water barrel.

In those days I was the logical person to spare for errands. Uncle would send me a mile and a half down London Road for mead I'd carry back across my shoulders. Two foaming buckets swinging, slopping and dribbling into the dirt, never mind how carefully I walked, the men at the smithy would keep a sharp eye out. And as I staggered onto Magdalene Road, their great cheer would go up and fill me like a good meal!

So young then, I got the jobs others didn't want. But as I grew, I would learn the forge, the bellows, the tongs and hammer, the anvil, the water barrel. And one day I was, trimming the curled hooves of cattle, sheep, goats--and horses, of course.

Now shoeing can be dangerous if a horse doesn't trust you or isn't treated well. More than one blacksmith has been killed by the sudden shifting of a flank or strike of a hoof. But Uncle Anthony used to say he could accomplish twice as much when I worked with him because he didn't have to fight the animals. I would speak to them in soft sweet words, and they would calm down--and get a better-fitting shoe as well. And they knew it. I could trade thoughts with any animal, for I loved their company; and often could share my thoughts with no one else.

One lucky fact raised me to heights no villein should ever reach: I was bright. And because Lord Cornwall thought so highly of my uncle, I became a student at St. Bartholomew Abbey along with the likes of Lord Cornwall's own son. Fifteen of us studied at lessons in the rectory of St. Anselm's chapel there. A second group of boys, slightly older, kept to a different room, although we came together for Latin and religious exercises.

Our learning room had a floor, not the rammed dirt of our cottages and other buildings, but of carefully cut stone tiles. The shine of those stones fit together so logically, the shush or ring of a foot upon them, told me this was a floor for the quiet, the orderly, the well-mannered. And to have access to such a place of discernment of the mind, gave me stature within myself. And this way I felt carried by fate, sensing some destiny that held in a protected way the very path of my life.

The classes at St. Bartholomew were long and tedious and was entirely opposite the highly physical life I knew. At first I would nod off any number of times, only to feel a little rap on the back of my neck from the master. And by the end of the day, I was thrilled to go home to feed the animals, chop wood, or muck horses at Uncle's shop.

School wasn't all learning Latin; sometimes it was French; and sometimes we spoke in a refined English, unknown in my daily life. Born a good son of Dev'n, I naturally dropped my front "h", replaced "v" with "f", "z" with "s" with raw expressions learned from Uncle's blacksmiths that sent the students into riots of merriment at my expense. I heard one whisper behind his hand, "Why is the beggar here? To become a lord, I suppose?"

But our schoolmaster Father Stephan, a slender young priest with dark tonsured hair, very straight, and a finely sculptured nose, was kind about my difficulties, his blue eyes holding good-humored understanding, even as he reprimanded me. And under the cloak of his kindness, I could keep some humor about myself. At home, I practiced my fs and vs on Uncle Anthony, and still remember in his face the mixed feelings that his nephew spoke to him in the tongue of his betters. "You do us proud, lad," he'd clap me on the back.

To soothe myself at my study bench, I often resorted to the sounds of the horses in the stable out back. Like the sight of the great tree outside the school for villeins on Martin Street, hearing animals large and small call to one another made me at home in myself and the world. Truly, there were many times when the whinny of horses saved me for a day.

One day, we'd finished eating and were about to take our bowls out to be washed when the cleric in charge of meals held up his hand.

"Never mind, lads; Jophiel will take care of these for us."

He kept his face, one that folded sallow upon itself, turned from me as he spoke; still I saw the dark satisfaction, and felt the pleasure that rippled through my classmates at this demeaning; for custom was that each boy washed his own bowl. I had worked hard to become more correct; but to those youths, my efforts were dust. They tolerated me because they had no choice; and let me know my new chore felt satisfying to them. Still, some carried their bowls and spoons out anyway; but most left their mess behind for me.

But such incidents strengthened me. And forcing myself to see the lesser and greater side by side was a practice that saved me.

And the cooks saved me.

And Brother Frederick saved me.

Outside in back was a well and a great cauldron that hung over a small fire, it was in scrubbing bowls that I took note of Brother Frederick hauling wood, his large face dripping. This was a bear of a man with sunken eyes of piercing blue tucked under a bulging forehead and peering over a large nose; a man with a hunch from stooping in that way of very tall people, yet still wearing the kindliest expression, nevertheless. And there seemed no unwelcome task others didn't feel free to assign to Brother Frederick who, like ancient Greeks I would learn of, held everything up with his back.

Brother Frederick always saw me as of equal value in the kitchen, and bright and belonging in the school. Because of his way of holding silence, my classmates thought him stupid; but I came to know a most dignified intelligence and kindly heart. When he became my teacher of long-standing, it dawned upon me that for both of us our outsides looked different from our insides; and that we both suffered from loneliness. Over the years I liked to think I gave some solace to my teacher, as he did to me.

Uncle's house was two-storied, the lower part one large room with an enclosed stable at the front, as most folks had. Above was the sleeping loft on the second story, though you could not stand up fully there. Packed tight we were. Indeed, I made sure after school I sat with the children of Aunt's house for a crust before my chores, as soon I would be a workingman, home at night not much before my uncle. I still had the power then to see through children's eyes and did not forget how, when you are very small, the dark can be fearfully peopled; or what an hilarity it is to announce the things animals may think or say to one another; and older yet, how satisfying to watch grown folks make mistakes. By taking time with the young ones, I could give Aunt a rest, though she never asked.

When I had finished my schooling, Uncle began teaching me all that must be known about the blacksmith business. Life now gave me even less time for myself. Still, busy as I was, I never lost my need for the comfort of shadows or an unlit space others might avoid where I could till my thoughts. Often I sought out a certain pond ringed by slender trees that leaned inward like maidens whispering. There I would play my whistle, draw or read; and at times wish for the company of another youth of like mind and humors.

When Uncle was not around the shop, men at the smithy liked to dig into me about caring more for solitude than carousing.

I had finished my studies at St. Bartholomew the Spring before. But Brother Frederick urged me to come by when I had time. Often I found him on a stool cleaning roots for the perpetual soup. Both sunlight through the open door and firelight from the hearth cast shadows of the cauldrons, spice barrels and cooking tools; and there would raise up among them his freckled and balding pate like its own moon. On a bright day, you'd discover the marvel of his red hair curling like fire. A certain Sunday in June, my head filled with ideas from ancient religions, I found Brother Frederick separating carrots from their tops in the kitchen garden.

"Tell me Scholar which would you prefer; a God of the Ancients or the God you have?"

I shook my head, laughed. "My understanding of the God we have is not great, Brother; but I would hazard those of others could not be more different." I dusted my hands, plucked up a strawberry.

His sloping forehead wrinkled. "Some argue all Gods are alike."

The clang of the Call to Supper parted the air--down-stroke, up-stroke, down-stroke, harsh at first, then feathering over the orchards of St. Bartholomew, the crooked streets of Exeter and the hills of Devon.

Later in my life, I would come to see that through our conversations, Brother Frederick showed me there is no wall into which a question cannot cut a doorway, then free you to cut more. And I call him "my great teacher" for he opened to me my own mind and set me to using it by taking me down the roads he himself had trod; and so readied me for much that life would demand.

Thus, from about eight to sixteen years, I would go back and forth from Uncle's blacksmith shop to the school. And it was within those walls I found the great teacher who gave me a sanctuary in which to grow my mind.

Probably you are already familiar with how our cathedral's massive towers were built by workmen erecting a hill of dirt to carry to the masons the stones split below. As I passed the cathedral one day delivering some fancy-worked door hinges, I saw something in common with that way of building and my own life: How Mamoon, Uncle Anthony, Father Stephan, Brother Frederick each raised me a step higher than I envisioned for myself. And there is one other person to whom I must also give credit for my enrichment. I had since I was a youth of fifteen years been in love at a distance with a golden-haired maid I would see from afar at Lammas. Her name was Sarah Dorset; and she intruded upon my dreams.

August first brings the celebration of First Harvest we call Lammas, a day sacred from pagan times; and one the Church now claims for herself. From among vendors' wagons and stalls, over bursts and trailings of music, you'll hear the racket from feats and contests of lances and shields, wrestling, running races, horse races, jumping tests, stone throwing, javelin hurling, archery as well as cheers and swearing from those who bet on them. Spaces are set aside for rest and pleasant distractions: juggling, tightrope and stilt walking, fire eating, puppet wagons, the singing and the playing of instruments and dancing on the Green by the maids.

And it was at Lammas I first saw Sarah Dorset.

As she walked, I remember, I watched her skirt tumble like wild grasses in the wind. I can see it to this day. I found something quiet and joyful in her step, and her face soft, but open, too, as a good day. A rope of fairy gold bound with rose-colored ribbons of nearly the same hue as her cheek hung down her back. her eyes blue as a summer sky. A fair, fair maid.

Those eyes first discovered me with Uncle and his friends booming by in the other direction. As she came along, I felt stopped in my tracks. It was as if she were a meadow I'd stumbled into and couldn't leave. When we passed, she raised her eyes to mine already fixed upon her; and in the space of a breath we silently bespoke ourselves of something not yet understood; then both looked away, confused.

I staggered up to the leathers stall and turned for a last glimpse of her, and saw her father stop to talk with my uncle. And how my heart leapt, then fell; for I was too far along to go back with no reason! All I could do was to pass the leather pieces through my hands, breathe the tanning fumes and miss my chance to meet her.

Before I knew it, Lammas had come 'round again.

When we got to the hay, where we harvest feed, I knew to look for the wagon where the puppets pounded one another silly and I hung at the edge of the crowd until Sarah came running, her brother behind him. They hailed me and dropped breathless to the ground among the audience to fix their eyes upon the wagon's stage.

I strolled the direction they came from and there, amidst this uproar of puppets and children, I sank into the very heart of peace; for always, near Sarah, peace stole upon me. And we saw the play three times through.

Then the bell rang for the Dividing of the Loaf, and we joined the circle where Sarah's parents, Aunt Mathilde, Uncle Anthony and my young cousins held a place for us. Each family brought a new loaf of bread with an unlit candle stuck in it to pass to another family there. And looking upon all those smiling faces, the candles burning, I could not help but think of the heavenly bodies above that abided one another in harmony; and now here were all of us below in harmony, too; and all of nature as well. And I prayed the stars to watch over us and to keep us always thus.

You can imagine I was aching to be alone with Sarah; and when the mothers and small children stretched out in the shade to nap while the older ones scampered off to explore the booths of ware, Master Dorset nudged Sarah and me.

"Go on, you two. The day will be over before you know it."

I caught up her hand and led her behind a stall piled high with willow baskets. Once, I had seen a woodcut of a love-stricken knight fallen onto his knee to his lady. Just so, and overflowing with urgency and terror (and without even knowing I had done it), I fell to my knee.

"My lady," I called her, "there is none in this world I prize greater than you; and none to whom I would more gladly vow my service and the strength of my body, so long as my breath shall last." These were not my words, believe me, for I had none; but Love poured through to speak for me.

The wind teased the wisps of her hair; and she looked long and deep into me. "I thank you for that, Jophiel," she said. And it seemed for a moment she would say more, for she hesitated; but then bent to raise me with that hand of hers I still grasped. "Come," she said, "we'd best get back. Our families will wonder where we are."

Back again with our families, then, too soon we packed our things and paused to say our fare-thee-wells. Then, horses and wagons swaying, and dust rising to meet the wheel hubs, I raised my eyes for a last look at Sarah; and found she had turned to look back at me. We gave a wave of departing while more wagons with children crying, dogs barking, wheels and harnesses squeaking and drivers shouting "Heigh. Heigh now!" crowded between us.

Oh fare-thee-well then, love. Fare-thee-well.

A week later, Master Dorset appeared at the smithy. A brutally hot day, the last of summer burning itself into the earth, I was at the water barrel dousing my hair when he pulled up in his wagon. I took the harness.

"Good to see you, lad. I have a favor to ask, if you can be free for an hour or so. I must collect some grains at the mill. I could use a hand."

"Let me check. We seem to be in a lag right now."

I was back before he could turn his head. He wheeled his horse about and we jolted along toward the river where the mill sits like a huge grey gnome, and pondering its grinding stone. Wild summer flowers thronged in the fields and we would spy a slip of blue water appearing and disappearing until it grew into the river Exe. Birds dropped from the trees to explore the wagon's bed, and an occasional dog bounded from a cottage to rave at our wheels until, as we crossed some invisible line, it would trot away satisfied, and lie down at its cottage door again.

Master Dorset cleared his throat. He wore no hat and the tops of his ears were bright pink from the sun. Without turning his head, he wondered aloud was there a subject I would like to broach but did not know how to begin.

Since my tongue had clearly frozen, he went on then, that after Lammas last, Sarah had told her mother she and I had come into agreement and would like to marry.

Unprepared for such news, my face flamed and heart, trapped between joy and fear, stopped altogether. I swallowed.

"Ay, Sir, we have bespoke our feelings."

"Well then, if there be a question of marriage, some things come up two men need discuss together."

I stammered I would do all I could to protect and provide--.

He waved me off. The care I would give their daughter was plain as day to everyone. "And there is none more welcome into our family than yourself, Jophiel."

Oh but my heart flew up with joy at that, and with a relief tempered by wonder and humility. While Uncle was held to be an important businessman in Exeter, Master Dorset was the latest in a line famous for its dairy that had served the nobility for generations. He whistled to his horses.

"When two marry," he went on, "families marry as well. You would see Sarah's needs met, yes; but how would you manage your work situation, for instance? We would welcome your skill and knowledge at our business; but what about your uncle?"

Since last Lammas, I had sometimes let my thoughts stray this far, but retreated always at the thought of deserting Uncle Anthony.

"I don't know what to say, Sir," I stammered. "It would be a privilege to bring my service to you; but my uncle has given over more and more to me in the running of his shop. He has sons, but they need some years yet before they can do what I do."

"And likely you are not sure what work situation you would want. His is an excellent place, the best smithy in Devon and hereabouts, no doubt of that," Master Dorset nodded deeply, "and Anthony quite a well-respected man."

Oh, and it did my heart good to hear this praise for my uncle.

"He has given me everything, sir. I owe him more than I know how to repay."

Now we could smell the Exe, see its dew upon the grasses. And for some time I had heard a rumble and felt soft trembling through the wheels of the wagon as we approached the mill, a great building of stone set beside the Exe where its huge wooden wheel scooped the wild water at a steady pace, and sent out a spray like fine rain that blew over everything.

We shook hands with the miller, Master Haverstock, who remembered me from two years before when we replaced the holds on the center pin around which the grinding stone turns.

"Things work out where all have best interests at heart, Jophiel." His eyes upon me were kind. "And if someone makes an offer and someone accepts," he waved a hand; "the rest unfolds to everyone's contentment. Let nothing be a hindrance to you, lad."

Relief washed through me. Now I needn't any answer but Sarah's. Sarah's father had thrown open a door; and the breeze through it awakened me from one dream and into the next: my proposal to Sarah.

A sliver of new moon hung over the meadows next day as I made for the Dorset farm. The family waited their morning meal until I arrived; and we shared cheese and bread and ale. I turned to Sarah and laid wool across her lap. It could have been my heart. Her mouth sprang open and she buried her hands in it, passed it over her cheek and then shook it out and swung it 'round her. And truly it appeared just as I had seen in my mind, glowing across her shoulders and under her flaxen hair.

Father and mother shooed us onto the path to the river that would provide a long walk and plenty of privacy. The sun made a halo of Sarah's hair. I spotted the ancient oak ahead, a landmark you can see reaching into the sky as you come along London Road. Sarah talked of the gifts, how perfect each one was; and the flutter of her fingers braided wildflowers as we walked, her soft face and the feeling of her gentle ease with me swelled in me until I thought the words I had practiced for days would burst forth before I ever got to my knees.

"Let's rest here, Sarah." I gestured toward the old tree with its branches low like rungs of a ladder and spiraling around and up. "Sit here among these leaves, Pretty Bird, and sing me a song."

Father and mother shooed us onto the path to the river that would provide a long walk and plenty of privacy. The sun made a halo of Sarah's hair. Hector came along, knocking his tail against our legs, snuffling the dirt; but after a time, he turned back.

I spotted the ancient oak ahead, a landmark you can see reaching into the sky as you come along London Road. Sarah talked of the gifts, how perfect each one was; and the flutter of her fingers braided wildflowers as we walked, her soft face and the feeling of her gentle ease with me swelled in me until I thought the words I had practiced for days would burst forth before I ever got to my knees.

"Let's rest here, Sarah." I gestured toward the old tree with its branches low like rungs of a ladder and spiraling around and up. "Sit here among these leaves, Pretty Bird, and sing me a song."

She laughed and let me put my hands under her arms to lift her onto the thick lower branch; and the perfume of her body and of the earth around made me dizzy. She looked across a far field for a moment, naming aloud songs she might sing. "He came upon his Horse" or "The World's bliss"?

She turned back and I had dropped to my knees.

"Mistress Dorset," the words came of their own, "I am but a humble man. Even so, I make bold to ask if we might unite. I would do everything in my power to make life good and fruitful for us; and, whatever may come, I can promise that our life would be one filled full with love and happiness, for you are my heart's treasure and delight. And toward your comfort and ease, I would bend every effort, as there is none other in this world to whom I wish to give allegiance or to serve."

They were not the words I had practiced; but they made their way onto the air from my heart, and as if chiseled into stone.

But Sarah had no reply. Her mouth trembled and tears began to spill down her cheeks. She buried her face in her hands, and my heart sank that I must have misunderstood all along; or that she had changed her mind. Then she took her hands away and shook her head slowly, her eyes lighted through the tears and fixed upon me.

"To be with you is all I have dreamed of since first I saw you, Jophiel," she whispered." And sunshine broke then upon her face, and she held her arms out for me to take her down. "Of course. Of course I will marry you. 'Tis all, all I have longed for."

And we kissed then. And I held her to my heart, my treasure, my betrothed. And not knowing for how long nor caring, we pressed against one another, kissing, each one's breathing moving against the other's body while the day arched over us, tender and verdant.

Then finally, reluctantly, we woke to the fact of Sarah's parents awaiting our return. Her father opened the liqueur. Mistress Dorset carried in cold chicken and late strawberries. Sarah sat close. Then her father raised his cup. "To the betrothed!"

Three weeks hence, her mother told us, was quick as everything could be set with the church, with relations and friends.

We nodded blindly. The sooner the better.

Then came the wedding morn. Our family arrived early at St. Vitalis, about half an hour by horse out of Exeter. Uncle brought a gift for the priest, a man his own age with a graying tonsure and patient kindly eyes who laid his hand upon my shoulder as if in blessing. Sick with anticipation to see my bride, I could only return a weak smile and a nod while we stood at the church doors where family members and neighbors would join us to affirm there was no impediment to the union; and to hear our vows and see me slide the ring onto Sarah's finger. I saw Brother Frederick's large frame stride across the church yard; he would assist the priest at the wedding mass.

The sound of plucked strings soothed my nerves and pleased our gathering guests.

When the music stopped and silence fell, the priest stepped out in front of the church doors and I turned, my heart pounding, to see the crowd part. And there Sarah was, an apparition coming through the crowd on her father's arm. Her gown was the blue of the summer sky set against the bloom of her skin; and the pale spun flax of her hair was wreathed round with star ivy and lily of the valley and small pink roses. The hair itself was loose at the front, and in back plaited with dark pink clematis and green leaves.

Uncle Anthony nudged me, then stepped away as I moved to join my bride before the priest. She kissed her father, and he gave her over to my keeping. And something about her spirit, as if she rose from the earth to command the fields and the flying of birds, took hold of me too; and whatever I still held to myself of being a youth fell away then; and I stepped out to meet her, to take her hand in mine, a man.

Then at the priest's bidding, I took up Sarah's hand and all grew still. Her fingers met mine soft and eager, and the gold ring captured the flame of the large candle her cousin held to the side; and a brilliant white star sprang 'round the ring as I slipped it onto her third finger, the one people say is joined to the heart. Then I looked deeply into her eyes and repeated the words that established our contract: "I, Jophiel, take thee, Sarah, to be my wife; and bestow upon thee all that I have for as long as we shall live." They were not adequate words for my heart; they did not say that I knew our two souls now to be one soul and one breath of life. Then I bent, though I had not planned to, and kissed that hand that gave itself to me.

So then the church doors were opened, and we followed the priest inside to stand before the altar to suffer the ordeal of the Mass where the smell of beeswax from the candles mixed with the perfume of roses twined about the old silver holders.

The final blessing then.

And Sarah and I, our faces flushed and eyes dancing, led our families and guests out from the church where we stood just beyond the door to receive their good wishes. And there arose from our guests under the trees a great babble of high spirits while Master Dorset's cousin the fiddler and several of his cronies tuned up and began to scatter notes from fiddle, mandola, harp and drum. And I thought this music to be like a happy heart raising up in joy to sing out everywhere.

We sat back a little from eating our fill.

Then the dancing. Sarah and I led a reel, and all of us with our stomping and clapping scattered squirrels and birds and made the air ring to fill the afternoon with such laughter and good times that even the cold grey stone of the church lit with color; and we thought we must surely cause to dance those in the graveyard just beyond, and indeed the very hills of Devon this September day to burst again into Spring.

In late afternoon, with most of the wine and beer drunk, and fruit tarts for fertility and wedding cakes toothsome with honey and hazel nuts devoured to the last crumb, some guests who napped now in soft piles with their children under the trees began to stir, to collect themselves and bid us fare-thee-wells.

I hugged and kissed every one. Aunt tugged at my cheek, her eyes brimming. Uncle clapped me into an embrace, kissed me through his wiry beard and told me in a husky voice I was always their family, and now Sarah too.

The evening star was up as we drove from St. Vitalis. And for our first night of love upon a pallet filled with fresh hay and lavender, we were blessed with a brilliant moon standing watch over us and our small cottage.

And so we lived our dream of love.

Epilogue

What of your ravishing beauty
under these great hanging lamps
does my barren heart now covet;
and what, unnoticed, long ago
absorbed? And my dear one, what
has he, like me, kept, hoarded?

But soon enough comes the winnowing,
terrible and glorious with its snagged flesh,
broken teeth, its empyting out of hot tears
until finally unfolding to embracing, sumptuos
feasting and uproarious laughter, then dancing,
singing and the merciful regaling with stories!

Printed in the United States
by Baker & Taylor Publisher Services